ADDISON J. CHAPPLE

WITH DANNY KRAVITZ & ELIZA MARSH

The author of this book is solely responsible for the accuracy of all facts and statements contained in the book. This is a work of fiction. Names, characters, places, events, and incidents are either the product of the author's imagination or used in an entirely fictitious manner. Any resemblance to actual persons, living or dead, is entirely coincidental.

Published by:
Level 4 Press, Inc.
14702 Haven Way
Jamul, CA 91935
www.level4press.com

Library of Congress Control Number: 2019944546

ISBN: 978-1-64630-768-5

Printed in the United States of America

Other books by
ADDISON J. CHAPPLE

The Man Who Would Be King
Rambling with Rebah
Santa Ana

To Harley Kravitz, who inspired and encouraged my love of books and stories.

— Danny Kravitz

To Ann, Lauren, and Grace. And in memory of Clark.

— Eliza Marsh

1

Prewitt Patry leaps over a four-foot gap in a metal gangway, brown water rushing below. His headlamp sweeps down the right side of a slimy cement wall illuminating a teeming mess of pipes. The New York City sewer tunnel is murky beneath the weak security lights and smells like a wet garbage dumpster left in the sun. The steady river of trash-laced water has inched up in the last fifteen minutes—*zero percent chance of rain, my ass.*

Prewitt finally sees the opening he has been looking for and jumps across the water into an alcove. He nearly sticks the landing but has to grab onto the rungs of a ladder to keep from falling back out into the wet tunnel. He climbs up, his headlight illuminating the steel rungs as he goes. At the top, Prewitt carefully balances on the ladder. With both hands free, he reaches above his head, pushes upward on a heavy manhole cover, and peers out. He only sees the glare of headlights of a massive truck barreling his way. In one swift move, Prewitt lowers the metal cover and brings his head back into the tunnel before a string of tires rumble across the manhole. He hangs in a backbend for a moment, rather nimble with his athletic dad bod, his few extra pounds worn well. Prewitt grabs the ladder, sets the balls of his feet against the outside poles, and slides down to the base. He angles his headlamp down and drags a hand-drawn map from his pants pocket.

He realizes he was looking at the map upside down and turns it. Prewitt steps back into the sewage tunnel, straddling the water, and there, on the opposite side of the main tunnel, he sees the ladder he should have gone up. He hustles.

Prewitt's black-clad form emerges quietly through the heavy metal grate at the top of the ladder into a large utility room. A check of his watch shows he's four minutes behind. He stows the headlamp, but his ski mask stays in place because every common room in this luxury midrise has security cameras. After his eyes adjust to the dim lighting, he looks past the ordered piping conduits and sees the tell-tale green light in a far corner. They'll know someone was here eventually, but he'd rather keep his identity to himself. He disappears out the door into the hallway and enters a stairwell.

Prewitt checks his watch while lunging up three flights of stairs. He's going to miss the gap in the security patrol if he doesn't get his ass moving. He eases the door open to the third floor. Just as he'd hoped, it's empty. He runs to the far end of the hall, where there is an impressive set of oak doors.

Two weeks of creative surveillance secured Prewitt the six-digit code he punches into the electronic door lock. He lets out a relieved breath as he sees it go green and hears the deadbolt click over. He steps in, closes the door, and hurries through the lavish condo to the corner office. After a quick search, he finds what he came for.

Under his mask, Prewitt grins at the safe.

"And hello to you," he says as he draws his safecracking kit from inside his jacket. The following minutes pass for Prewitt in a flow state of focused yearning, unchanged from those first tries as a kid when one rainy night, a bored, escape artist carny at the traveling fair taught Prewitt and let him keep trying until long after the rides quieted, and the colored lights shut off. The talent is still there, but his confidence is shaky. It's taking too long. "Come on, baby."

Finally, there's that sweet click as the lock yields. Prewitt reaches in, past several scant stacks of papers, and pulls out a bank deposit bag, zipped and locked. He slips it into his jacket beside his kit and straightens as he looks around the office. Prewitt scans the rows and rows of elegant shelves, searching. He recognizes many of the volumes as classics of literature, large format art books, and collections on histories of the world.

Then he sees it. One slim leather book sits alone on the desk. Prewitt knows it was placed there in a staged, casual manner. He also knows it's the most valuable book in the whole room. It's why he took the job in the first place. Well, the second place. He took the job because he needed the money. But as he always does, once his research revealed the mark was a legitimate bad guy and in possession of something Prewitt valued, he was game for real. In an instant, the book disappears into Prewitt's jacket.

After another quick check of his watch, Prewitt dashes back through the condo and out into what should have been, at least for another ninety seconds, an empty hallway. But the chime of the elevator announces the arrival of two guards. The shock of seeing a guy in a ski mask running down the hall freezes them in place for a moment before they break into a sprint. Prewitt has to beat them to the stairwell, or it's game over. He'll be going away if he gets caught now. Prewitt gives it all he has and barely gets through the stairwell door before the guards can get their hands on him.

But he's not in the clear yet. Flinging himself down the steps like a competitor on middle-aged American Ninja Warrior, Prewitt bypasses the utility room and another romp through the sewer in favor of a sprint through the building's ground floor parking garage. He can hear a guard yelling "Close it!" into his walkie-talkie. Soon enough, the garage attendant has punched the button on the heavy metal door, which is now shuddering its way downward. Prewitt has a moment to consider the bruises he'll have on his ass for the next two weeks before throwing himself into a feet-first baseball slide and just clearing the garage door as it hits the ground.

Hauling himself back to his feet, Prewitt can't stop to catch his breath as he takes off at a jog. Running of any kind was not what he'd planned for tonight's adventure.

Prewitt keeps a steady pace as he pulls his mask off and wipes his sweat-drenched face, rounding 78th Street onto Lexington. The rain is now barely a drizzle. He jams the mask in his pocket, keeps the jog up for a few blocks, then slows to a brisk walk and rubs the sting from his right butt cheek. He continues up Lexington against traffic, past little shops under sidewalk scaffolding, past an old drugstore with a vintage RX sign and a case of pinned butterflies in the window, past a little hippie espresso shop with smells of coffee and incense wafting from its open front door, and past all the red awnings and dirty roll-up storefront doors until the rain stops. The street is empty of cars for a moment until an old Honda Civic, its back bumper scraping along the pavement, claws by and turns onto 87th sparks rolling and bouncing around the corner. At 88th, Prewitt turns west then heads up the sidewalk to a break in the buildings and finds his way to the back door of The Gaf, the Upper East Side's finest late night dive bar.

"Gonna need a drink," Prewitt says, as he drops the deposit bag onto a desk.

Dripping sweat in front of this banged-up metal desk in a room full of liquor boxes, Prewitt kneads the familiar tightness at the small of his back with his right hand, his face a grimace of pain.

Behind the desk, Judith "Mace" Duncan reaches over and picks up a cigar from the lip of a black marble ashtray. A once hardcore party girl, she went out clubbing a lot in the late '80s, and her hair got so spiky with thick, silver barbs that her head looked like a medieval weapon, thus the nickname. Mace takes a full draw and blows out the smoke with a little retrohale from her nose that makes her look like a dragon.

"Get whatever you want," she says as she waves an arm toward the other door in the office, the one that leads to The Gaf's long, tidy, and always-filled bar. "It will take me a sec to get this bitch open anyways."

Prewitt stares hard at Mace for a moment. She fits every middle-aged, female dive bar owner cliché, down to her blunt haircut, men's jeans, and flashy high-tops. But Mace adds a tough, punk-era flavor to her strut, and to the way she barks at Prewitt. She flips the bank deposit bag over and starts rummaging through the drawers for the right tool to open its lock.

Wiping the last of the sweat from his forehead, Prewitt heads out to the bar and helps himself to a glass, ice from the chest, and water from the gun. He drinks half the glass, adds more, then heads back. Shutting the door behind him again in the office, he sees Mace picking the lock. She's capable. He watches her as he sits, noting a little gray at her scalp where her hair has grown since the last dye job. Trying to ignore the growing pain in his lower back, he thinks about how Mace has aged in the fifteen years since he's known her.

What one wouldn't suspect just looking or listening now, Prewitt muses, is that Mace happens to be one of the most adept criminals and con pimps in the country. Mace has run jobs and managed crews with the best of them. Her work as a bottom-feeder, as of late, is just how the ball bounces in life. A sting that stung back, a heartbreaking break-up, and the personal problems and bullshit that comes with it. Watch out, hubris, 'cause bad luck is always looking to crack a winning streak. Mace went down hard. Real hard. With tears. It was a year before he saw her in person and another before she did anything other than watch drag racing while sipping whiskey at her bar. Which is why she and Prewitt are simpatico right now. But Mace is also one of the toughest cats Prewitt knows. She sprung back into a low hunter's crouch, and redemption, in the form of a great con, a back-in-the-game grand grift, has long been on her mind. The lock clicks open. Mace reaches in and pulls out an unimpressive stack of bills.

"Fucking dumb bastard," Mace says. "What happened to keeping dirty money at home?"

Prewitt's shoulders slump. *Two weeks' work.* The owner of those solid, oak doors sells stolen goods on the street through a network of hustlers, one of whom is in hock to Mace. That hustler was her narc, just another of the degenerate gamblers Mace carries and milks like sick cows. This mark supposedly makes five figures monthly and launders the cash through his laundromat business. But the money doesn't move until the end of the month. The cash was supposed to be in the safe.

Mace's lips move as she divides the haul in half. "$2,430 each," she says.

"Are you shittin' me?"

"That's all that's here. Maybe I got the dates wrong."

"Great."

"Well, what can I tell ya?"

"I've become a petty thief," he says, shaking his head in disgust. "Just give me my money." Prewitt stands and places his half-empty water glass on the desk and holds out his hand.

Mace barks out a laugh. "For now. Stay sharp, Prew. The big one's coming." Mace hands him his cash. "And answer your damn cell phone when I call."

Prewitt shoves the cash in his jacket and pushes open the back door.

"Not staying to chat?" Mace calls from behind him before the door slams shut.

2

As he walks along the puddled sidewalk, Prewitt wonders if it was wise not to call out the four C-notes he saw Mace palm. It's so pathetic, and why embarrass her? Even though he knows he needs the money more than she does.

Prewitt hears drunken laughter. A group of kids in their early twenties, dressed like they come from money, are taking up the whole sidewalk and heading right for Prewitt. They don't notice him until it's almost too late. The closest guy sees Prewitt and doesn't change course. Instead, he purposely hits him, then bounces off Prewitt's firm shoulder.

"Damn bro, what the hell?" the kid spits out as he raises a hand to his own shoulder like he's wounded.

Prewitt says nothing. He just stands there at his full height of five feet eleven inches. Even at fifty years old, he's still got most of the muscle that helped him in more than one high school parking lot fight and has no interest in backing down to some punk whose entire generation boggles Prewitt's mind with their "I'm the shit, so look at me" attitude. Gone are the days when a guy might risk getting punched in the face to make a point or manifest some machismo. And those are days Prewitt misses.

"Come on," whines one of the girls. She pulls at the punk's hand and almost falls off her high heels, which makes her grab at his arm and laugh. He allows her to drag him past Prewitt and down the sidewalk to catch up with their friends, who didn't even stop.

Prewitt watches them go, not because he's thinking about a fight, but because of the girl's loose-limbed elegance. Her lean frame and honey hair reminded him of someone. Like a ghost from a previous life. That someone had floated down these sidewalks once, holding *his* hand as they laughed their way from bar to bar.

A window display catches Prewitt's attention as he turns back around. He's standing in front of Sotheby's Auction House on the out-of-the-way path he chose to take home tonight. He steps into the foyer and looks at the catalog for an auction of English and Continental silver and furniture from the estate of Andrew Hartnagle, including a matched pair of late Louis XV gilt bronze-mounted kingwood and Chinese lacquered bibliotheques. They start at $100,000. And an Italian silver flamingo starts at $80,000.

"Have yet to see an Italian flamingo," says Prewitt.

He reads the next auction announcement for the McCallan fine and rare collection of single highland malt scotch whiskey. He finds a bottle listed with a starting bid of $30,000, distilled in 1971. "You and me both." *And I'm worth about ten bucks without the score from tonight.* Of course, Prewitt isn't counting the thousands he is in hock to Mace.

Prewitt wishes he could laugh at it all like he did when he was out in Manhattan past midnight with his ghost. But that was long ago. As he leaves Sotheby's Auction House behind, the city sheds its wealth, neighborhood by neighborhood, until a long while later, Prewitt works his key into the grimy exterior door to his rent-controlled apartment building. He kicks a mountain of moldering newspaper circulars out of the way as he heads to the stairs. Like always, it smells like cat piss and the corpses of a million dead cigarettes.

Four flights later, Prewitt's back has had enough of his unusually active night. He lets himself into his cramped studio and manages to lock one of the deadbolts before he walks past the tiny kitchen area, with its one counter and peeling 1970-era wallpaper, and collapses on the tidy bed against the back wall.

Eyes closed, Prewitt lays there for a few minutes. Then he starts hearing it. It's a slow creaking at first, above his head, the complaints of a worn-out box spring and commiseration of old floor joists. As the beat on the ceiling increases in tempo, muffled moans sink through until Prewitt can make out a voice yelling "baby, baby, baby." He forces himself to sit up. His back is not pleased with the decision, and he closes his eyes for a moment against the pain. He's lived with sciatica for so long; it seems like an unwanted roommate: won't move out, always loud when you're trying to rest, always annoying. He heads into the kitchen. There is a lone plate in the sink and an empty glass on the counter. He fills the glass with water from the faucet, takes four Ibuprofen from a bottle in the cabinet, and throws back the pills. He finishes the water and puts the glass down.

The kitchen counter serves as his table and divider from the bedroom slash living room slash office. A cell phone, plugged into the charger, sits right where he left it. Prewitt picks up the phone. There are three voicemail messages.

Two are from Mace. "Prew, why haven't you called me?" and "Answer your damn phone." The third message is from the laughing, lanky, honey-haired ghost girl. Though that girl is long gone. In her place is his angry ex-wife scolding him for missing yesterday's support payment. But she's wrong about why he missed the payment. It wasn't because he didn't want to; he couldn't afford it. He isn't making that kind of money anymore. He's lost his mojo. But Honey Hair, he still thinks of her by that pet name, has refused to believe him since the day eight years ago when she lawyered up and left.

Prewitt exits voicemail and clicks through to the photo album in his camera roll. There's a picture of Honey Hair holding their baby boy. The next image is all three dressed up for someone's wedding. Their boy is a five-year-old in a tuxedo holding a little pillow with pride even though there aren't rings tied to it anymore. They really were all stunningly handsome back then. *Even me.* People had said it all the time. What a beautiful family.

No one knew, not even his wife, that that was when he was the happiest he had ever been. But it was an unsustainable high. He was playing the longest con of his entire life, keeping his wife convinced that he wasn't a criminal. And why? Why would he do that? He just never knew she'd actually fall for him, a guy who didn't deserve to take her for a drink, let alone take her arm for life . . . and keep falling for him. She was so out of his league, the dogs in the park knew it when he would take her there, and they'd look at him as if to say, "Dude, are you serious with this? There is no way. You're pushing your luck," and all he'd say back to them with his happy eyes was, "I love her. I really love her. More than I love myself, I love her. And I'll make it work." He just had to hide what he thought he'd never have to explain because he never thought she'd love him too. But she did. Until she didn't anymore.

Back then, he was living in two worlds: a family with the love of his life, and a secret existence of artistic thievery, the life of the con. And Prewitt had woven his two worlds together with an impressive and intricate web of lies. But it couldn't hold. As much as he'd wanted them to stay together, at any moment, she could discover who he really was, and those worlds would float apart, zero gravity, lost from each other and drifting.

Prewitt looks at his texts. There's a message from her too:

Listen to your voicemail.
Your payment is late, and
don't forget his birthday.

Shit. His son's birthday. It's tomorrow. Prewitt checks the time on his phone: 1:25 a.m. Correction, it's today.

There is a knock on the door, which startles Prewitt. Prewitt goes over and looks through the peephole. It's Ed from across the hall. He's always hauling film equipment up and down the stairs and occasionally burning food, but he's not a bad guy.

Prewitt opens the door a foot and sticks his head in the gap.

"It's a little late, Ed."

"Sorry to bother you, man, but I heard you come home. I was up rendering some footage of . . ." Ed realizes Prewitt probably doesn't give a shit about what he was doing. "Anyway, I thought I should tell you some scary-looking dudes were here banging on your door a couple of hours ago. One of them had a screwdriver and went at a few of your locks, but they gave up pretty quickly and left."

Prewitt swings the door all the way open, and sure enough, one of the locks has scratch marks, but then there are two more, the ones Prewitt installed himself that can't be broken through so easily. Those are fine.

"Thanks, Ed. I appreciate you letting me know. They must have the wrong address, because there's no reason anyone would want anything from this place." Prewitt puts on his most wholesome smile and gives Ed the gentle laugh of complete innocence.

"Okay, man, just wanted to tell you . . ." Ed's already heading back into his apartment.

"Thanks for keeping an eye out. Have a good night," Prewitt says quietly as he gives a little wave.

Prewitt closes the door and locks all the deadbolts. *Who the fuck?* He arches his back and feels pain shoot down his leg. Prewitt pulls out the meager earnings from his little caper. What a disappointment. He's not sure how he's going to come up with the money to pay his rent and the ex-wife. He isn't looking forward to seeing her in person with a balance on the books. He shoves the money away into a drawer. Why suffer more tonight?

Then Prewitt sits on his bed, reaches into his jacket, and pulls out the small leather book he liberated from the office earlier in the evening. *Evangeline* by Henry Wadsworth Longfellow. First edition. His research showed it went for $11,500 at Sotheby's Rare Books and

Manuscripts auction last year. It wasn't hard for Prewitt to discover the mark had bought it. It turns out Laundry Man had a history of purchasing all manner of things at auction with no specific areas of interest. Also, Prewitt knew from the sale records that the mark over-paid for everything he won. Prewitt has spent a lifetime learning the value of rare pieces, not to steal them, but because he loves few things more.

He reaches over to the compact, deep-hued walnut bookcase beside his bed. The top half is a lawyer's case, each shelf protected by a piece of glass that louvers open from the top on slides like a tiny garage door. The bottom half is a series of drawers, graduated in size from top to bottom to a pleasing effect. Prewitt had bought the thing when he was in college from a nearly forgotten junk shop in the small town of Mt. Lebanon, outside of Pittsburgh, where he went to school. Shortly after that, he dropped out of school, fell into his current line of work, and started filling the bookcase with little treasures.

Dropped out. It's a term he's used when the conversation can't be avoided, but only because it's easier to say than "forced out" or "kicked out." Of course, even "kicked out" can't fully capture the utterly fuckedness of what happened just before; as a twenty-six-year-old grad student, he was set to defend his dissertation for the Dietrich College of Humanities and Social Sciences at Carnegie Mellon. At the finish line. A doctor-to-be in Art History and Museum Studies. An academic star who came from the gutter.

At CMU, Prewitt had indulged his love of foreign languages, early modern European culture, furniture, and architecture. He'd been paid to do it. And he'd found a mentor. Professor Dylan Watkin Standish taught, inspired, and cared about Prewitt. He'd supported him and encouraged him and gave leeway for Prewitt to make artifacts his main area of study.

Prewitt pulls open the top drawer of the bookcase. On a wool pad sits restoration tools. Also capable of being used for forgeries, but not this time. Prewitt selects two linen cloths from a neat stack and carefully wipes clean all the surfaces of the book to remove any oils from his hands or the careless paws of the previous owner. He holds the book tenderly with a cloth and flips through a few pages. He smells the paper and examines the ink, and the edges of each page, gauging the amount of foxing.

It was Standish who'd introduced Prewitt to society and privilege. He'd shown him wealth, and the wealthy. Real wealth. Prewitt grew up dangerously poor, and Dylan Watkin Standish, being extraordinarily rich, was the only well-healed person he'd ever known. Prewitt always thought the wealthy were aliens, snobs. Standish appeared to not be. He took Prewitt under his wing. And he made him feel loved. Until he'd destroyed Prewitt's career and shredded his heart for good measure. Professor Dylan Watkin Standish was a pillar, and he was a con artist.

Prewitt closes the book and holds it another moment. *Evangeline.* Then he opens a shelf on the bookcase. Prewitt nestles it in with several other volumes he has rescued over the years.

Carnegie Mellon. Prewitt knows he was pushing back against some karmic plan by even believing he could be a winner in the other people's game, let alone a professor. And when it was all over with Standish, Prewitt had been left right where he always knew he belonged, outside. Except he'd let his guard down and had believed otherwise, so there was a sting now. *How did I not see it coming*?

He looks at the little digital clock by the bed. The red numbers read 1:46 a.m. Time to say goodnight to his modest collection of purloined artifacts, his books on philosophy and politics, and subjects like architecture and world history and flowers from the different continents. Prewitt crawls into bed, turns out the light, and returns to his worries about the support payment conversation coming tomorrow and what fresh hell will be visited on him by his ex-in-laws, all shit he will put up with without hesitation so he can see his son on his birthday.

3

Prewitt is almost to his breakfast meeting with Johnny when, before opening the door and entering My Lovely's Cafe on the corner of Waverly and Washington Square East, he stops to look at the throngs of folks walking past, skateboarders and college kids playing guitars in the park. Prewitt still marvels at the instincts of the city planners who knew this trash-strewn city would need all the gorgeous green space it could spare. And that arch, to celebrate the hundred years since Washington became the first president, classy move. Who cares if most people don't realize why they built it. History always brings a sort of chill to Prewitt, how easily America could have lost the fight for independence. To him, this whole city is a picture book of the events that made a free America. It's the best thing about walking Manhattan.

Inside My Lovely's, Prewitt sees Johnny already sitting with a full plate of food in front of him. *But what the hell is on his head?* Johnny is wearing a blue velvet hat and a navy-esque jacket that makes him look like an Irish Captain Crunch. My Lovely's is the new favorite breakfast spot of Johnny, Prewitt's almost-retired parole officer, and recently very changed man. Divorce seems to have unleashed a happier, more eccentric version of Johnny. He has since moved to Soho and taken up ballroom dancing. He's swapped his once austere and cop-like look for flip-flops and beaded bracelets. According to Johnny, divorce worked out just fine, better than fine. Best thing that ever happened to him.

Johnny was Prewitt's friend long before he became his parole officer. They first met at Willow Country Day Elementary School, which Prewitt attended for two years before moving on to the next foster home two towns away. They had written letters to each other until high school, when a driver's license made getting together more doable. They hung out as often as they could. Johnny never claimed to know what Prewitt was doing after leaving academia. Prewitt always suspected Johnny knew, but to Johnny, the value of childhood friendship was a separate thing from laws written in black ink on white paper. A suspicion that was confirmed when, busted, Prewitt spilled all, and Johnny just kind of smirked, got himself assigned to be his parole officer, and got on with the business of watching Prewitt's ass. Maybe it was that Johnny had been a cop in NYC and had seen too much nasty shit to be in judgment of people and their odd, winding journeys through life. Or maybe it was that Johnny has always been a good egg, from day one. Prewitt simply knew Johnny was a real friend, one of the few people who cared about him.

That day Prewitt had been caught, the day his life finally got a knock on the door from the karmic bill collector; it was sweet innocent Honey Hair who answered and got it handed to her. Prewitt tried explaining it, that his entire life was a lie but that it also really wasn't, just the part about how he made money. That he could still love her as much as he did and was still the same man she thought he was, and there was a way for this to all be okay . . . that message was dead on arrival. Prewitt tried to sell it, but Honey Hair didn't see it that way, couldn't see it that way, and by no fault of her own. A bucket of shame from her rich-kid, be-perfect past got dumped so heavy onto the little girl in her psyche that when the news hit, it crushed her happily ever after beyond repair. And any voice trying to explain the gray areas of life was heard as a foreign language, the language of bees, nonsense, indecipherable. It wasn't himself he cared about, though the thought of losing her was searing and awful. It was that he had hurt her. He'd harmed what he held most precious. And her wet eyes and that disbelieving look on her face as she stared silently at him, wondering what was wrong with her to have made such a mistake . . . his heart shattered in a way he'd never felt before. *Sweet, sweet Honey Hair. My girl. And I lost her. Did I ever really have her? No. No, I didn't. I just conned myself into thinking I did. That was my best con.*

"I couldn't wait. Too hungry," says Johnny.

Prewitt sits and grabs the menu, quickly settling on the first omelet option he sees, "My Lovely's Four Egger Denver," he tells the waitress.

"You're not pulling any bullshit, right?"

Prewitt stares at Johnny.

"Just say it out loud," says Johnny.

"No bullshit," says Prewitt.

It's the little game they play since Johnny knows that Prewitt is always ankle-deep in it. Johnny hard-pressed the potential consequences only once, at their first official meeting as parolee and parole officer. Prewitt never served time, but since then, Johnny mentions it now and then to remind them of what could happen should Prewitt get felony pinched again. Other than that, they just talk about life. If forced to answer, Prewitt trusts both men would agree that they are best friends. This has accompanied their every interaction before and after Prewitt's fall from grace. And that is also why Johnny still makes him say it.

"There's a warehouse job I could get you tomorrow if you want it. You could work your way up from C.O.N. to C.O.O. with the brains you got," Johnny says with a wave of his hand, his bracelets flying by in a blur of color.

"I'll think about it," says Prewitt. "What's with the pirate hat?"

Johnny smiles. "What? Should I wear a fucking Yankee's cap instead?" Johnny says.

"If you don't want to be confused with someone who's having a mental breakdown," says Prewitt, chuckling.

After getting his meal, Prewitt listens to Johnny talk about his ballroom dance class. He's met a lady whom he's "courting," and he's seeing her again for dinner later.

"What are you doing today?" Johnny asks.

Prewitt explains how he has to see his son and his ex at her parents' place and how much that is going to suck, which includes his father-in-law sharing how he thinks Prewitt is a worthless piece of shit. It's nothing Johnny hasn't heard before.

"Why do you still give a shit what that asshole thinks of you?"

"I don't."

"Sure you do. You let what he thinks, actually her too . . . You let what they all think about you get under your skin. Like it fucking matters what anyone thinks."

"Nice that you don't have that problem."

"Well, I sure used to. And I finally said fuck that. You know why? Because fuck that. That's why. I *like* ballroom dancing. A lot." Johnny scoops up the last of some kind of steak and eggs dish and fills his mouth.

"It's not like my life is all that rocking right now, Johnny."

"Oh, bullshit. What a bunch of bullshit that is. You're full of shit."

"Tell me what you really think." Prewitt smiles.

"Okay, here's what I think. I think you know a lot about history and books and art shit. And if someone told you one of those things you steal was worth nothing, you'd know they were wrong, and you'd say, 'Fuck off, you idiot.'"

"I'm not following."

"Alright, well, follow this. If one of your paintings, like a fucking painting by the guy that did the scream thing, if it were alone on a wall in some cluttered library in Germany, and people walked by it every day, but no one knew what it was really worth, would the painting know what it was worth? Yeah, it would. Because it's a great damn painting. It don't matter that the janitor thinks it's ugly. He's probably color-blind. Beauty is not actually in the eye of the beholder. It's in the heart of the fucking guy on the wall. You follow? So quit feeling sorry for yourself, lift up your chin, and get on with it, man. You live once. Once."

In his own way, Johnny was a poet, or some kind of artist. Prewitt always knew that about him, loved that about him. If Johnny hadn't been born into a family of Irish cops in Hell's Kitchen, he might have become a . . . well, something other than a cop-turned-ballroom-dancer.

And sure, Prewitt appreciates where Johnny is coming from. But what help is it, really? He still has to go and face the music.

"I gotta go. I'm gonna be late."

"I ain't keeping you here."

And with that, Prewitt gets up and walks toward the door. He doesn't leave any money. Johnny hasn't let him pay for a meal in ten years.

4

Prewitt hustles off the train car at Great Neck and hauls ass up the stone stairs. He doesn't bother finding a cab, just takes off at a light jog through Firefighters Park, passing families on the playground. Like a carriage horse in blinders, Prewitt keeps his eyes straight ahead. He doesn't want to be haunted by memories today. Jogging down Grace Avenue, he passes St. Paul's Church and its striking old-world façade. There's an elegance to the sweeping stone buttresses that form a colonnade on the street side of the building. Once upon a time, he walked there with a beautiful girl in a white dress. *All of Long Island, ruined.*

Grace Street dead ends into East Shore Road. The houses he'd passed so far were hulking but still huddled together in that New York fashion. Now the neighborhood gives way to expanses of manicured lawn and park-like sections of wild growth and small woods. The estate he approaches is cordoned off by a massive wrought iron fence. Prewitt tries to catch his breath and rings the gate buzzer. He stares blankly in the direction of the security camera and waits to be permitted entrance to his ex-father-in-law's kingdom.

Honey Hair is waiting in front of the double oak doors at the maw of the oversized central hall colonial. He feels like he's entered a film about some asshat publishing magnate with a family fortune behind him, right down to the obnoxiously large portrait of said asshat waiting inside the foyer. Honey Hair. Although, Prewitt has to call her Sharon now in person. Still so damn gorgeous. But she's so mad. Prewitt can tell even though he's still a fair distance away. It's a long driveway, and he's taking his time, partly for the breathing. Partly so he can enjoy her presence before it becomes trickier.

"You're an hour late," Sharon seethes. Her hand is tenting her eyes as she looks into the sun from under the teakwood-clad portico.

Prewitt could make an excuse, tell her a lie, cast the blame on someone else, but where would lying to her get him at this point in their relationship? Instead, he just climbs the few steps onto the porch until he's standing in front of her. "Sorry. How's Josh?"

Sharon seems pissed he didn't participate in the argument she was angling for. She takes a step back and a moment to respond. Prewitt continues to read her body without appearing to be looking her over. Underneath her expensive sheath dress, it's all toned. Sharon always loved a good workout. But her hair is still her most striking feature. It pours off her head in thick waves almost to her waist. She has it pulled all into a coil and draped forward over her right shoulder. He watched her do it as he came up the driveway. He's sure she's not conscious of how much she plays with her hair. Even as they've been speaking, several tendrils have slipped loose, and she tucks one behind her ear. *Does she know what that still does to me?* Prewitt hopes she still loves him. Sometimes, he believes she does, but he knows she can never *really* love him. Not anymore, not from where she comes from. It just wouldn't fit. Somewhere in her subconscious, that battle was fought and lost.

"Josh is fine," she huffs. "Of course," to indicate years of anger and that left under her care, Josh is as well as any boy could be. But it's anger that can't hide the sad.

Prewitt watches her shake it off, the last sign of any real emotion she'll share with him today, and glide back into the mansion. He tries to put on a carefree demeanor as he follows her into their son's birthday party.

***

Sharon's heels strike the marble tiles in staccato bursts as she crosses the grand entrance hall. And there's that damn portrait of his ex-father-in-law, high up on the wall looking down on everyone. *Well-painted though, I'll give him that.* The echo of her footfalls makes the house seem empty, but Prewitt knows there are caterers in the kitchen and other staff lurking about unseen. He follows Sharon into the breezeway that runs the entire length of the back of the house. The property has a commanding view of Manhasset Bay. The façade is colonial, but Prewitt recognizes the back of the mansion as Italian villa. He takes in the resort-style pool and hot tub with an invisible edge, then passes a massive pergola currently housing dining for twenty. There's also a tasteful smattering of bar tables, and lounges are arranged on the flagstones around the pool. Several serving staff pass among the partygoers.

Prewitt sucks in a breath, steps through the open doors of the breezeway, and heads down to find his son. Just as he sees Josh talking to his grandparents, Prewitt's phone vibrates in his pocket. He slips it out quickly and sees it's a call from Mace. He ignores it.

"Ah, Prewitt, you finally made it."

Prewitt locks eyes with Geoffrey Sterns. Josh's grandfather is a short man but has volume in girth and voice. He's like an overstuffed howler monkey. Prewitt has always hated him. Even when he loved Sharon, he hated her father. Not just because he was a world-class jerk, but because somehow Geoffrey Sterns sensed who Prewitt was, and that he was unworthy. Prewitt pitied Sharon's mother Beatrice an equal amount.

"Did the train schedule trip you up? Beatrice, we should have sent a car for Prewitt. Why didn't we send a car?" Geoffrey says.

Beatrice, the Queen Bee, as Geoffrey often calls her in jest, responds with worry, "Was I supposed to have sent Driver to fetch Prewitt from the city? Oh no, I've done something wrong."

"Of course not, Beatrice," Prewitt turns to her and takes her hands, all clutched knuckles, and smooths them. "How have you been?"

Before she can answer, Geoffrey howls so everyone in the yard can hear, "Dinner is served," and drags Josh off to the pergola before Prewitt can even greet his son. Josh looks back at him as he gets pulled away.

As Prewitt escorts Beatrice to the dining table, barely visible beneath two overabundant floral centerpieces and all the plates and placemats, his phone vibrates again. This time Mace has texted:

The big one!!!

The exclamation points annoy Prewitt. *The big one, my ass. Who does she think she's fooling?* If it is such a big one, it can wait. Big ones tend to take time. Prewitt settles Beatrice into her seat and surveys the remaining options for himself. Josh is watching him. There are no seats next to Sharon, no seats next to Josh. The only empty seat is at the far end next to one of Sharon's cousins, Martha. Even Josh's friends Ronald and Toby are further up the table. Josh watches him with those kind puppy eyes Prewitt marveled at in the delivery room at New York Presbyterian in Manhattan. Even then, Josh looked like a softy, a precious, kindhearted soul. Prewitt had never felt the kind of instinct to protect anything that clobbered him the moment the nurses placed Josh and his little blue hat and his dark brown eyes in his arms. He still feels it.

Part of Prewitt would love to scream, "Hey you fuckers, I know what you're doing with the second-class seating move you pulled here," but Prewitt decides he might enjoy his meal better from the cheap seats. It'll be easier to ignore Geoffrey from the far end of the table.

"Oh, Prewitt, nice to see you again," Martha says with the smile of someone in an annoyingly great mood. Martha has never been in a relationship before, ever, as far as Prewitt knows, and has always been excited and bubbly about one thing or the other. This time it's rats.

"Excuse me?" says Prewitt after she shares the fact with a simple, "I'm into rats now." The next thing he knows, the phone is out, the photo app is open, and he's being shown pictures of two rats in matching fuchsia rat sweaters.

"Handknitted," she says. "It's so hard to have pets in the city . . . and who the hell wants to be a cat lady?"

Prewitt can't resist, "When you can be a rat lady."

"Exactly," she says, seemingly oblivious that someone might poke fun because she's too happy to see a problem.

Prewitt wonders what it's like to be Martha.

"Do you smell that smell?" she asks.

Prewitt does not know how to answer, worrying the rats might be in her handbag.

Martha leans forward and shoves her neck into his face. "It's eucalyptus with a note of licorice. I'm this month's top seller in Brooklyn, and sixth in all the five boroughs."

It smells nice to Prewitt, the licorice, just as she said. "Is there much competition?" he asks.

Again, she doesn't notice the snark. "Essential oils are big, real big. You wouldn't believe how big. And sales just keep growing. But I like to wear my products too. That's why I'm good at sales. Because I believe in my . . ."

Prewitt drifts off for a moment, fantasizing about sitting in the bathroom for the rest of the meal, brought back when he feels her hand on his leg.

"Do you smell the licorice?" she asks, leaning into him again.

Prewitt shifts in his chair, away from Martha and toward the sound of Geoffrey laughing at one of his own jokes. Prewitt looks next at his son. Josh is peering at something on the screen of Toby's phone. They have their heads tilted together. It's so easy and comfortable. Prewitt's heart swells for Josh and his friendships, unique to this age when life can't dilute all that is so precious about friendship. And because Josh has everything open before him. *What I've learned about love from having this boy.*

Just then, a huge chocolate mousse cake hits the plates. Geoffrey stands and clangs his knife against his crystal water glass. "Joshua, happy eighteenth birthday. A fine young man you've become. Now, everyone, Joshua has a few words to share with you all."

Josh clears his throat and scans out into the faces. *That kind smile. His mother's smile.*

"Thanks. Umm . . . thank you all for coming. And I'd also like to thank my grandparents. Grandfather, Grandmother, it's great you're having this birthday party for me."

Looking out, Prewitt can see the slight breeze playing through the tops of the trees along the edges of the property. As his son's voice eases into his ears, Prewitt's gaze settles somewhere out over the bay. The light on the water is an orange line, stuttering and broken but leading off to backlit clouds and rays of sunlight. Prewitt thinks back to summers past when Josh had played in the pool outside all day long. Josh would drag his dripping body out onto the deck long enough to gorge himself on a hot dog before plunging back in to carry on with some game of toy boats and water monsters.

"Tell everyone the best part!" Sharon urges

"Oh yeah, right. You guys! I got into Harvard!"

Prewitt is tugged back to the present by Josh's last sentence. Applause follows. Prewitt sees Sharon hugging her son. Josh gets high fives from his friends. Prewitt feels a warmth as a smile grows on his face. *You did it.* But how is he going to pay for it? He can hardly scrape together enough for support payments right now. Then the pride pours in more, and Prewitt feels only that. *Way to go, little man.*

The warehouse job? Prewitt is going to have to go legit. He'll finally take Johnny up on the offer to punch a brown plastic clock somewhere. $18.00 an hour? How many hours for a semester at Harvard? Years' worth of all the hours he can find in a day. Many, many, many years.

"Dad! I did it," Josh calls to him from the other end of the table. "Can you believe it?! I wanted to surprise you today."

"Amazing. That's just so . . . amazing," Prewitt says, sounding to himself like the least articulate man to ever congratulate a son. Prewitt pulls himself together and gets up to hug Josh, beaming.

"Yes, *amazing*! What will be truly amazing is the magic act you'll have to pull to pay for it," Geoffrey says. His voice booms loud enough for everyone to hear. "Josh has done all the hard work. Only to have his dream school dangle far beyond his father's financial reach."

Dick.

Prewitt feels the bile rising, and the cold, ready-for-action tingling in his body as he resists the urge to take a dangerous step toward Geoffrey. Even with the ruinous consequences, Prewitt wants to starch the man with a nice open-hander. But he hides it under a mastered smile. That lesson Prewitt learned around the same age he'd first tried riding a bike. Can't let 'em see it coming.

"Walk with me, Josh," Prewitt says, pretending not to have heard.

Josh settles into the same stride as his dad as they start a slow lap around the pool. Prewitt can feel his gentle energy. Josh is so likable. Eighteen now. A man. Soon to be a Harvard man. *I remember him falling asleep on my chest as we looked out at the ocean in Cape Cod.* Honey Hair did a hell of a job.

"Dad, I know Harvard costs a lot of money."

"Don't worry about that. Just think about what *you* did. You did it. And you should be proud of what you've accomplished."

There were terms to the divorce regarding shouldering the cost of school payments which Prewitt insisted on.

"But I do think of it. I don't have to go there."

"Sure you do. You earned it. It will be a great experience. And going to Harvard creates life-long opportunities *you* will put to good use. We've talked about this."

And they had. Starting when Josh had first learned what college was one day in his third-grade class at Pepper Pike Elementary and came home excited to share with Prewitt, surprised to learn his parents also knew what college was. And having been told by Mrs. Kusich about the different types of colleges and how Harvard was considered the gold standard, then immediately deciding he'd be attending, Josh shared that detail too. And it never changed as he got taller and more curious about life. And as the college conversations became more realistic, it only became more attainable to him. Prewitt always told Josh how great that was. How they'd get there together. It was their plan. Honey Hair too. And with every test and every activity, Josh had kept earning the increasing odds. And it wasn't just to get in. Josh liked learning. And cross-country, and investment club, and student-directing theater productions, and volunteering to build houses on weekends. Mostly. But Prewitt saw something else was going on with Harvard now. It was Josh's way to stay connected to something they once were. It pained Prewitt to even hear Josh's concern. And it sickened him that Josh knew he didn't have money.

"But it's more than you can afford."

"Hey, Josh. I can pay for this. I always told you I'd pay for it. And I can."

He'd done that too, because it was important to Prewitt his kid got to feel what Prewitt never did, that someone had his back. For the long haul. And maybe Prewitt shouldn't have talked about money with Josh when Josh was dreaming his Harvard dreams and Prewitt his perfect dad ones, but he had. Told him he'd pay. Said it was because Josh mattered to him. Planted that lovely fragile flower, never thinking he'd be where he is now.

"I got you, buddy."

They hadn't spent nearly as much time together as Prewitt had hoped they would when the divorce began. He just never realized how busy a kid's life could get or how the moments missed when you're not in the same home would add up. He also never counted on how little Prewitt would have to offer. It became easier just to let Josh skip nights and continue with Honey Hair than to make up the couch in this studio again and feel like a pathetic, forty-year-old camp counselor. He told himself that it was only until he got into a better apartment, one with a room for Josh and endless food choices in the fridge. But the heavy debts and the financial inertia had been brutal, the confidence starved for oxygen, and luck off on a bizarrely long sabbatical. The temporary avoidance became the way they did it. Maybe it was pride, but Prewitt had begun to think it might be best for Josh. By the time he'd realized it felt like rejection to the kid, the damage had been done. A big fucking mess he'd made. And he'd hurt his boy. He wasn't going to hurt him ever again.

Josh hugs Prewitt, and when Prewitt brings a hand up to the middle of his back, Josh holds on tighter. Prewitt reaches up with his other hand and rests it on the back of his son's neck, almost his height.

"I got ya," Prewitt repeats.

The "Thanks, Dad" just melts him.

5

After goodbyes, Prewitt walks back to the entrance hall. It's dark outside, and a massive chandelier throws prismatic light through the whole center of the house. It's nice. His phone rings. It's the third call from Mace. He finally picks up. "Can't talk."

As he shoves it back in his pocket, Geoffrey walks up behind him.

"I need to speak to you in my study." Then Geoffrey heads off without checking if Prewitt is following him. He does.

Geoffrey's study is a cavernous room on the lower level. Prewitt has been in here before, when he was first married, but it was never fun, and he quickly realized his father-in-law was a colossal dickhead. The study was in *Architectural Digest,* an article entitled, "Best Personal Libraries and Clubrooms of the East Coast." Prewitt has heard it all before. The walls are paneled in Dalbergia, a ludicrously expensive hardwood; the rugs are imported from Istanbul. Behind Prewitt, a massive stone fireplace is flanked by two Chesterfield sofas. In front of him is Geoffrey's huge wooden desk. There is a Degas behind the desk Prewitt would love to rescue. One item in the room is new. It's an Italian silver wall mirror. Prewitt notices custom lighting has been installed to set it off. It reminds Prewitt of the silver flamingo from the Sotheby's Auction House catalog.

"Do you like it?" Geoffrey asks as he seats himself behind his desk. He's holding a snifter of something dark. He doesn't offer Prewitt a drink.

"Yes," Prewitt offers.

"Silver. Solid silver. Worth about $65,000. Not what I paid. Got a good deal, of course."

Geoffrey sloshes his drink in his snifter as he toasts the wall mirror, spilling a little.

"So, about Harvard," Geoffrey says. "I know you can't afford it, not in a million years. Sharon is always on you about support. I've told her to remove you from her life, but she is stubborn on the boy's behalf."

Geoffrey takes a healthy sip.

"Go ahead, Prewitt. Take a good look in that mirror. Is that a man who can put his son through Harvard? No, but I can. Easily. Sharon has been happy to take handouts from me her whole life, even during your marriage, and she'll continue doing it now."

Prewitt knows Sharon did not like taking handouts from her father. She'd be pressured into it through the emotional blackmail of knowing her mother could be bullied if her father was angry. She'd given all the money to the New York City Food Bank. Prewitt had been bringing in enough to keep them, if not in the lifestyle she was accustomed to, in acceptable comfort.

"Joshua is a young man, his future's bright. Doesn't need the disappointment that comes with trusting you. Sharon neither. So, I'm taking them over. I'll pay all the bills and more from here on out. As long as you don't contact them anymore. I've had my lawyers draw up an agreement. No one will ask you for money again. I know it's what you want. You don't know how to love anyone. You'll get your freedom, and I'll take care of my family."

The words hit a nerve, and for a moment, make Prewitt consider perhaps he is more than just a failure but actually flawed. Anger rushes to save him. Prewitt isn't sure if Mace really does have the big one lined up or if he'll be slinging boxes around in a warehouse or flipping pancakes at a 24-hour diner, but fuck Geoffrey. Fuck this pompous jerk with all his money and the captive art in his stupid Long Island lair.

Prewitt takes a breath to calm himself. "I'll tell you what I told Josh.

I can pay for Harvard. Keep your money, and I'll keep my son." Prewitt turns and walks to the door. "And your mirror is worth thirty, max."

On the train home, Prewitt slumps on a seat in the back. The train car is nearly empty, and his brain feels tired and drained. Usually, it's energizing to play parts and say the right things while moving among the wealthy. But tonight's players just sucked. And now there's a realization creeping in that he's got to get a foothold and fast. The cliff is sheer, and his grip is slipping. Geoffrey wants to take his son away forever. *What's the next move?*

His phone vibrates. Mace again.

Prewitt answers, "Alright, tell me about this stupid job."

6

But it wasn't a stupid job. Not at all. This was the possibility of a real play, a bunco, a sting. A big one? Maybe. *The* big one? Prewitt listens.

"Some rich French asshole. He comes into the bar looking around like he's completely lost," Mace tells Prewitt after sharing she'd stumbled onto the potential mark with an old-world accent and old money bonafides. She'd insisted Prewitt come on over to The Gaf. "Too good to discuss further over the phone," she'd said. So now he's sitting across from Mace at a scratched-up wooden bar table. She's got a shot in front of her she hasn't touched since he sat down two minutes earlier.

"So, Frenchy takes the first stool he can find that doesn't have anyone sitting in the seats to the right or the left and barks out: 'Barkeep!' I had to grab onto Otto to keep him from charging down there and throwing the pompous guy out on his ass." Prewitt keeps listening. Mace loves to spin out a story for the sake of talking.

"So, I introduced myself to his lordship and explained this was my bar. He called me ma'am and said his name was Ranger du Countercurse, the Red Baron of Pizza, or some shit nonsense. The man has more names than I have beers on draft."

"I'm pretty sure the Red Baron of Pizza is Italian."

"Just wait, smartass. So, Ranger Rick tells me he's come from Sotheby's, and he was trying to get some air by walking back to his hotel. But he'd gotten lost and was needing a drink. I served him an over-poured highball of scotch neat, and he downed it, then went on to tell me he was soon going to 'collect' his bags from the hotel concierge and get a car to Newark before he missed his flight to Paris. I over-poured him another and asked if he'd won any prizes at the auction. I know how you like those antiques, Prewitt."

"I'm listening."

"So, he downs the second glass of scotch and doesn't answer my question. So, I ask again. Again, he doesn't answer. He just stares out, thinking. And all *I'm* thinking is I gotta keep this scaly bastard here. I got a feelin', right? So, I poured him a third. Guy doesn't even say thank you. Just keeps staring out as he sips on it. Then he finally says, 'I sold something. That I'd only bought last year. More than doubled my money. Yes, I did very well.' He takes another sip and adds, 'Very well.' He says it just like that. Twice. The stuffy fucker. 'You should only do so well,' he adds. What a dick. So now I'm really getting wet. But then, before I can find out what it is he sold and for how much, his stiff ass pulls a wad of fifties from a red leather wallet and asks how much is needed to cover the drinks and tip and if we would order him a car. I asked him to stay, but there was no charming this turd-head. So, I took three hundred and told him Otto was my driver and it would be no trouble to run by the hotel for his bags then to curbside check-in at Newark. What could I do? The guy had a plane to catch."

Mace slaps a tan leather business portfolio onto the table. "He left this behind in Otto's car. I was trying to get ahold of your stupid ass so you could intercept. You know, find out what he's really working with. Seemed like a real prize-winning jackass, Prewitt, you know, right up your alley." Mace smiles, all proud of herself. "Nifty, huh? Yeah, pretty nifty," she says, nodding her head.

Prewitt watches Mace revel. She's like a candy-cane-loaded little girl in her glee.

"So, are you with me? I gotta feeling here, Prewitt. A real juicy fish-over-the-fire feeling."

Prewitt picks up the portfolio, just a folder, really. The leather is high-quality and new. He flips it open and sees a Sotheby's Auction House catalog and what looks like a travel itinerary in French. He looks at Mace, nodding at him, brows up, eyes wide, like she's wondering when Prewitt is gonna start doing a happy dance.

"Well? Well?" Then a third time with a nice big lean-in. "Weeeellllll?"

"What's his name, Mace?" says Prewitt.

"I told you."

"His real name."

"Right."

Mace leans back and finally downs the shot.

"Courtemanche. Ranger du Courtemanche. I looked him up on the ol' internet. Did a ton of research. He's worth a bundle. Eight figures, the way I figure it, Prew. That's right. The Big One."

It's well past dark by the time Prewitt gets to his apartment. He walks to his only window and looks across the narrow street to the apartment buildings opposite while thinking about paying for Harvard.

Prewitt is excited to check out the "Rich French Asshole." He sits down, opens his laptop, and gets to it quickly, learning Mace was spot-on about the rich part and the long list of titles. The potential mark is Ranger Augustine Benedict du Courtemanche, Earl of Orleans, and Viscount of Blois. At one point in time, over a century ago, the Courtemanche family was one of the wealthiest in France.

The first results Prewitt finds also reference a boating accident that took the lives of Ranger's wife and their two young children. At the time, Ranger wasn't in France. He was vacationing with a mistress, the European news said. There are a lot of articles about it, comparing the current scandal to rumors of how the Courtemanche fortune was made back in the early 1300s. *Hmm.* Prewitt reads every word, and not because he is into gossip. It's while he's reading between the lines Prewitt's gut will make up its mind on whether this is the right kind of mark. A guy who cheats on his wife, friends, or anyone else who trusts him. A guy who has every advantage and takes more, stepping on all he can along the way. A guy who thinks he deserves separate rules from the others and certainly the less fortunate because, to him, they are less deserving. That's the only kind of guy Prewitt will con. Because guys like that cheat, and if you cheat, you're fair game for whatever might be coming. That's Prewitt's code. And it's important to him.

From the first time he ever conned anyone, the code is something he's held to. If you deserve it, you get taken. If not, you don't. Life and karma are identical twins separated at the big bang. Bonded. And they'll work toward the same purpose. That's dangerous juju. Besides, anyone can be a thief. But how many thieves can live with themselves? Prewitt always wondered about that. Many probably can. But Prewitt could never be just a thief, never had the stomach to do a decent person wrong. Hated it. Even as a kid in the streets. The bullies? They can suck on knuckles. The rest? Do unto others.

There is always the chance Ranger is a good guy. For Prewitt, it's seventy-thirty that with that kind of wealth comes that kind of jerk. And he's being nice with the odds. Just his experience. But there is always that chance. A good guy? Honest and hardworking, cares about people other than himself? A good guy is not a good mark for Prewitt.

After an hour of reading, it's clear this Frenchman is a real dirtbag. And his ancestors are even worse. Aristocratic arch criminals of some sort. Mixed up in a plot with the king of France that got a whole lot of people executed. Prewitt reads the words with wide eyes and, without thinking, tucks away some of the history that could be useful for a con. Then he learns Ranger and his two sisters are the last of the line. No surviving heirs. That boat accident. He reads more about it and Ranger's affair. Lots of pictures of Ranger with his mistress. Seems he didn't even try to hide it. Prewitt also discovers Ranger got into it with a wine exporter over the Courtemanche brand and was forced to sell vineyards after a drawn-out legal battle. He lost.

Going further back, Prewitt reads news articles about Ranger's top finishes at equestrian events in boarding school, then news about championships won in polo matches played when he was a young man. And at one time, Ranger paid the highest bid price ever for a team of ponies. The quote in the article read: "I wanted them, the price was irrelevant, they were the best."

Prewitt shifts his search criteria a bit and turns up some articles that reveal more about the scandal that kicked off the family history. He learns Ranger's ancestors came into their titles and money during the reign of King Philip in the 1300s. That's where it gets ugly. Historian after historian connects the Courtemanche family to the burning of members of the Knights Templar for heresy in 1307. The family made their fortune from it. A quick check-in with his gut, and Prewitt knows he'd have no problem working a con on this guy.

Prewitt begins sifting through an international database of auction sales. He discovers the Courtemanche family has bought and sold millions worth of art and artifacts. Though in the last half century, they have been selling more than buying. Ten years ago, a single chair from the original Thomas Chippendale workshop in London sold at Christie's for over $500,000.

Digging more, Prewitt learns in the generations immediately preceding Ranger Courtemanche, entire chunks of the family's massive landholdings had been sold off, too. *Must be sittin' on a lot of cash.* Prewitt will do more research on the Courtemanche assets when he's in France. After he meets this guy, he'll know just where the chinks in the armor are; then he'll work his way in until the caches of cash are revealed.

"Mace, you may have come through on this one," he says softly. *Imagine that.* A big fish Prewitt can hook and cook to put his son through college.

Prewitt keeps searching on the computer. He loves the detective work. It's just like his academic research. And as he is learning, his brain is fitting together pieces of a puzzle, testing them, shifting them, watching them as they form an image that swirls and spins and moves through time, watching the image become more and more clear, watching, until finally the image has stopped moving. It's finished, framed, pretty enough to hang on a wall. The con.

Prewitt goes outside, walks to the corner, and enters A Little Slice, the tiny, wood-paneled take-out pizza shop with pictures of Madonna and Don Mattingly hanging over the register. He orders two slices of mushroom and black olive pizza and eats them both while standing outside his apartment building. Prewitt waits outside another ten minutes, relishing the night air and the slight wind and the fact they feel worth relishing, a sign he has been in a flow state.

Once back inside his apartment, Prewitt continues reading for another hour, learning more about the family's wine business and the family tree all the way back to the 1300s.

Then he finds it. It's just a small paragraph toward the end of an article about Ranger's maternal grandparents and a wedding in 1907. But it mentions something Prewitt is looking for, that he's always looking for on any job. Something special for him. Hanging, almost as an afterthought in the second to last sentence of the paragraph, is the word jewels. "Though they haven't been seen worn in two centuries, the Courtemanche jewels have never publicly been sold," the sentence reads.

For a moment, his eyes lock in on the word, and his breath catches.

Prewitt googles "Courtemanche" and "jewels" together. A name pops up. Amarante du Courtemanche. There are two results. One is an *ArtNews* article on the painter François Boucher that lists Amarante du Courtemanche as one of the aristocrats who posed for a portrait. Prewitt writes down the artist's name and the title of the painting: *Lady Without Her Jewels*. The second result is from a more obscure art journal, *The Painter's Practice*. It, too, is an article about Boucher and the painting of Amarante. It includes a tiny picture, but it's hard for Prewitt to see details. The writer tells of a rumored exchange between the lady and her painter about the abundance of jewels she was wearing. "Take them off. Put them away," Boucher said to the lady. "It is you who is priceless."

"Priceless," Prewitt rolls his shoulder and flexes his tired fingers. Taking a deep breath, he lets his gaze adjust through his window to focus on the green branches outside.

But some things have a very clear price, like Harvard, or the airfare Prewitt needs to get to France, or the extra hands he'll need to pull off a con like the one he's got in mind. Mace will front the cash. And perhaps this caper will pay for Harvard. If there's money to be had, he'll get it. And if there are jewels, he'll find those, too, and keep just one for himself.

A moment of doubt hits Prewitt in his stomach like a small jolt of electricity that rises from his intestines to his heart.

He turns back to his computer screen and looks at an image of the Courtemanche castle in France. Prewitt has known more than a few con artists in his time, including the one who stung him sharp and taught him the most important lesson, don't trust, ever. But Prewitt also knows he's as good as any. Better. Just a little rusty right now. He closes the laptop. Soon he'll be meeting this Courtemanche family. And if Prewitt has his way, they'll be opening their cupboards and not just showing him the cheese but offering it up on a fancy plate.

7

Prewitt is wide awake with the sun. He needs a loan for the support payment he still owes Sharon, so he'll add that in when he asks for the plane ticket to France and the cash to get the con rolling. He sits at the kitchen counter and dials Mace.

"You're up early."

"This is good, Mace."

"I told you it was good. We on?"

"We're very on. I want to leave for France tonight."

"Great. Though I heard something last night," says Mace. "The word on the street is somebody's looking for you, and they're not selling cookies."

Prewitt remembers his neighbor Ed pointing at his jimmied door lock and telling him about the two guys who came by. Prewitt doesn't have a clue about who it could be. He only owes money to Mace, and he never ratted anyone out to the cops.

"I don't know who it would be. Maybe I'll leave today."

"Well, they know you. Yeah, best you get going before they catch up with you. I'll have Otto drop by with the cash you need in two hours. Go straight to the airport. You can't gut the big fish if you're in traction." Mace hangs up.

Prewitt wonders who would want to hurt him. Nearly every con or theft he's ever done has been flawless. He's only been busted by the cops once. The marriage killer. That job haunts his dreams, but it didn't leave him with any mortal enemies. Sharon doesn't want him hurt. Maybe her father does. Would Geoffrey go so far as to hire hit men? No way. He plays by different rules. Or does he?

Prewitt gets up from the kitchen counter, walks past the bed, and opens the sliding doors to the apartment's only closet. As Prewitt begins packing and selecting the right tools for the job, he realizes he won't get to see Josh again before he leaves town. He will be in France for weeks. And miss his graduation. Prewitt wasn't looking forward to another party at Geoffrey's estate on Long Island, but seeing Josh again, and Honey Hair . . . *It is what it is.* Time to go.

Prewitt makes a call from the cab on his way to the airport. Just when he thinks it will go to voicemail, Josh picks up.

"Hey, Dad." Josh sounds like he's expecting bad news.

"Hey, kid. Fun seeing you yesterday."

"You too. Is everything okay?"

"Yes, but some unexpected travel has come up for work."

Josh doesn't know about Prewitt's past. Or his criminality. He's been told some vague, near truths about Prewitt's employment. He knows he works for a New York businesswoman in the restaurant-ish industry, and he's her Jack of All Trades. Like a glorified gofer. He *is* Mace's gofer. She finds jobs, fronts the money, and he goes and gets meager profits. Working with Mace has been such a slither down the shit slide from where he used to be when he pulled cons that were complex and hit fat payoffs, which is why he feels more alive today than he has in a long while. Sweet Josh thinks everything his dad does is on the up and up. He doesn't know Johnny is his parole officer. He just thinks dad's best friend is a cop. Cool. It is cool. And it's also all Josh can ever know. Prewitt can't break another heart. One was enough to hate himself for a lifetime.

"Ms. Duncan is sending you on a trip? What, some kind of conference?"

"It's more like she's loaning my services to some clients of hers in France."

"Awesome."

"Remember when you went there with your grandmother and grandfather?"

"What, do you think I'd forget?"

Of course, Prewitt didn't think that. He just made the mistake he always makes, thinking he was speaking to his beautiful young boy. He wonders if he'll ever stop seeing Josh that way.

"Sorry, I know you didn't forget."

"I'd like to go back."

"Maybe we can go together."

"How long will you be there?"

"Not sure, but the thing is, I'm going to miss your graduation."

Josh is quiet for a moment, and the silence tugs on Prewitt's heart.

"I understand, Dad. I know you work hard. That you do the best you can. I know Mom and Grandfather don't always believe that, but I do. They just don't know what it's like to not have a bunch of money." Josh laughs. "I guess I don't either. But Mom says I have to get a student job on campus. Just a few hours a week, so it doesn't get in the way of studying. But she said I'm supposed to feel what it's like to have money I earned all by myself."

Prewitt loves the times when Josh shares things with him and pauses to savor this one.

"Okay, kid. I'm getting to the airport now. Congratulations in advance," Prewitt finally says.

"Thanks, Dad."

"Bye, Josh."

"Bye, Dad."

***

Prewitt steps out of the cab at Newark and gets his luggage from the trunk. As he passes through pre-check, something starts shifting in him. He is no longer a dad. Dad is being tucked away now. Settling into his middle seat on the Boeing 757, he is no longer some past-his-prime, down-on-his-luck New Yorker. That's leaving too. And by the time the aircraft has risen to cruising altitude, he is no longer Prewitt Patry. He is someone else. A persona. *The* persona. The perfectly formed character he's crafted over the last ten hours. The one that will move amongst the puzzle pieces as he sets them in place. He's breathing and blinking and seeing as the persona now. Soon he'll sleep. But he'll awaken in France, fully able to step off the plane, travel to Blois, then say hello to the unsuspecting Courtemanche clan and take them for the ride of their lives.

8

On the approach to Paris, when his back pain had gotten to be too much, Prewitt took the persona for a trial run and used fluent French to sweet talk a flight attendant into handing over a few doses worth of aspirin. Then he spoke perfect Italian as he made his way through the usual long lines of Charles De Gaulle customs.

As Prewitt makes his way through the airport exit, he is surprised to see a mustached man, sixty-ish years old, in a tailored suit holding a sign with PREWITT lettered on it. *Thanks, Mace.* Long and lanky, he stands in front of a classic dark red automobile. Prewitt places it as a late 1950s Facel Vega Excellence.

"Hello, my name is Boniface," says the man in dripping French-accented English as he reaches out and shakes Prewitt's hand. Boniface looks Prewitt over. "Just like Mace described you. Shall we?"

Prewitt nods, and Boniface places Prewitt's bags in the truck. They get into the car, and Boniface starts up the engine.

"Mace asked that I provide a place for you to stay tonight."

"Thank you."

"And to help you out, whatever you need. I have good people."

Prewitt notes the perfectly manicured fingernails and the nicely waxed ends of Boniface's mustache. "So, what's your uh, area of expertise?" says Prewitt.

Boniface looks over his shoulder then pulls out into traffic. "The usual shit."

Soon Boniface exits the A1 onto the streets of Paris, which are busy with cars, buses, bikes, walkers, and pets on leashes. The sun is setting, and its light shines on the pale limestone buildings, the black wrought iron balconies, and their distinctive blue-gray slate roof lines, giving everything that warm glow Prewitt loves in the evening. He feels comforted by the noble beauty of it.

Prewitt hears a ring tone of "She Works Hard For The Money," by Donna Summer and looks over to see Boniface take a hand off the wheel, pull his cell phone from his jacket pocket, and answer. He hears a woman's voice, speaking loudly in accented French for a while.

"I said I would work on myself. I've just been busy lately," Boniface says. "My mother was sick."

Boniface listens.

"No, the other one. But I have your list, and I'm actually with my therapist right now. A new one. American expat," Boniface says as he stops at a red traffic light. "He says your feelings are valid, but mine are, too." Boniface looks to Prewitt expectantly and holds the phone out, nodding. The light turns green.

Prewitt says in English, "Yes, your feelings are valid."

Boniface shakes his head disapprovingly.

Prewitt tries again, "I mean, his feelings are valid."

Boniface nods and brings the phone back to his ear. "He said it. And he's a doctor."

The female voice speaks loudly again. Then there is silence.

Boniface slides the phone back in his pocket and puts both hands back on the wheel. He makes a few turns, driving in silence, then, "I've been dumped."

"I'm sorry," Prewitt says.

"You should be. You just ended my relationship."

"How long have you known her?" Prewitt asks.

"Doesn't matter. When the lightning bolt strikes, it could be a week, a year. It doesn't matter; when it's real, it's love."

"So, how long was it?"

"Two weeks. And she's Spanish, so maybe I dodged a bullet."

Boniface guides the Excellence along the residential streets of the 3rd arrondissement. Finally, they ease into a parking spot.

"Here we are," Boniface says.

Prewitt looks out from the car to a classic Paris apartment building. It's a nice one with ornate balconies holding potted geraniums. The mansard roofline has large dormers and big windows. He knows the rent on one of these places wouldn't come cheap even if they weren't in the wealthiest part of the city. Boniface is already heading toward the blue-painted front door, leaving Prewitt to gather his suitcases.

"Come on, Prewitt. You can meet everyone."

They climb stairs to the second-floor apartment that opens onto a large foyer. Light streams in through large windows. There are several exotic-looking plants and two people who are either together or about to be. The woman is leaning against a marble topped credenza. She's tall and all legs that stretch out of her short black dress. The man twirls a section of her wavy red hair around his finger. Neither of them seems startled by Boniface and Prewitt coming in on their private moment. The man kisses the woman on the lips before they turn.

"Bonsoir, Boniface," she says with an air kiss.

"Bonsoir, Kat, this is my friend."

Prewitt gives her an air kiss as well. "Bonsoir."

"I am Benny," the man says. He wears several gold necklaces, their large links nestled into his chest hair. Benny is dark-skinned, fit, and very handsome.

Prewitt introduces himself in flawless French.

"Follow me," Boniface yells as he disappears down a long hallway. Kat and Benny return to each other.

Prewitt pushes his two suitcases next to a white leather couch as out of the way as he can manage and follows Boniface down the hallway toward the sound of many voices.

"Bonsoir, bonsoir!" everyone calls out as Prewitt emerges into a kitchen crammed with bodies. The counter is covered in bottles of wine and liquor. A gleaming white gift box sits in the center of the mess, flouncy ribbons streaming over the sides.

"Someone's birthday?" Prewitt says. No one answers.

Boniface greets his way through a crowd that, to Prewitt, looks like a circus troupe just off work and still in costume. One woman wears a silver sequined bodysuit. Another looks naked under an oversized silk suit jacket with wide blue and red stripes. He is handed a glass of wine from a petite woman in a black leotard hemmed with silver tassels at every seam. She has on a matching hat. Prewitt accepts graciously.

Prewitt looks beyond the kitchen to a large living room. In between a few chairs and couches, at least two dozen people are engaged in conversations.

"Prewitt," Boniface walks out of the kitchen and into a knot of guests, "Here are Michel and Louis." Michel is tan, clean-shaven, and wearing a slate blue suit with a white shirt, open at the neck. With hair a perfectly coiffed airplane wing of platinum blond, he looks like a swimsuit model turned investment banker. The guy next to him, Louis, might be his brother, Prewitt muses. There is enough of a resemblance. But Louis looks like he just came from the gym. Buzz cut hair. He's kitted out in track pants, trainers and a sweatshirt with the sleeves cut off, revealing both arms completely covered in colorful flash tattoos. And he's big, someone you'd want with you in a bar fight, Prewitt thinks.

"Bonsoir, Michel and Louis. Great to meet you."

Michel steps forward to shake Prewitt's hand. "American, yeah," he says in English. "I want to practice my English. So, Prewitt, how am I doing? Not a trace of French accent, no?"

"You sound like Pepe le Pew," Louis says, chuckling.

"Shut up," says Michel.

Louis reaches up and goes for Michel's hair.

"Not the hair," yells Michel, pushing Louis's hands away.

Louis keeps swiping at the now messy locks, his arms a swirl of muscles and color.

"Not the hair, we had an agreement," Michel yells again, tackling him to the ground.

The tussle quickly ends as Michel stands and walks to the mirror. "I'm telling grandma," he says, deadly serious and pouting.

"Prewitt, this is Lorelei." Boniface says as if nothing happened, gesturing to the young woman approaching.

"Bonsoir," Lorelei says with a beautiful smile. Fit and wearing a body-hugging green dress, she looks barely in her twenties. "So, this is the home plant guy?"

"No, I'm not—"

Boniface interrupts him. "*Aime tes Plantes* will be here tomorrow, Lorelei."

Farthest from the kitchen, a husky man wearing a powdered wig who looks at least ten years older than Prewitt is giving what sounds like a political speech. As the man concludes, the two women closest to him turn from their conversation to applaud, and the man takes a deep bow. Prewitt does nothing, but then, feeling eyes on him, puts his glass of wine on the mantel to clap. A few more guests join in.

"That's Duke Wellington," Boniface says to Prewitt. "He's just done an excerpt from the four-hour Lloyd George budget speech to Parliament. He has the whole thing memorized." When Boniface sees the skeptical look on Prewitt's face, he clarifies, "according to him."

Prewitt meets eyes with Duke Wellington and gives him a nod which Duke returns before launching into more. Prewitt is tired from traveling but entertained by the energy here with Boniface's friends. It's refreshing to see professionals, which Prewitt has no doubt every single one of these people are. And he will need many of them for the con.

After a few more introductions, Boniface has led Prewitt full circle and back to the kitchen. "I must run out, Prewitt," Boniface says, and shakes Prewitt's hand. He heads into the hallway. "Have fun!" he yells.

After picking up a second glass of red wine from the kitchen, Prewitt makes his way back to the living room and leans against the wall to just . . . be. *Step one down. I'm here.* He takes a sip, looks around, and takes in the people, admiring their glee, their in-the-moment *joie de vivre.* It's a far cry from the life Prewitt has been living. And worlds away from anything he saw as a kid. It's what Prewitt always thinks about when he witnesses adults at play. And it's one of the reasons he likes living in a city. There's more of it.

Prewitt remembers five different foster homes before turning eighteen. He'd seen violence. Felt it. And he stole like the rest of the scrappy little wolves. How else do you eat? By sixteen, he'd become quite good at it. But then life settled a bit for Prewitt. A new foster home with a kind, older woman and her seven other kids, who had given him a bed and hot meals for the last two years of his childhood. Finally, he'd had a moment to breathe. Prewitt knows many of the people at this party would understand his story or have a similar one to tell. Maybe that's why he feels at home too.

Lorelei, the handsome young woman in the green dress, approaches again, her eyes locked on his. Her short dark hair shows off toned shoulders and strong, lithe arms.

As she stops in front of him, she stares another moment. Then Lorelei puts her hand around his arm and squeezes his bicep. "Very nice," she says and smiles with mischief.

9

Prewitt wakes up on the couch, where he remembers closing his eyes and dozing off as two of the party's lingerers were chatting across from him. He'd wanted to stay up later to shake off some of the jet lag, but three glasses of red wine put him down like a baby with a pacifier. He sits up and winces at the slight headache, more blame to the red wine, but at least his sciatica has let up a bit. Prewitt walks down the hallway into the kitchen and is surprised to find it spotless. But the gift-wrapped box is still on the kitchen table. Prewitt opens the refrigerator and takes out a mini bottle of orange juice. Drinking, he looks into the living room. Not a throw pillow out of place.

Prewitt pulls his phone from his pocket – 8:30 a.m. in Paris. Good. Time to get moving. There's research to be done now that he's on French soil. Prewitt walks back into the hallway. He eases doors open and finds several empty bedrooms. The beds are all made. He finds the master at the end of the house. It, too, is empty. Prewitt takes a quick shower and puts on a clean shirt. Then he puts his suitcases by the front door and sits down on the nearby couch to call Boniface. His butt has barely touched the upholstery when the front door opens, and a young couple comes in with their own suitcases. Prewitt can tell they are the homeowners. The woman screams.

"What the fuck are you doing in our house?" the man yells at Prewitt.

Oh shit.

"Answer me, you fucker!"

Prewitt's mind whips back to the unwrapped gift box, the question from Lorelei asking if he was the home plant guy. Boniface's response that it was scheduled for the next day. *Ah, hilarious, guys.*

Calmly, Prewitt responds in perfect French he's glad they have returned home safely. He explains that they had signed up for the gold level of the home plant care service, Love Your Plants, of which he is the owner. The building's manager let him in.

"*Aime tes Plantes,*" Prewitt repeats as he caresses a leaf of the nearest monstera plant and murmurs to it affectionately. Then he tells them if they give him the names of three more friends and neighbors, they will have a credit on their account for two free care visits from Aime tes Plantes the next time they go out of town.

The couple stares at him. Then they turn to each other and ask which of them signed up for plant care. Prewitt listens to them bicker until the woman goes on what Prewitt assumes is a quick valuables check then returns as Prewitt is rifling through the pages of his notebook, "Yes, here is the name: Estel Brinkley. Not you?" They shake their heads. "She's a new client. The manager must have let me into the wrong apartment. I was supposed to water Estel Brinkley's plants. This took me two hours."

"Why is there luggage here?" the woman asks.

"Leaving straight from here to the airport, my first vacation in a year. I'll send my assistant to Estel's plants."

"Can we still keep the gift?" she says.

"Yes, please."

"Why, thank you."

"You're welcome."

According to the woman, there are two handmade mugs and a new French press in the box on the kitchen table with a card saying, "Thank you for your business."

"Where are you going on vacation?"

"Greece."

"Very nice."

"So I've heard."

Thirty minutes later, after being treated to a fresh coffee from the new French press, gathering the names of six friends and neighbors who should become clients of Aime tes Plantes and telling them more than they could ever want to know about their fiddle-leaf fig tree and monstera deliciosa plants, Prewitt gives air kisses at the door and promises to visit the next time he is in the neighborhood.

When Prewitt gets outside, he sees Boniface's car is still parked in its spot. Along with a ticket, there is the PREWITT sign Boniface was holding at the airport. Prewitt pulls it out from under the wiper blade and turns it over. It reads: "Use the car!"

Prewitt sees the keys are on the floorboard. Is the Vega hot? Might be. The last thing Prewitt needs is to get pulled over by the Paris police on his first day in France. He folds the sign and puts it in his jacket pocket, then opens the map app on his phone, grabs his suitcases, and rolls off in the direction of the nearest library.

10

Prewitt lucks into one of the last available desks at the Bibliothèque Kandinsky, in the modern glass Centre Pompidou building. With his suitcases at his feet, he pulls out his laptop, connects to the free Wi-Fi, and books a few nights at the cheapest hotel he can find. He looks for a rental car agency within walking distance and chooses a standard car.

Next, Prewitt connects to the library server, which allows him access to records from all over France: real estate files, police blotters, obituaries. Though he can retain everything he reads, Prewitt makes notes in his Moleskine notebook so it can be used as a prop in the con. It had been a high school teacher who'd informed him of how rare his photographic memory was. Mr. Malkin, the history lover from Israel who plucked Prewitt from the shit life he'd known. Mr. Malkin saw past the same clothes worn day after day, and the wounded indifference and noticed all the books Prewitt read in class about kings and knights and castles revealed an actual person, not a to-be-forgotten loser floating past the eyes of the rest of the burnt-out teachers who hated any student who made them realize how tired and overworked they were. Mr. Malkin didn't scold Prewitt for reading Rosemary Sutcliff's *Sword at Sunset* in class. Instead, he handed him *The History of the Kings of Britain* one day and asked Prewitt to tell him what he thought. It was Mr. Malkin who, in a saint-like intervention that followed the day after throwing Prewitt up against the lockers and threatening to turn Prewitt's lights out because Prewitt had, moments earlier, picked a fight with the very large football monster Brad Saul after Brad had called Prewitt a "gear," a fight Prewitt was winning, guided Prewitt to an exit ramp off shit street Prewitt never knew was there. That next day when Mr. Malkin insisted Prewitt sign up to take the SAT and the ACT, and paid him to do it, Prewitt didn't understand the gift as anything more than idealistic teacher bullshit. No one cared about him. When the tests came back aced, and Mr. Malkin told Prewitt he could have a good life, Prewitt thought Mr. Malkin was insane. Good life? What the hell does that even mean? But then Mr. Malkin reached out to a friend at Carnegie Mellon, and Prewitt was accepted on scholarship, with room and board. And Mr. Malkin had talked to him for hours over weekends and turned on a lamp and showed Prewitt a map of a life that ends not in jail but in a life. And Prewitt had begun to listen.

Prewitt returns to his research and finds Courtemanche real estate records. They only have one property presently, Chateau Loir-et-Cher. In Blois, France. The heart of the Loire Valley. He reads the deed. The only name listed is Ranger's. Prewitt writes the address down in his notebook.

Next, he does a search on the property address. A local news article with public notifications of suits filed with the court comes up. The address of the Blois property plus the words: "parcel 16. Ownership Dispute, R. Courtemanche." Ranger du Courtemanche seems to be suing someone over a patch of land.

Next, Prewitt searches for Ranger in the community rosters. He's not in any local clubs or on any committees. He is not listed on any boards. Prewitt can't even find a picture of the guy more recent than the early 1980s. He searches for both sisters' names but finds no photos or articles about any of them since the boating accident and scandal forty years ago. It seems the family is not involved in society in any public way.

Prewitt continues his search through the library records for hits on names of the Courtemanche family members from the past. He finds the same results for Amarante, the Courtemanche who supposedly had the jewels a few hundred years ago and who is the subject of that Boucher painting from 1745. He decides he wants to see a better picture of it. He jots down the call number and makes his way to the reference desk.

"Bonjour, mademoiselle, your help please?" Prewitt slides the slip of paper torn from his notebook across the desk.

The librarian, looking late thirties with a tidy ponytail and a modest white blouse buttoned high on her small frame, smiles up at him. She's cute. With kind eyes. *Too kind.* And no ring on her finger. Prewitt can imagine the string of non-deserving dickheads she's loved more than she should have. Or maybe it's just one big dickhead. He smiles back as she settles her reading glasses onto her nose and picks up the paper. "A large format art book. Heritage collection. Just wait here a moment."

She disappears into the stacks behind the desk and, in less than a minute, is back with a book three inches thick. Prewitt thanks her. Another smile. Women in France are so far being friendly to Prewitt. It's not lost on him "the persona" is more confident than the guy he's been of late. Prewitt opens the book right there on the desk.

He finds the page numbers for Boucher in the index, and soon he and the librarian are looking upon Amarante's portrait. The painting is almost angelic in its harsh light, soft curving lines, and gentle color palette. True to the Rococo style, Amarante is depicted realistically, reclining on a couch in a turquoise gown festooned with bows. She holds an open book in one hand. Her other arm is draped casually off the edge of the couch. Her gaze is vacant and falls somewhere off to the painter's left. Though interested in the jewels, as Prewitt scans the painting, he finds himself thinking about other things. Was this painted in the artist's studio or the Courtemanche castle? What time of day was it with light coming in like that? What was the season? Prewitt wonders how

Amarante was feeling in that moment, or on that day, or even that year. Was she happy? He looks closely at her face. She's giving nothing away.

Prewitt looks at Amarante's ears, her neck, and her wrists. Naked. He looks around the portrait. Below her hand is a small chest of drawers. The top drawer is open several inches, and there is a dark velvet cloth draped over the lip of the drawer. Inside the drawer are several daubs of paint in jeweled tones. The artist has added a few tiny spots of white paint, the jewels catching the light. *There you are.*

"Are you planning to see the original work by Boucher?" asks the librarian. "I could look up the museum information?"

"Perhaps," Prewitt responds. "Though I am more interested in his subject."

"May I?" The librarian turns the book around and reads the description. "Amarante du Courtemanche. I believe there may still be surviving members of the family in France."

"I believe you are right. I'm studying the historic ones."

"Are you a teacher?" asks the librarian.

"A writer, actually." Prewitt, without thinking, deploys his own charming smile.

She blushes slightly. "That's exciting. I'd be happy to continue to assist."

Oh, this one is very sweet. A real giver, Prewitt thinks, as he notices an instinct to protect her. From what? *All of it.*

She turns over the slip of paper. "If you leave your email address, I can search a bit and contact you if I find more records of historic Courtemanches?"

Prewitt writes down the address of his personal email account. "That would be very kind of you, mademoiselle. Anything from 1300 on, as well as any of their standout moments, connections to historical figures, scandals, the juicy bits of history."

She smiles again. "I'll see what I can find."

"Thank you."

"Of course."

"You're very kind," Prewitt says, meaning it.

The librarian lingers just a moment, then turns her attention to another patron who has just approached the desk.

Prewitt returns to his computer and opens Photoshop. He sees the librarian steal glances in his direction from time to time as he goes to work forging one more ID for the con.

The next few hours pass quickly as Prewitt stops by a local copy shop and, using the work he saved to a thumb drive, prints and laminates his new ID. He drops his bags in his hotel room, picks up his rental Peugeot, and drives out of Paris on the A10, heading toward the Loire Valley.

While he has never gone all the way down the rabbit hole of rare and valuable wine, Prewitt knows something about the history of viticulture in France. It had been just a year before the Reckoning when Prewitt and Honey Hair had a Paris getaway so soaked with love it's still dripping everywhere he looks. And in a rare free moment between any-hour-of-the-day hotel room lovemaking and their exploration of all the cozy off-the-beaten-path shops, cafes, or two-meter wide streets like the Rue de Venise, where he took Honey Hair so he could kiss her while they leaned against the remains of one of the oldest fountains in Paris, Prewitt had read a great book about the Loire Valley and it being its own special place for wine. Maybe not as fabled as Bordeaux, but the wines of Sancerre in the Loire are as tasty as they are pricey, the river land's limestone-rich soil producing some of the most complex sauvignon blanc flavors in the world. Juxtaposing the emotion of that trip with this one? Prewitt wants to gag, but who said life was perfect? No one. No one told Prewitt life would even be any good at all until Mr. Malkin and his college sales pitch, or until Honey Hair's love turned the world technicolor for a while. Prewitt got lucky, that's all. And he got a son out of it, too, which makes him lucky for life.

His research back in New York revealed the Courtemanche family estates used to include hundreds of hectares of mature Loire Valley vines. Prewitt can only imagine the valuable bottles Ranger has in the dank cellars of the castle. The family home, Chateau Loir-et-Cher, is the largest of almost a dozen castles in the area. The southern estate boundary borders the Loire River for a kilometer.

The drive from Paris is two hours, and Prewitt soaks in every sight and every breath of the fresh air. Marveling at the old homes with their stone walls, steeply pitched roofs, and the overgrowth lining the roads of the countryside, Prewitt wonders to himself what his life would have been if he'd been born in one of these charming farmhouses nestled in the hills, a young farm boy growing up in the same house his grandparents built. Maybe they'd have lived there with him and his parents.

When Prewitt arrives at the address and makes the turn for the driveway, the Courtemanche chateau comes into view. He stops the Peugeot and gapes out the window. He read about it and saw some photos. But *holy shit. This castle is a beast.*

The structure rises from the center of the tree-lined drive like Versailles' pretty little sister, the main chateau shimmering like a soft mirage of white limestone in the late morning light. From each side, wings and outbuildings stand like sentinels.

Prewitt continues down the drive cobbled with limestone, studies the massive sugar maples that line the drive, and notes they must be more than 250 years old. More silent spectators of life. Many have branches no arborist would let grow so wildly. But Prewitt likes the trees just as they are. He thinks of the 300-year-old English Elm in the north corner of Washington Square Park in his beloved Manhattan. *Traitors swung from that sucker during the Revolution. It watched gangsters truck bootlegged hooch from the East River docks during Prohibition, and now it sees us with our backpacks and motor scooters and iPhone selfies.* Prewitt wonders what these trees have witnessed.

Prewitt drives through a massive iron gate. He notices, in the deep black of wrought iron, more than a few areas of rust among the detailed finials and dramatic crests in the center. Prewitt drives past the first of the buildings that flank the central garden in front of the castle. The limestone cobbles have run out, and now the Peugeot crunches gravel under its tires. Prewitt sees the central garden is a field of grass with a plinth in the center that, at one time, would have held a sculpture or fountain. Now it's just something the mowing crew has to dodge.

He parks right in front of the main doors, gets out of the Peugeot, walks up the stairs, and knocks. A butler-type in a black suit opens one of the doors. He is slight of build with dyed black hair, slicked back, and large ears. Prewitt puts him in his late fifties, though his face looks boyish.

"Bonjour, monsieur," says the butler, smiling kindly.

"Bonjour."

"How may I help?"

"I am Prewitt Marcellus, and I am with the *Santa Alleanza*." He flashes his new ID. The butler's eyebrows rise in concern. "That's the Vatican's intelligence service. It is important I speak with Ranger du Courtemanche."

The butler begins to wring his hands. Prewitt notes the lack of stoicism he'd normally expect from a butler. "Is it urgent?"

"Very."

"Oh dear," he says. "Please follow me." The butler leaves the door open after Prewitt steps in. But then he notices, rushes to push it shut, and starts quickly down the central hallway of the castle. He looks back at Prewitt a couple of times, his nervous expression growing. As Prewitt follows, he takes in the white limestone flooring with black marble insets in a harlequin pattern. They pass Italianate columns. Between each is either an opening to a room or a piece of art, mostly portraits, *perhaps long-dead Courtemanches*. Soon there's a suit of armor holding a shield with the coat of arms.

The rooms Prewitt glimpses as he follows behind the fast-moving butler are huge. Though in some, the furnishings seem sparse. He peeks into a sitting room with ugly mauve damask wallpaper and one lonely side chair. There is a library with half-empty shelves. Another room has several faded patterned rugs scattered across the floor, an upright piano, and a slouchy couch with a guitar leaning against it.

The hall intersects another, and the butler turns right. There are upholstered chairs every fifteen feet, and the wall opposite is full of windows. Prewitt notices a plastic bucket half full of dirty water sitting under what must be a leaky spot in the roof.

Eventually, the butler stops at an oak door and opens it outward.

"The Earl du Courtemanche is at the pool, monsieur."

Prewitt hesitates.

"Right out there, monsieur," the butler says, pointing a slightly shaking hand.

Prewitt steps through the door, which the butler shuts behind him. Prewitt heads down the stone stairs in front of him and toward a hedge garden and the sound of a splash.

Time to shine.

11

After Prewitt steps off the last of the stone steps onto a gravel path, he stops to look back at the castle through overgrown lilacs. The stone walls, with their clumps of moss and lichens, give the manor an ancient grayish permanence Prewitt finds alluring. More giant trees, unpruned, range about the property. He follows them, scanning out to the Loire River in the distance. At Prewitt's feet, boxwoods make a formal hedge along the path, and one huge cement urn overflows with ivy.

Prewitt continues down the gravel path until he comes to an opening in the hedges. He looks through to a rectangular, in-ground swimming pool surrounded by cement and white, plastic lawn furniture dating from the 1980s. It's here that Prewitt finds the Courtemanche siblings passing what has become a bright sunny day.

The fact that they're not expecting anyone gives Prewitt a moment to spy before being noticed. Closest to Prewitt is one of the sisters, reading a magazine, tucked as far back as she can get into the shade of a red patio umbrella. Her face is hidden by a massive white hat and Audrey Hepburn sunglasses. Her white linen suit is straight out of a vintage Hollywood film. The bare hands, bare feet, and few inches of neck that he can see are pale and thin.

Over by the rose bushes lining the far side of the pool, Prewitt sees a man who must be Ranger. And Ranger is pretty much what Prewitt expected. Gray hair pushed back, and he's wearing a light blue suit with a crisp white shirt underneath, topped with an ascot. No socks, feet clad in driving loafers. The same look Prewitt has seen in pictures of Prince Charles back in the day. Ranger seems about the same age as the now king, too, a bit past seventy and just as debonaire. Ranger reaches into the roses, plucks off a wilted bud, and drops it to the ground. He goes in for another.

Then Ranger is hit from behind with a splash of water.

"Amelie! Merde!" he yells, as he turns to the pool.

A hedge guards Prewitt's view of the far end of the pool, but he now sees a human shape under the water's surface, swimming toward the shallows. Then a woman emerges, water sluicing off her naked body. She climbs out slowly, laughing. *Sister number two.* With a wide smile, she looks Prewitt right in the eyes.

Prewitt blinks. Is it the sun playing tricks, or is a soaking wet, statuesque, nude woman staring at him? He looks at the other sister, nose in her book. He looks at Ranger, wiping the pool water off his pants. Apparently, this one swims naked regularly.

"Ranger, a person is here," she finally says as she saunters to a chaise lounge and retrieves a towel. She keeps her eyes locked on Prewitt.

Ranger has turned his attention back to the rose bushes again, but he squints in Prewitt's direction.

"Really? Where? I see no one, Amelie."

Amelie. Then the clothed one is Pensee.

"Oh? Look again," says Amelie. "Someone is definitely here."

"Is it Cary Grant?" Pensee says, looking over her magazine at Prewitt. "He looks like Cary Grant."

Prewitt watches Amelie, casually drying her legs. She wraps the towel around herself with a smile that he takes to mean she's doing it for his sake.

"I don't think so," Amelie says to her sister. "Sorry."

"Can I help you?" she asks Prewitt.

"Prewitt Marcellus from the—"

"Someone *is* here!" Ranger, finally seeing Prewitt, bounds around the edge of the pool like a crane, his thin, long body striding toward the stairs. "Monsieur, what is your business?"

Now that Ranger has finally engaged, Prewitt watches Amelie spread the towel out on the chaise lounge and lay down on her front, one arm hanging off the chair, fingers grazing the ground.

Prewitt thinks of the portrait of Amarante du Courtemanche, the casual drape of her white fingers over the edge of the couch, just inches from the jewels peeking out from the drawer. Fast forward 300 years. Prewitt realizes he is looking at the last branches of the du Courtemanche family tree. Three flush siblings, sunning it up in the backyard of their castle.

"Bonjour, Earl du Courtemanche, official business of the Vatican." Prewitt says. He extends his card. "I am Prewitt Marcellus, and I am with the Santa Alleanza."

"Oh . . . ? Oh! Santa Alleanza, the Vatican intelligence service?"

"Yes."

"You come unannounced, monsieur."

"I do."

"Is it important?"

"It is."

"Too important to call ahead?"

"I didn't want to use the phone."

Ranger considers this.

"Fine." Ranger glances at Amelie's bare butt then, seeming more annoyed than mortified, marches toward Prewitt, yelling, "Bertrand, show this man to—ow!"

Ranger has stubbed his toe on something decorating the entrance to the pool area. Prewitt looks down and sees an antique bronze diving helmet.

"That looks real."

"Of course it's real. It was Simone's," Ranger says.

"Who is Simone?"

"Jacques's wife."

"You don't mean Jacques Cousteau?"

"Who else would I be speaking of?" Ranger changes the subject. "Have Bertrand show you to the blue salon." He heads off toward the far wing of the chateau.

Prewitt looks around. Bertrand, the butler, is not there. Prewitt retraces his steps back into the castle and encounters Bertrand waiting nervously in the main hallway.

"Earl du Courtemanche would like to see me in the blue salon."

Bertrand shows Prewitt into the receiving room with the blue damask wallpaper. "Something to drink?"

"Water is fine, thank you."

Bertrand hustles out.

While waiting for Ranger, Prewitt looks around. In a window, a pair of faded upholstered chairs flank a marble-topped table. Two couches center the room with an ebony coffee table between them. The couches are Le Corbusier, twentieth-century modern. The table is just old.

But it all kind of looks shabby. A few pictures hang here and there, original oils, but nothing exceptional about them. And there is a very cheap floor lamp next to the window. Even the designer couches look like they belong at a garage sale. Prewitt is put off by the lack of taste and can't help but judge the disregard for the castle's upkeep.

Bertrand returns and hands Prewitt a glass of water, stares at him nervously, then leaves without a word. Prewitt takes a sip then looks around for a place to put the glass down. There are no coasters.

Soon Bertrand is back through a different door, announcing "Ranger Augustine Benedict du Courtemanche, Earl of Orleans and Viscount of Blois." Ranger comes in as Bertrand leaves.

"Now, what is your name again?"

Learning how to be a con artist after being conned by Standish was like taking a 400-level course without bothering with the prerequisites. And Prewitt was smart enough and angry enough to hit the ground running. He got what he could from what Standish had done to him, by then realizing Standish had been doing it to others. He tried his hand, teamed up a few times, found his footing, then augmented it all with his own set of rules. But keeping as much of your true self in the persona as possible, that was all the professor. "Prewitt Marcellus."

"And you barge into my home like you are somehow welcome? Into our private back garden?"

"I'm sorry about that. The butler—"

"*Va te faire foutre.* Oh, I'm sure you're very sorry. Why are you bothering us? Here for a donation?"

"I'm not here for a donation."

"Then what the hell do you want?"

Ranger strides over to one of the couches and perches on its worn armrest. "Go on then. Or did you forget why you came?"

Prewitt does a few short laps in front of the fireplace as if pacing will help him get it out. "We have long kept watch over the important families in France. And maintaining our protocols is essential. To that end, there are questions I must ask." Prewitt whips out his Moleskine notebook.

"What kind of questions?"

Prewitt bends over and peers up inside the fireplace as if looking for something. Prewitt clicks a pen against the notebook several times. "Have you been followed any time in the past two weeks?"

"Pardon me?"

"Have you?"

"Why is the Vatican asking if I've been followed?"

"Please answer."

"No."

"Has there been suspicious activity here at your home? Any break-ins?"

"No."

"Unusual calls?"

"No."

Prewitt makes a note in the notebook.

"Has something happened you're not telling me?" says Ranger.

"I am not at liberty to say."

"Why not?"

"Have you recently left the country?"

"No!"

"You've not left the country in the last two weeks?"

"Did you not hear me the first time? No!"

Why is he lying about that?

"What is this about, dammit?"

"We are still gathering information. I don't have the authority to share yet with you, Earl du Courtemanche. So as not to alarm you."

"Not to alarm me? What the hell do you think your questions are doing?" A look of satisfaction comes over Ranger's face. He points a thin finger at Prewitt. "Duran sent you."

"Duran?"

"My neighbor. You're here because of the lawsuit. The property."

"I do not know Monsieur Duran."

"Bullshit."

"I am with the Santa Alleanza. We don't care about lawsuits. Please make note of anything suspicious. I will return in a few days." Prewitt nods and turns to the door, tucking his Moleskine back in his jacket pocket.

"Wait."

But Prewitt heads to the door.

"Don't walk away from me."

Prewitt continues to the door.

"Stop, monsieur. Get back here. Do not walk away from me."

Prewitt has already let himself out of the salon and is heading down the hallway to the front door. Ranger hastily follows. "Monsieur!" he calls out.

Prewitt walks back to him. "Earl du Courtemanche, I must leave. Just make a note if anything happens between now and then. You have my card."

***

As he drives away, Prewitt feels satisfied. The hook has been set. Ranger was rattled, and that's all that was needed. The fact he was so prickish only deepened Prewitt's confidence; this is his kind of mark. Reeling in this marlin will be a simple, systematic turning of the handle, one crank at a time. Prewitt's moves have always been smooth and assured. This will be no different. He'll keep turning, the water flowing past his line, until all that's left to do is lift the tip of the rod and watch his prize rise right up out of the water.

Driving past more old trees along the road, he relaxes into a hopeful calm. It feels good to be back at something this big and this worthy of his talents. He breathes in the country air, loving the smell.

Prewitt's thoughts turn to the sisters at the pool. What was the story with those two? Especially the naked one. Odd ducks, for sure. *The richer they are . . .* Prewitt leans back and pushes the Peugeot a bit faster. As he lowers both windows, the warm wind ruffles his hair. And as the breeze whisks past his arms and face, he feels like he's flying.

12

That afternoon, Prewitt finds Boniface in the Place Saint-Sulpice, drinking espresso at a little metal table in a square buzzing with people. A server removes plates from what looks to have been a massive lunch. Prewitt sits across from Boniface and compliments him on the plant guy prank. Boniface smiles, takes out a toothpick, and casually works it in what seems more like a habit than the need to unstick something.

"But she is a gorgeous car, no?" Boniface says a few moments later, seemingly bummed Prewitt hadn't risked driving the Vega Excellence around Paris.

"Yes, Boniface, but I'll stick with the Peugeot," says Prewitt, now sipping his own very good espresso.

"Urgh," Boniface mimes being ill. "Peugeot is a wife. But the Excellence is a mistress."

"What will it cost to employ your team?" Prewitt says, getting down to it.

"We are professionals, Prewitt. We provide Excellence work, not Peugeot work."

"Give me a number."

"Many dollars."

"American?"

"Sure . . ."

"A number please?"

"Twenty-two thousand up front, recouped. The dollar is weak right now. And twenty percent."

Prewitt knows the twenty percent is in line with non-Peugeot work. And it's what he expected.

"Oui?" says Boniface.

"Oui."

Prewitt takes a quick look in an envelope with the stack of bills Mace staked him with, then hands a good chunk of it to Boniface.

Boniface slides it into his linen jacket. "We're worth every penny."

"Mace vouched for you."

Boniface eyes Prewitt. "You know you can't trust her, yes?"

"Thieves. No honor. I know all about it."

"Except for me." Boniface stands from the café table, still noodling with the toothpick. "Okay, I am off to tell the team."

"Can you get them together today? We'll go over the first steps."

"Sure," Boniface waves to the short woman clearing a nearby table. She waves back, and Prewitt recognizes her as the one wearing the black tasseled outfit at the party.

"Your meal is on me. I have a tab," says Boniface as he walks off.

Prewitt watches him go, then turns to the tasseled woman. She is smiling at Prewitt. He thinks about his next steps. No time to eat here. He'll return to his hotel and get Boniface a working list of the skills he needs for the con. Prewitt stands to leave and smiles back at the server, wondering if she'll be in on the job. He's looking forward to seeing Boniface's colorful troupe again. And he's looking forward to watching the parts of the machine he has dreamed up come together and start moving.

The sun is dipping behind the buildings when Prewitt, drinking a coffee outside the patisserie on the corner, gets a text from Boniface with an address. He looks it up on his map app. It's right off the Bonne

Nouvelle stop of the Balard Metro line. He walks a few blocks and takes the train.

Soon Prewitt is standing on a street corner dominated by a restaurant, Chez Jeannette. The place has huge windows and a bold red awning. He double-checks the address and walks through the door, straight into Lorelei, who is taking off a server's apron.

"Howdy, house plant guy!" she says in English as she squeezes his arm again. Then she laughs. "We're in the back. Follow me."

The bustling restaurant has a retro vibe from its Formica-topped bar and diner-style booths. Lorelei walks through the dining area, smiling and greeting customers. They pass into the kitchen briefly before taking a right turn into a private room with a big family-style table. Boniface and others Prewitt remembers from the party greet him as they pass around plates of salade Niçoise, leg of lamb with green beans, and cassoulet. Lorelei grabs a seat and motions for Prewitt to take the empty chair next to her. Duke Wellington, wearing a beret instead of a parliament wig, is on Prewitt's other side. He smiles and passes Prewitt a platter of boeuf bourguignon.

As everyone makes small talk and eats, Prewitt observes each member of the team Boniface has assembled. In addition to Lorelei and Duke Wellington, he recognizes gold-necklaced Benny, and red-haired Kat, the canoodling couple from the entryway of the townhouse.

Prewitt re-introduces himself. "Bonsoir, Kat. Hello, Benny."

From down the table, a voice calls out. "I'm Louis," says the tattooed bodybuilder gym guy, "and this is my brother, Michel. We met at the party."

"Hello, guys."

"My good people," Boniface says. "As you remember, our friend Prewitt has just arrived from New York with a job to do. Big job." Heads nod. "He requires our unique talents to pull it off. I told him we are the best."

"In the world?" says Michel proudly, sweeping his blond bangs from his eyes.

"I didn't specify," says Boniface. "Prewitt, the floor is yours."

Prewitt leans forward in his chair. "Everyone, thank you for joining me on this adventure. As Boniface may have already told you, the group's take will be twenty percent. Understood?" They all nod, then the nodding turns into whispers, then chattering, then back into silence.

Prewitt gives a quick rundown of the mark and the mechanics of the con. And he brings the team up to date on what he's done so far. Next, Prewitt pulls a stack of papers, folded in half, from his coat pocket. "And here are the roles I need you all to play." He straightens the stack on the table in front of him.

"Who's your climber? And can they also handle power tools and handyman stuff?"

"That's me, and yes," says Lorelei.

"I'll need you to get a work van, a TV antenna, security cameras, motion sensors, and two climbing ropes. And one of the climbing ropes should be dark green to blend in with ivy."

"No problem."

"All the details are on here." Prewitt hands her the top two pages from the stack.

"Next, who's your impersonator? Uniforms; local police, utility work, etc.?"

"I have all the uniforms," Benny says.

Prewitt hands a paper to Duke Wellington, who passes it down the table to Benny.

"Do you have a drone operator?"

"That's me," Boniface says.

Prewitt passes a page down the table to Boniface.

"A coder? URL rerouting, fake web pages, all-around tech?"

"Me," Kat says. "But I like to play in costumes with Benny, too." She gives a sexy shimmy of her shoulders, and everyone at the table laughs. Prewitt hands her a paper.

"And who are our best actors? I might need people to act as specialist staff on loan from the Vatican. If anyone has additional languages like German or Italian, that would be ideal."

"Also me. Four languages," Boniface says.

"I'm fluent in eight languages, and I can speak to dogs, horses, and several species of birds," says Duke Wellington, standing.

"That's bullshit. Maybe four, not eight," says Michel. "And bullshit on the birds too. The birds are bullshit."

"I will prove it anytime."

"But you believe him about the dogs and horses?" says Louis, followed by laughing.

"No. That's bullshit too," says Michel.

"It is not bullshit, my young friend. I don't speak a language to them. But we communicate. It's been studied. And you all know, if I might speak honestly, there is no one more qualified where acting is concerned. Any role. I'm your man. Or woman, if required."

"Blah, blah, blah," says Lorelei, smiling at Duke.

"Who is better? Who alive is better? Besides Daniel Day-Lewis, of course. He's quite good."

"Blah, blah, blah," says Lorelei, pulling Duke back down into his chair.

"He can do whatever is needed," Boniface says.

"Thank you, Duke." Prewitt hands out the pages. "We might not need everything there, but be ready just in case."

There's only one sheet of paper left in front of Prewitt.

"And the last one?" asks Michel.

"Catch-alls, maybe getting a little dirty, available at the spur of the moment."

The brothers look at each other. "That's us. Pass down the paper," Michel says.

"As long as there are no spiders," says Louis. "My brother Michel hates spiders. It's a real problem."

"Shut up, asshole!" Michel punches Louis in the arm and gets punched in return.

"We are going to be at a thousand-year-old chateau. I suspect there may be spiders," says Lorelei.

"Then my brother is fucked."

Everyone laughs.

"Fuck you," says Michel.

"No twenty percent for you, brother." More laughing.

"Why do you embarrass me?"

"Everyone already knows this about you. Just not Prewitt."

"Well, you didn't have to tell him."

"Where is the fun in that?" says Louis as the group laughs even harder.

Looking around, Prewitt wonders what he will know about these people by the time the job ends. He knows he already likes them, these nutty outcasts, these colorful, con crazy weirdos. But why? It's hard for him to describe to anyone who hasn't spent time on the grift. They're off, all of them. They don't fit anywhere. Couldn't live square if they tried. All broken. Broken and self-glued together. And not a self-pitying bone among them. More trustworthy than pretty much any of the straights he has ever known, even when they're not. And they laugh. At life, at the rules. They cry too. But not for very long. Prewitt feels at home with them. He breaks into a smile.

"As you can see, Prewitt. We are ready," says Boniface, raising his glass.

They all follow suit. "Santé!" and toast in unison.

Prewitt feels his smile growing.

"Santé," he says to them all.

The next morning, after a night robbed of sleep by needling pain, Prewitt is on the floor of his tiny hotel room, back flat against the cold floor tiles, begging the muscles to relax their biting grip on his sciatic nerve. Above him is the old French hotel version of annoying neighbors fucking. The springs of the bed frame squeak with a distinct

French accent. Prewitt wonders about what he did in past lives to deserve this karmic reminder of how long it's been since he's gotten some.

Prewitt's phone rings. He leans up just a smidge, and the hurt hits like a Taser. He grabs the phone and looks at the screen. It's Ranger. Prewitt lets it go to voicemail. Ranger's call was expected. Boniface's troupe is right on schedule with the first of some pokes Ranger was sure to notice: Michel and Louis dressed in black cloaks moving around in the gardens at nightfall. Setting the hook just a tad deeper. But the back pain is not what he needs today.

Prewitt goes to the bathroom. Shaving in the mirror, he sees more gray in his beard. *Or maybe it's just the light in here.* During his shower, his thoughts drift to the Parisian plaza, imagining Honey Hair sitting nearby, alone at a table, sipping her espresso, as if he should have looked around but didn't think to. She is beautiful, sitting there, her hair coiled over one shoulder, her soft hands cupping the drink. It's nuts, and he knows it. But he can't shake the feeling he screwed up. That he should have looked around. *Not now.*

He gets out of the shower, grabs his phone, calls Boniface, and it keeps ringing until it goes into a voicemail with a female voice offering the option to leave a message.

"Call me. I need something," Prewitt says after the beep.

13

Prewitt walks down the corridor to the rear exit of his hotel. He has noticed the manager has a big, black SUV used to shuttle around hotel guests. Prewitt crosses the narrow back street and tries the door of the shiny vehicle. Unlocked. Prewitt knows right now the manager has to mind the lobby. The guy is in his cramped front office smoking, watching TV, and listening for the bell on the check-in desk. Hopefully, he won't move for hours or miss the car keys Prewitt lifted. But Prewitt's got a story should a cop get called, and this won't take long.

Prewitt starts the SUV, and soon he's headed to the castle. The message Ranger left was pretty much what Prewitt expected. "Why in the hell aren't you answering? It's Ranger du Courtemanche," Ranger had said before hanging up. *Because it's not time yet.* The trip to Blois feels shorter this time. Even with the shooting pains. Pulling into the castle drive, Prewitt stops under the maples just beyond the iron gate and points the nose of the SUV straight at the front door. He waits a few minutes to give the staff time to notice. Then he takes out his phone and calls the castle.

Bertrand picks up and gets Ranger on the line.

"Earl du Courtemanche, I am sorry for the delay in returning your call. There is much work for Santa Alleanza. I am at the airport now to return to the Vatican."

Prewitt rolls the car forward, revs the engine loudly, and executes a slow turn under the arch. He rolls a few feet, then brakes. Then rolls forward. Then brakes. Revs the engine again. Then rolls forward again, brakes, then revs the engine one more time for good measure. Finally, he guns it and speeds out of the end of the drive, taking the turn fast. Loose bits of limestone and dirt fly from the tires.

"You're leaving?! Someone has been on the property, in the garden. They destroyed the roses and . . ."

Prewitt hears a voice in the background describing what a suspicious black SUV has just been doing. It sounds like Bertrand.

Then Ranger's back on the line. "And just now, a big black car has harassed the drive and gone speeding away from the front gate."

When he is beyond any view from the castle, Prewitt pulls over.

"Are you sure the black car is not just turning around?"

"Yes, I am sure. Are we some kind of idiots? Something is going on here that is not normal."

"This is what I feared."

"You feared this? What's this?"

"I can tell you in person."

"I am calling the police."

"That won't help."

"Why not?"

"Trust me. I can explain later. And not on the phone."

"Then you need to come back here and tell me what is happening, you incompetent worm."

"I'll cancel my return to the Vatican and be there first thing in the morning. Don't call the police."

Prewitt takes the SUV back into Paris and parks it in the hotel lot a couple of spaces over and next to a bus so anyone who'd been thinking it was missing would assume they'd overlooked it. Then he walks to the Metro. Before going down, he checks his phone for the address Boniface sent. It's followed by: Back door knock twice.

Prewitt tries relaxing into the vibrations of the train as it makes its way to the other side of the city. It's not happening. Every jostle is a needle into the nerve down his leg. While riding, he visualizes the next interactions he plans to have with Ranger and imagines the various responses Ranger might have hearing Monsieur Marcellus explain what these strange things might mean. He prepares for any of them.

The back door to the pharmacy is painted white to match the bricks of the building. The street number Boniface sent is stenciled in black. Prewitt knocks twice. Soon, Duke Wellington opens the door. He smiles broadly when he sees Prewitt.

"Boniface told me."

Prewitt looks surprised to see Duke Wellington. "Where's the pharmacist?"

"I was a medic in the army. I know enough."

Duke shows Prewitt a small paper bag. "For the pain. But if it's your back, then you need physical therapy. Strengthening, stretching. Dry needling works very well too. Painkillers won't solve the problem. I could show you some exercises."

Prewitt stares at Duke, not hiding the annoyance. "I'll get some physical therapy when I'm back in the states," Prewitt finally says.

Duke offers the bag, but when Prewitt grabs it, he doesn't let go. "You are not an addict?"

"No."

"Of any kind?"

"No. I barely drink."

"Okay, this will help for now."

"Thank you."

Duke smiles and lets go of the bag.

14

The pills work. Prewitt only needed two before he found some relief. And he spends the last hours of the afternoon napping, then grabs a quick curry for dinner. He's asleep again by ten. In the morning, he takes two more pills, then he's on his way to the castle.

Arriving just after 9:00 a.m., Prewitt drives through the gate and sees someone on a riding lawn mower. As the Peugeot passes by, Prewitt sees it's a young man, probably early twenties. Huge headphones on, shirtless, tan, leanly muscled. *Good-looking kid.* Prewitt parks in front of the castle doors again. This time, Bertrand is there to open them before Prewitt can raise his fist to knock.

"Monsieur Marcellus. I'll take you to see the Earl du Courtemanche in his office." Bertrand seems even jumpier now, Prewitt noticing a subtle quiver of his lower lip. And he moves through the castle almost as if they're late. Prewitt follows Bertrand up to the second floor. Then, just as Bertrand stops in front of a closed door, the door opposite eases open a few inches with a seemingly unintended creak. Prewitt feels eyes on him. As he turns his head, he hears a voice whisper "*Le chat!*" The door quickly closes, but not before he catches a glimpse of a lemon-yellow suit and large black sunglasses. Pensee.

Bertrand ignores Pensee and, opening the door, announces Prewitt. Ranger sits in a chair behind a huge desk. Prewitt's brain flashes to his ex-father-in-law preening like a vulture behind his massive slab. Rich guys and their desks.

Much like Geoffrey's basement lair, the office in this castle is paneled in detailed woodwork. But it's the original thing, not the nouveau riche imitation. And behind Ranger there is a stunner of a marble fireplace. Prewitt's eyes are drawn to the mullioned windows along one wall, letting the softest light stream in. He imagines light coming through the same way centuries earlier and wonders about all the conversations that have taken place here over lifetimes. Prewitt walks over to Ranger's bookcases, wondering if there are volumes here as old as the castle. He stops in front of the shelves, half of them empty. There's an old white and blue encyclopedia set from around the same decade as that swimming pool, and stacks of magazines. He focuses on a shelf of novels when a particular mustard-yellow spine catches Prewitt's eye. His love of artifacts gets the better of him. He pulls it out and turns gently through the first pages. "The Silent World by Jacques Cousteau. 1953. This is a first edition."

"Of course it is."

"It's signed," Prewitt says with a rough edge slipping into his voice because here's another rich jackass who doesn't appreciate the treasure he has.

"Of course it is. I told you; I knew Jacques Cousteau."

Prewitt is curious. "How so?"

"Our families were close. My mother and Simone went scuba diving in Monaco all the time. That's where the helmet came from."

Prewitt feels the vast chasm of privilege separating his childhood from Ranger's. He puts the book back. "To the reason why I'm here. You say there has been suspicious activity?"

"Yes, there has been. I have seen at least two suspicious persons lurking about the grounds. Bertrand witnessed a large black vehicle driving about the front gate. And my roses have been butchered."

"I see."

"Are you going to tell me why this is happening?"

Prewitt casts his eyes around for a place to sit.

Ranger waves his hand at an old armchair by the door. "Just bring that chair over here."

Prewitt moves the chair in front of the desk and sits.

"Give me the details," says Prewitt. He opens his Moleskine and writes down "Details."

"After you came here, I was in this office at 8:05 p.m. when I heard a noise in the back garden. It couldn't be a groundsman so late in the evening, so I thought it might be my sisters. It was not. It was two male persons wearing dark cloaks. I made sure to check the time. The sun was not completely gone, so I could see them. Hooded cloaks. They walked around in the gardens and went off into the trees. Then I saw them again farther away, heading toward the river."

Prewitt mutters, "religious rite," and writes dutifully. "What else?"

"That next morning, every rose on the north side of the garden had been beheaded. It was awful. Then, yesterday, someone in a black truck supposedly sat watching under the gate then sped away, leaving ruts in the gravel. This was happening just as I called you."

Prewitt writes and mutters, "Surveillance" and "Psych-ops." He notices Ranger's agitation growing as he hears these words.

"The murdering of the roses is the most telling," Prewitt says.

"Why?"

"It means they want you to know who they are."

"Well, who are they?"

"*Pauperes commilitones Christi Templique Salomonici.*"

"The Knights Templar?" Ranger asks.

"Your family has done you a disservice if they have not taught you your intertwined history with the—"

"I know who they are."

"The Santa Alleanza have made it our duty to root them out and protect Europe from their schemes."

"But they're here? At my home? Chopping the blooms off my roses?"

"I have no doubt."

"Why didn't you tell me this before?"

"I didn't want to worry you until I was sure the threat was real. The roses are a calling card—a reference to the French king who destroyed them in 1307. You know the founding of the du Courtemanche estate was in 1307?"

Ranger's attention seems to drift off.

"Are you listening?"

"Yes, I am listening!"

"Their order was headquartered at the Vatican until King Philip IV had them arrested and executed. The Vatican fully disbanded them in 1312. But this is all connected . . . The Knights Templar, your family . . ."

"Marcellus, I'm currently engaged in a lawsuit with my neighbor over property lines. He's probably hired ruffians to intimidate me."

"Ruffians who cut the heads off roses? Earl du Courtemanche, your family is being targeted now because of the role they played in the destruction of the Knights Templar. The debt has come due. A price must be paid."

"Oh, come on. What does that even mean?"

"It's hard to know."

"You're the expert."

"Still hard to know."

"I'm calling the police."

"I'd advise you not to do that."

"Why? This is trespassing, and destruction of property. I'm sure it's my neighbor."

"The Knights Templar infiltrate police at all levels. Even the local ones."

"Is that true?"

"It is."

"Okay then, if the Knights Templar *are* attacking me, what do I do? Tell me, with your Vatican expertise, you aren't just here to give me history lessons. You have an answer, right?"

"I'm not sure I do, monsieur. You must find out what they want. In the meantime, you will have to protect yourself."

"Without the police?"

"Yes."

"That sounds impossible."

"And you should inform your family. You have two sisters who live here?"

"Pensee and Amelie."

"There is no one else in the family who needs to be made aware of the danger? No one else who needs to be protected? Is there anyone else the Knights Templar might target, a mistress, any children?"

"I don't have a mistress!" Ranger sputters. Then his voice takes on a grave tone, "Or a wife. And there are no children."

That wasn't just anger there. There was pain in Ranger's answer. Prewitt considers it, but his thoughts are interrupted when a door opens, and Amelie walks in. Clothed, this time.

"Ranger. Monsieur, bonjour. I heard we had a guest, and now my brother is yelling and agitated. Ranger, you wouldn't tell me anything the last time. So, what's going on here?" Amelie walks across the room, and when she stops in front of the windows, the sunlight throws her body's curves into relief. She wears a pair of slim, thin cotton pants that rise to mid-calf, a silk sleeveless blouse, and a pair of simple leather flats. Amelie's hair was wet the last time Prewitt saw her, dark and slicked back from the pool. Dry, it hangs in loose waves around her face, the ends just brushing her collar bone. It's thick and perfectly auburn. Prewitt admires the symmetry of her face and her soft, high cheekbones. Her beauty feels elegant and old worldly to him. He puts her in her mid-fifties.

"Nothing you can help with," says Ranger.

"Earl du Courtemanche, it would be a good idea to inform both of your sisters of what is happening," says Prewitt. Prewitt needs Ranger the most, but he should have all the Courtemanche siblings in his confidence if everything is to go smoothly.

Amelie looks back and forth at each of them. "So, which one of you are going to tell me?"

Ranger looks down.

Amelie takes several purposeful steps toward Prewitt. He stands tall, but she gets right up in his personal space, her eyes demanding.

So Prewitt tells Amelie everything he told Ranger.

There is a moment of silence then, walking back toward the window, Amelie starts to laugh, a beautiful, joyous laugh.

"You can't be serious," Amelie says.

"About the history?"

"About it concerning us."

"I'm afraid I am."

"Are you?" she says, followed by another laugh.

Prewitt knows Amelie could be skeptical. Or even in denial. But the way she's looking at him . . . *She thinks I'm full of shit.*

"The Vatican takes the business of the Knights Templar very seriously. We have been tracking and recording their activities for centuries. They have a personal vendetta against the Courtemanche family. It was only a matter of time."

"A matter of time for what?" Amelie asks, smiling.

"Before the Knights Templar sought their revenge."

Amelie looks Prewitt over before her gaze settles on his eyes. "That's a shame. Life is so much easier when ancient sects aren't seeking to destroy you. Well, it sounds like you two will get this under control. Ranger, leave it to me to tell Pensee. Now, I have my yoga to get to. I'll see you at dinner, brother."

Amelie stares at Prewitt for a moment. She keeps staring, and her curious stare feels like she's asking who he really is, and if he were to tell her, she'd sit and listen. It's as if she's staring right through the persona all the way to the young boy who first realized the girl looking at him was making him nervous. Finally, she heads for the door without another glance at either of them. "Goodbye, Monsieur . . . Marcellus? Yes, that's right."

Prewitt waits a moment, then turns back to Ranger. "I advise you to make sure your staff also know what's going on. And I will come back tomorrow at 9:00 a.m. to further discuss this after I have spoken to my colleagues."

Prewitt lets himself out of the office, and Bertrand escorts him through the castle to the front door. "Is everything okay, monsieur?" says Bertrand, lip quivering. Prewitt wonders if he was eavesdropping.

"I'm not at liberty to say," says Prewitt as he walks toward his car.

From the driveway, Prewitt looks up and sees Ranger looking at him from a window on the second floor. He's holding a cell phone to his ear.

15

"I can hear you fine," Prewitt says. He is back in his hotel room, Mace on speaker, wishing Duke's two pain pills would kick in faster.

"So, got an ETA for our big payday?"

"Yeah, exactly four days from now at 8:33 p.m. East Coast time."

"Don't be a smartass."

"Everything is moving along. Boniface seems to have a good crew."

"That's what he told me. Boniface and I did some cool crap back in the day. Remind me to tell you the story of why I'm never allowed back in Amsterdam."

"When we're done with Ranger."

"I can't wait to hear how much money the old coot's sitting on."

Prewitt's looking forward to that information too. Then he considers Amelie. It may take a little extra work to deal with her. He's nervous just thinking about it. It's not the worst thing when a mark doubts you at the beginning. But the confidence with which she shit on his parade? Luckily Amelie is not the ultimate mark. But she could cause trouble.

"You know I'm right, Prew. Big money," Mace says. "And who knows, maybe a trinket or two to boot."

Prewitt notes the enthusiasm. Mace is giddy, but she's almost too excited. He knows she needs this as much as he does. And he feels sympathy for his old, lonely, recent partner in crime. In that moment, he wants success as much for her as he does for him and Josh.

"I think we'll do just fine."

"Keep me posted, Prew. You're the best. Always were."

When Mace hangs up, Prewitt pictures her sitting in her office at The Gaf, a glass in front of her and a cigar at her lips. He wonders if she might have a date later, or if she's at least back on the dating websites, maybe flipping through pictures on her phone right now. He hopes so.

Prewitt opens his email and finds the drone footage he requested from Boniface. *Good.* He runs through his mental checklist of tasks assigned to Boniface's crew, including the upcoming fake break-in. That should convince Ranger it's not just an angry neighbor. Then there are plans for the anti-hacking solutions, motion sensors, and security cameras. The goal is to create a sense of security then show it's not quite enough. Prewitt's own next step is to get knowledge of Ranger's accounts. "Anti-piracy" software will do just that. Soon he'll know how much he and Mace stand to profit.

Then Prewitt thinks of the prize he has earmarked for himself, his private indulgence, the Courtemanche jewels. He'll find them too. Mace never knew about those, so she doesn't need to know about them. Besides, selling them off would be its own crime. He wants to know more.

Prewitt considers the clues to date. He knows Amarante was not the first Courtemanche to own the jewels. According to one of the articles he read, she told the painter Boucher in 1745 they had been in her family for over 200 years. That places the time of their acquisition in the early 1500s. He decides he'll do some additional digging and starts with internet searches on what was happening with the aristocracy in France at the time, as well as what was going on in the Loire Valley.

After reading a while, Prewitt makes an interesting discovery. It turns out the king had a chateau nearby. In an article from the Smithsonian website, he reads in 1515 the king of France invited Leonardo da Vinci to live at his chateau in the Loire Valley.

Prewitt pulls up a map. The king's Chateau d'Amboise is just up the river from the Courtemanche castle. Googling Chateau d'Amboise, Prewitt soon learns about secret tunnels used for leaving the castle, da Vinci's architectural plans for a utopian French capital in the town of Blois on the Loire, and that he brought the Mona Lisa with him and continued to work on it. He reads da Vinci died in his bed at Chateau d'Amboise, a very wealthy man whose grave is on the estate there. He also learns da Vinci was a generous benefactor to his personal secretary, Francesco Melzi.

Indulging himself, Prewitt reads about Leonardo da Vinci for hours, his searches narrowing to the last four years of his life, the ones he spent just down the river from the Courtemanche family. Da Vinci kept diaries, and many of the pages have been scanned and added online to university libraries. He tracks them down and reads through in Italian. Then he comes to an entry from one of da Vinci's diaries that makes him curious:

> August 4, 1518
>
> Francesco is keeping me entertained as I recover from my recent episode with the confessions of his heart. He has fallen deeply in love with the daughter of our neighbor. The lady is of marrying age, but her father keeps her out of society. Francesco tells me the father insists his daughter must marry of noble class, but no one has yet come forward with a candidate. The gossip is this neighbor is despised behind his back for being elevated to lands and titles by treacherous betrayal of men who trusted him and who lost their lives as a result. I have counseled Francesco to be cautious, but he is young. Francesco tells me he loves her, and they meet in secret under the trees in the moonlight. He swears to me he is never followed, and he takes the king's secret tunnel out and then rows a small boat unnoticed up the river. I worry he will get the lady with child, and she will be dishonored and disowned. I think of my own mother . . .

Surprised to discover da Vinci was from an illegitimate relationship, Prewitt keeps reading and learns da Vinci's mother was bedded by a young lawyer named Ser Piero da Vinci. This man married more than once, producing seven brothers whom da Vinci argued with over the father's estate. Prewitt then reads on in another journal entry.

April 1, 1519

Francesco is the cause of pain in my heart beyond what physically ails me. I am again too weak to leave my bed, and he is my constant support, and for that, I am deeply grateful. I care for him as if he were my own son. Francesco weeps openly, fearing with all too much proof his secret lover is with child. The folly of youth that they do not listen to warning. But I love him and have determined I will not see the child he and his love may bring into the world suffering the rough aspect of life I did.

It is my firm resolve to give them a start, and maybe if luck is on their side, a rich life away from the judgment of her father and the veil of shame she has endured with that family name.

April 25, 1519

Francesco tells me I have not been myself for several days . . . another episode. I am of sound mind at the moment and have called for my lawyers. I will revise my will.

That is the last entry. Prewitt looks up da Vinci's bio and reads he died on May 2, 1519. He wonders if Francesco's lover was a Courtemanche. Then he wonders if the jewels were part of the inheritance Melzi got from da Vinci. The possible provenance gives him all-over-his-body goose bumps.

If Prewitt can connect the jewels to da Vinci and his secretary

Melzi, then Melzi to Courtemanche, it would be the most important discovery of his life. But until he can prove it, it's just wishful thinking. Prewitt decides he'll need to track down more information about Francesco Melzi.

He leans back from his computer.

For a moment, Prewitt considers what this would mean were he still an academic. If true, it would more than make his career. He'd also be rewarded with the gift of being able to continue his work, respected for it, and excited to share it. Unlike now, where divulging any of this would get him locked up for being there in the first place. He imagines what it would be like to share this discovery with Josh. If it would make him proud to be Prewitt's son. What would Honey Hair think, or Geoffrey? It would all be so different.

Prewitt pictures his little corner desk in the shared office on the third floor of Dietrich at Carnegie Mellon, overgrown plants hanging down from the old green windowsill, how quiet it got at night when he'd stay working long past when anyone else was still on the floor, his little antique desk lamp shining yellow light like a burning candle. Prewitt had loved working there. And he'd loved walking home in the early morning hours, down winding paths, past old buildings and small starlit yards and fields quiet and quaint and perfectly manicured.

It had been late fall when things crumbled beneath Prewitt so fast the shock had him wondering if it was a bad dream. Standish had been running a fiddle game con on two members of the board of trustees at the university. He'd arranged for them to be presented with a possible donation to the school, an old antique secretary desk. They asked Standish to authenticate. He sent them to an appraiser who told them it was worth upwards of twenty million dollars, a Goddard-Townsend he had said. And being greedy, they planned to buy it for themselves from the supposed donor, who they didn't know was Standish, offering a cool million and hiding their intention of then turning around and selling it for a huge profit, which they would never have gotten because the desk was worth $500 at most, the appraiser working with Standish.

The only problem with Standish's plan was Prewitt, accidentally seeing the desk and fearing someone was pulling a scam, told Standish it was a fake. He thought he was being helpful. The next thing Prewitt knew, he was summoned to the university president's office for a meeting that lasted barely fifteen minutes. Standish, realizing Prewitt would eventually see it all clearly and could bust him wide open, had gone to the board members two hours earlier and told them they were being conned, and it was Prewitt who was responsible for the whole thing. He even said Prewitt had admitted it to him. Prewitt stood in front of President Kimmel and the board members and was advised he was caught and not to deny it.

To Prewitt's surprise and immediate understanding, they explained Standish was the one who turned him in. In return for no criminal charges being pressed, Prewitt could quietly leave. It would look too embarrassing to the university for people to know actual board members were scheming like that, let alone that they'd been tricked. Later that night, Prewitt had a face-to-face with Standish in his massive wood-paneled office. Gun in hand, Standish explained he was a prolific con artist, he wasn't sorry, and he'd kill Prewitt if he ever needed to. He blamed Prewitt for being a bit too smart and said he never really cared about Prewitt but was, in fact, grooming him as a pawn for some future, not-yet-devised swindle. He regretted he wouldn't be able to use him now. He'd pulled out an envelope from his desk with five grand in cash, which Prewitt reluctantly took because he was ruined, and he knew it, and he barely had two nickels. He'd packed and was gone the next day.

Prewitt comes back to the here and now, a cold flutter dull in his chest, wishing he could just forget. Then he thinks of the jewels again. *Are they still in the Courtemanche family?* That's the other important question. He uses the same stolen credentials he always uses to get into international auction sales databases. It takes over an hour, and he follows multiple search results before walking away from his laptop.

Ranger Courtemanche hasn't sold the jewels at auction, ever. But that only eliminates one possibility. Prewitt sends an email to an old friend. There is more digging to be done.

Prewitt opens his eyes. He rolls over in the lumpy hotel bed and grabs his phone. It's 4:07 a.m., which is 10:07 p.m. in New York. He sits up, feeling dull pain in his back and butt, then gets out of bed and walks over to the window. Prewitt's comfortable here in this hotel room in Paris. The street noise, partiers yelling, drunks singing, very New York. It's a lullaby he can fall asleep to. But it's all quieted now, and looking out at the empty street and sidewalks, he imagines everyone back in their homes sleeping. Prewitt is not awake because of his sciatic pain. It's the jewels. And how, after the excitement from his research settled down, they led his brain right back to Honey Hair. The story he learned about Melzi has him thinking about her and his own peasant background. He looks at his phone. So close he could nudge her. But why bother? He knows Honey Hair would rather sleep than have to deal with anything about him. He has these moments, always at night, when the dissonance hits like a boomerang you forgot you threw the day it all went sour. Then *bam*, right in the head. It's easy to remember what it felt like to share your heart with someone who shared theirs. And it takes work to keep those thoughts away. Too much to ask at 4:00 a.m. He hears a dog snap out two angry barks that echo, then leave the street seeming quieter than it was before. *My problem, not hers.* Prewitt walks to the bed, his pain sharper, then lies back down. He curls onto his side and puts a pillow between his legs. Staring at the wall, he listens for the sound of someone else's life. Anything to feel that theirs might be more screwed up than his. A truck drives by on the street beneath his window. He listens for a voice, another bark, anything. Nothing. He pictures Honey Hair, sleeping in her bed. Sleeping, but sad. *I'm so sorry, Sharon.* Then Prewitt closes his eyes as his heart sinks. Too quiet tonight.

16

It's dumping rain. And the wiper blades making thumpy sticking noises across the windshield seem louder to Prewitt on account of his lack of sleep. He's on his way back to Chateau Loir-et-Cher for another meeting with Ranger, but his mind is full of history. Not his history with Honey Hair. He has resolved to do a better job with those thoughts today. He's back to Melzi and DaVinci this morning.

Prewitt looks out at the dripping gray landscape of the Loire Valley and its houses, sleeping peacefully, soaked with rain they've known a thousand times, a million. He thinks again of trees, this time the ones under which young Melzi met his secret love along the same Loire River shores that hide behind these farms. That the jewels may have some rich ancient provenance to them . . . he can feel his heart in his chest, the rain thumping counterpoint on the metal roof of the Peugeot. In this moment, he trusts he'll find the jewels. For some reason he doesn't want to question, he believes it. Prewitt remembers just days ago, he was scraping the hoofs of Manhattan, hoping to find a dime. He can't drive fast enough.

Bertrand answers the door looking sleep-deprived himself, his eyebrows furrowed in concern that's over-wrinkling his forehead.

"Bonjour," says Prewitt after a moment of nothing from Bertrand.

"Bonjour, yes, of course."

Bertrand takes Prewitt into the dining room and points to Ranger at the far end. "The Earl du Courtemanche."

Prewitt's footsteps echo across the expansive dining room with its stone walls and floor. The low-hanging chandeliers must have once dazzled when they illuminated grand dinner parties. Though notably missing is a long table. Prewitt passes several ornate fireplaces as he makes his way to where Ranger stands near a small buffet as breakfast is being laid out.

A matronly member of the staff deposits a silver chafing dish onto a stand. Prewitt notices her smiling face is chubby and smooth, her full cheeks resting atop deep dimples. Her uniform has been starched and pressed, and her apron is spotless. She snaps the lids of the chafing dishes open and closed, then disappears back into the kitchen.

Ranger heaps eggs on his plate then adds a slab of ham.

"Bonjour, Earl du Courtemanche. May I call you Ranger?"

"You may not. You're late."

Prewitt looks at his watch. 9:10 a.m.

"I apologize."

"I spent the night wandering around checking doors and windows with Bertrand. Each of us was armed with a pointy cooking utensil. Bertrand jumped at every shadow."

"My colleagues and I do not think you are in physical danger. If you were, you'd have been attacked already."

"You could have saved me some grief if you'd told me that yesterday. And by the way—" Ranger shuts up when a side door opens, and Pensee enters and wanders toward the buffet. She's wearing full navy trousers and a crisp white blouse. Her large summer hat with feathers has Prewitt picturing the Kentucky Derby. Seeing her without sunglasses, Prewitt estimates Pensee is several years younger than Ranger, late sixties. Pensee picks up tongs and opens the lid of the first chafing dish.

"Good morning, Pensee," Ranger says, then looks to Prewitt with an expression that suggests whatever Ranger was about to say is not going to be discussed in front of his sister.

Pensee turns. "Le chat's here again?" Pensee waggles the tongs at Prewitt. "And spending all his time with you, Ranger." She gives Prewitt a once over. "Maybe if my throat were dripping in jewels, I could catch his eye. But I can't stand the feeling of something so cold against my skin."

Bemused, Prewitt watches as Pensee turns back to the food, wondering why she just mentioned jewels.

Just then, a ringtone version of "Luck Be A Lady," by Frank Sinatra begins to play. Pensee fishes a cell phone out of her pants pocket and swipes at the screen.

"*Enculé de ta mère!*" Pensee says to the phone once she has opened her screen.

"Pensee, really—" Ranger begins, but he's interrupted.

"Oh no you don't!" Pensee yells at the screen.

Prewitt watches her peck at it with her bony finger as she leaves the room in a hurry.

"What was she saying about jewels?" Prewitt asks.

Ranger shakes his head. "It's nothing. Nothing that makes sense. I trust you have already eaten. I don't want to have to feed you too."

"I'm fine," says Prewitt, putting thoughts of Pensee aside. "Can we go to your office?"

Just as Prewitt and Ranger sit, there is a timid knock at the door of Ranger's office.

"Earl du Courtemanche, the police have arrived," says Bertrand.

"Oh good," says Ranger.

"I warned you not to involve the police," says Prewitt, sounding frustrated.

"I thought otherwise." Ranger stands. "Are you coming?"

Ranger and Prewitt follow Bertrand down to the hallway inside the front doors, where two officers in blue uniforms stand.

"You're finally here," Ranger says.

"Oui, monsieur," Benny says, as he presents his badge to Ranger. Prewitt recognizes the female officer as Benny's girlfriend, Kat, her red hair tucked back in a low ponytail.

Ranger looks at the badge, "Blois Municipal Police."

"Oui, monsieur. I have already studied the complaint you filed. When we arrived, my partner and I conducted a quick investigation of the flowers that were damaged on your property. They really cut off a lot of flowers. It looks so empty now where the flowers were. Just stems. Not good."

"I'm glad you disapprove."

"Do you have anything new to tell us?"

"No. Nothing new," Ranger says, annoyed.

"Well, who is this man?" Benny asks.

"I am Prewitt Marcellus with the Santa Alleanza." Prewitt hands Benny his ID badge and a fake Italian passport.

"You are with the Santa Alleanza?" says Benny, sounding impressed.

"Yes. You know of us."

"Of course. I am a good Catholic. Though I am mad with the Pope that he congratulated the Italian football team after they defeated France. Seems unfair to me he would do that."

Prewitt can't think of a response.

"Do you think that is fair?" Benny says, looking first to Prewitt, then to Ranger.

Ranger stares back at him.

"I don't," says Benny.

"I am here to assist Earl du Courtemanche with some of his affairs," says Prewitt.

Benny hands the ID to Kat, who steps outside as she speaks into her radio.

"Well, anyway, there is not much we can do for you at this moment," says Benny. "If you figure out who vandalized your roses, we can go speak to them and tell them not to do this. It is probably some kids. A prank, I would think."

"It's not my job to identify criminals. That's why I called you," Ranger says, sounding pissed.

Benny shrugs, "Eh." He then takes a few steps in and scans the foyer, looking up and down and to both sides, then shaking his head as if in approval. "Is the whole floor marble?" says Benny.

Ranger looks confused.

"This is not a question about the case. I am just very interested in chateaux."

Kat comes back in, "He checks out." She hands the ID to Benny, who hands it back to Prewitt.

"Is there anything else you need help with?" says Benny.

"Anything else?" says Ranger, his tone heating up.

"Did they hurt other flowers?"

"Would that matter?"

"No," says Benny.

"And what of the men?" says Ranger.

"What men?"

"The men I saw."

"I think they were kids."

"They did not look like kids."

"Why?"

"They were big."

"Kids can be big."

"We will call you if we need anything else," says Prewitt. "Thank you for your time."

"Of course. Very nice castle. I always wanted to see it."

"I'm happy for you, then, you young, stupid imbecile . . ."

Prewitt places his hand on Ranger's arm to stop him from continuing. "I can walk them out," he says.

Prewitt follows Benny and Kat out to two motorcycles parked in the drive.

"We were pretty useless, huh?" Benny says.

"Just right."

"Boniface says there have been no other calls to the police, but he will continue to monitor and intercept. And if there are, we can come back and be useless again."

"The soccer was a nice touch," says Kat.

"That was no touch. I really am mad about that. Did you hear about this, Prewitt? How is that fair to the French Catholics? Does God play favorites? No. Why did the Pope?"

"I'll ask him."

"Haha. Okay. See you soon."

Benny and Kat get on their motorcycles, and Prewitt watches until they pull onto the street at the end of the drive. He starts back inside. A little goofy, yes, but they inspired no confidence, which was exactly what they were supposed to do. Prewitt is reminded of the surprising joy he feels on a con when a team starts working together. He hears the motorcycles growl off in the distance. *Nice job, you two.*

Ranger and Prewitt sit across the desk from each other.

"I felt the need to call them," says Ranger.

"But as you can see, the police will not be helpful. I don't think there is any risk of those two being agents for the Templars. But again, I must stress there are many within the ranks who are loyal. They cannot be relied on to help you."

"I haven't interacted with the police in decades. I suppose I was wrong to think they were capable of more."

"This situation requires specialization." Prewitt takes his laptop computer from his bag and places it on the desk. "I brought my computer to aid in our discussion. Can I have the Wi-Fi password?"

"Marcellus, I should explain something to you," Ranger says as he sits back in his desk chair and pinches the bridge of his nose as if he has a headache.

Prewitt's not sure what is coming, but since Ranger isn't fighting the argument, he is encouraged.

"Yesterday, you mentioned my ancestors had done me a disservice by not passing down the family connection with the Knights Templar. You were wrong. I know all about the family connection."

Prewitt leans forward. *Good.*

"I know France's King Phillip was deeply in debt to the Templars and couldn't pay."

"I know there was a man in Philip's court who had joined the Knights Templar. He gave Philip the identities of many members of the Order in France. They were arrested and tortured and burned at the stake which took care of the debt problem. I know all about this," Ranger says. "As do many in France," he adds, annoyed.

"And that courtier was your ancestor," says Prewitt, thinking back to the night in New York when he, while researching the du Courtemanche family history, discovered what Benedict du Courtemanche had done and how that became the seed of the con Prewitt would craft.

"Yes. Benedict du Courtemanche, raised by King Philip IV of France in the year 1307," Ranger says as if narrating. "All of our lands and titles plus an allowance was given, apparently, in return for Benedict's assistance in bringing down the Knights Templar and freeing our wise King Philip from his debt. So yes, I understand that part of history and my family's role in it very well."

"It's a less than noble way to gain land, wealth, and title."

The comment seems to annoy Ranger more than anger him. "No different than the way many noble families rose to prominence," Ranger says, looking off. "Is ours the only family with someone who once committed an act . . ." Ranger hesitates as if realizing how tired he is of making this argument. His energy sinks a bit. "It's simply that most family's histories aren't as well-known as mine. So you can reserve your judgment. Or don't. It doesn't matter." Ranger stays quiet another moment, then looks to Prewitt. "And you believe this is why the Templars are targeting me?"

"Yes," says Prewitt. "I'm not here to judge."

"You'd be the first."

The words catch Prewitt's attention again. It's the way the family's history seems to poke at Ranger. Not what Prewitt expected. This is all exactly what Prewitt has set up, and the timing of Ranger's admission is perfect. Even the anger is important, since a mark can't see a con through the fog of emotion. But it's not only anger. There's something else there. Prewitt knows he'll find it at some point.

"So why now?" Ranger asks. "If they've been angry at my family since 1307, why are they only getting around to it now?"

"You told me you are the last of the Courtemanche line. I'm sure they sought revenge in centuries past but were unsuccessful. You remain, and this is their final chance to bring ruin to the Courtemanche name."

"Well then, it is my duty as the last Courtemanche heir and regent of this family to protect my home. And my sisters. Which I plan on doing."

Prewitt opens the laptop. "The Wi-Fi password? So I can join the network here, and my laptop can access the internet."

"I know what Wi-Fi is."

"Then you know it's an access point for the Knights Templar."

"So they can hack into my computer and what, take my money?"

"Of course."

"Could they do that so easily?"

"Not so easily. But they can try. Though the Santa Alleanza can protect against that type of hacking."

Ranger pulls open a desk drawer and draws out a piece of paper. He reads off a string of numbers and letters to Prewitt, who enters them into his laptop then his phone. Ranger tucks the paper back into the drawer.

"The Vatican too has a history with the Knights Templar. And we have a sworn obligation to prevent them from doing harm. Now that we've agreed the motive for the Knights Templar is to seek revenge, we can work together to help you."

"You're offering help?"

"I am."

"Then I accept."

Prewitt pulls up one of the drone pictures Boniface took yesterday and turns the laptop to face Ranger.

"What's this?" Ranger leans in to look at the picture. It shows Amelie standing in the back garden talking on a cell phone.

"The picture of your sister appears to have been taken by a drone. Have you noticed any drone activity?"

"A drone? That flies in the sky? No. I've not seen a drone in my life. Where did you get this?"

"The Santa Alleanza intercepts emails from the Knights Templar whenever we can. The emails are encrypted, but what my agency has deciphered already shows they are ramping up activity. Your chateau is being surveilled."

Ranger thinks for a moment. "Marcellus, are you sure they don't mean to harm us?"

"From what I know of them, the Knights Templar want money and, in your case, personal humiliation. It is highly unlikely they would try to hurt anyone. They can't enjoy their revenge if they empty the world of victims."

Prewitt notices a scared look come over Ranger, but there's something else in it Prewitt can't quite pinpoint. Shame, perhaps? Prewitt isn't sure.

"In similar cases only intimidation, blackmail, and theft occurred. There was once a kidnapped child who was ransomed, but that was more of an outlier, a rogue element in the order."

"Kidnapped?"

"Fifty years ago. Not a concern in your case."

Prewitt knows he could have gone the other way on that one, but against the instincts he normally has for these types of rich shits, he decides not to torture Ranger with some fear of violence or death.

"You say there are other cases?"

"You are not the first family to be targeted by the Templars."

"So then, what can be done?"

"To start, I can install a PJP cyber shield."

"A cyber shield?"

"It is a technology, developed at the Santa Alleanza, which will create a firewall, encrypt all your data, and secure your internet activity. The PJP will protect your files from prying eyes."

"PJP? As in Pope John Paul?"

"He's still a favorite. It's sophisticated technology but can be installed easily, like a TV antenna. But it is critical the cyber shield has an uninterrupted view of the Vatican satellite. A technician will have to go up on your roof. And we should install it as soon as possible."

"Tomorrow, then."

"Okay. I will have them come tomorrow."

"Monsieur, in my experience, what I have seen is once the Templars have tried and failed enough, they will feel thwarted, and all will cease. Sometimes we can catch one of the players. Barring that, we simply have to hold firm, and succeed in protecting you. Then hopefully, sooner rather than later, it comes to an end."

"Hopefully."

"Inevitably."

"And what if it doesn't come to an end?"

"It will. Our job now is to be formidable."

"Fine." Ranger thinks for a moment. "The Vatican has its own satellite?"

"Of course. How do you think the Pope hears from God?"

Ranger seems to find no humor in the joke. But then, after a few seconds, his face shows the tiniest smile. It's the first smile Prewitt has seen from Ranger, and it's the smile of a boy, and to Prewitt, it looks sweet. Prewitt wonders how the hell he is even thinking Ranger's smile is boyish and sweet until he realizes it reminds him of Josh. And whether it looks like Josh's smile, or he simply has his son on the brain, Prewitt doesn't know. He just knows he's now thinking about childhood innocence when he would normally be thinking about fileting his flounder and fat stacks of cash. The distraction annoys him. He wonders if maybe the persona is a little tired. Prewitt says his goodbye, then leaves Ranger's office and walks down the central staircase to the first floor.

As he walks toward the castle's front door, Prewitt hears music and continues down the main hallway toward it. Through an open door on his left, he looks into the room with the piano he noticed his first time in the castle. But the music he hears comes from a small speaker on a side table. Amelie sits on the front edge of the slouchy couch, holding a guitar. Her eyes are closed, giving Prewitt a few seconds to watch her.

Amelie's lips move, but it's too quiet to hear if she is singing or just mouthing the words. She strums a chord along with the music, and one bare foot taps against a red and yellow zigzag patterned rug. Prewitt doesn't recognize the song. It's a male voice, singing in French, folky and melancholic. Amelie opens her eyes and stops singing, then looks Prewitt's way. *Busted.*

"Monsieur Marcellus."

"Madame du Courtemanche, I'm sorry to intrude. I heard you playing."

"Do you and Ranger need my help with the Knights Templar?"

Prewitt doesn't bite. He walks toward the upright piano in the corner, noticing the red wood of the cabinet. "Is this piano a Pleyel?"

"Yes, it is. How did you know?"

"The spruce is sourced only from Italy."

He gets to the piano and looks closer at the worn ivory keys and the patina on the stand where sheet music, dusty and yellowing with age, sits as if untouched for a hundred years. He turns a page to read the front cover, Frederic Chopin Compositions for piano.

"Are you going to play for me?" Amelie says.

"Not today."

"Oh? When then?"

"When I learn how."

"So, you're into wood?"

"I suppose. I like old things."

"Strange hobby for a security guard."

Prewitt just smiles.

"Wish I liked old things. I'm surrounded by them here."

"I have a few questions."

"I may have a few answers."

"Have you noticed anything suspicious in the last several weeks?"

"No."

"When you come and go from the chateau?"

"I don't come and go. The staff runs our errands."

"In general, then."

"No."

"I see."

"That's all kind of one question, isn't it?"

"I suppose it is. I have nothing else at the moment."

"You didn't have any questions for me. You were just walking by and heard the music."

"That is true."

"Why didn't you say so?"

"I didn't have a chance to. But I was curious about what you've seen."

"Clearly."

This woman is sharp. Prewitt starts wishing he hadn't walked by. Sure, he's confirmed she's doubting, but he has done nothing to help himself. Time to back out of this.

"As I said, I'm sorry I intruded. If I have other questions, I'll find you."

Amelie stays silent, staring again, looking Prewitt up and down. But there is a mischievousness to the look she is now giving him.

"I think I'd like that," says Amelie.

As she returns her attention to the guitar, Prewitt registers the flirting. Then he wonders why. There's often flirting when a game is afoot. *Is there a game here?* He turns and walks out. Moving away from the room, he replays her last words and her eyes and the way they lingered on him as her head tilted down. *She's very charming.* He's more curious than worried. Though that could change quickly. He continues toward the front door and lets himself out.

17

The next morning Prewitt wakes to his phone alarm. He sees an email response from the friend he asked to hunt for any record of the Courtemanche jewels on the dark web. It reads: Call me.

Prewitt dials. "Anything?"

"Your jewels have never come up anywhere. Not on any black-market auctions. Not among any of the dark dealers or collectors. I checked under every rock. No one has those jewels or knows where they are other than with their original owners."

"Thank you."

"How grateful are you?"

"There may be a little something for you at the end."

"Like what?"

"Like a beer and a meal."

"Don't be a dick."

"I'll peel off a couple Gs."

"My man."

"Gotta go."

Prewitt ends the call, then texts Lorelei.

Meet me at the chateau at
9:00 a.m.

***

"The roof access is up on the third floor," says Ranger pointing to a small stone staircase that spirals upward. He has brought Prewitt and Lorelei along the second-floor hallway to the opposite end from his office.

Lorelei, here to install the cyber shield, is dressed in a baggy coverall. She wears sunglasses, her face has smudges of dirt, and her hair is pulled back into a tight ponytail. The look is badass, and Prewitt notes the attitude she's brought with it. Prewitt takes a step and feels the pain down his leg. He shifts the huge tool case he's carrying from one hand to the other. It's got a modern-looking, foldable TV antennae in it, tools, cables, cords, and a small, black plastic box. Lorelei drops the purple rope she has coiled over her shoulder and pulls on a climbing harness.

"So, this isn't the roof access?" says Lorelei.

"Up these stairs, you will find a hallway with a dozen rooms. The last room on either end has a ladder and a trap door to the roof," Ranger answers.

"That's a lot of rooms."

"It's a large chateau," says Ranger, looking annoyed.

"How will we know if we've found the right one?"

"It's the last one on either side. Do I have to go up there with you?" says Ranger, still annoyed.

"No. We'll be fine," says Prewitt.

Now up in the room on the third floor and standing beneath the trap door, Lorelei passes a purple rope through the safety loop in her harness and ties a figure eight knot in it. Then she secures the other end of the rope to the bottom ladder rung. Prewitt gives a forceful yank on the rope to make sure it's tight.

"Don't you dare touch the rope when I'm climbing out on that roof. I'll kick your ass if you make me lose my balance."

"I won't touch the rope."

"You better not, or I'll fuck you up," she says, straight-faced.

Prewitt takes a cautious step back.

"I'm serious," she says.

"I believe you."

"Don't touch it."

"I won't touch the rope."

She puts her hand to her stomach and leans forward a bit.

"What?" says Prewitt, alarmed.

"My period. Cramps."

"Oh, I'm sorry."

"Menstrual bleeding is God's stupidest idea."

Prewitt doesn't know how to respond.

"Men get to enjoy having babies too. But they don't have to put up with pain every month. You have a baby?" says Lorelei.

"I do, a boy," says Prewitt.

Lorelei doubles over more. "You don't deserve him," she whispers through the pain.

After a moment she straightens, then leans over again.

"You could not handle this. Not every month."

"Can you take medicine?"

"Shut up and squeeze my hand," she says, holding her hand out.

Prewitt hesitates.

"It helps me. Just do it."

Prewitt takes Lorelei's hand and squeezes. "Is that too hard?"

She squeezes back. "It's perfect. Shut up."

Lorelei closes her eyes and takes deep breaths. After four of them, she releases Prewitt's hand. "Thanks." She grabs the ladder and puts a foot on the first rung.

"So, you'll attach the antennae to the roof and run a length of white cable and green power cord from it back into this room. Hook the white cable up to this router-looking box, then we'll plug it in."

"Yeah, yeah, yeah. And I'll leave the second climbing rope, hanging down the back of the farthest chimney where it will blend in with the ivy."

Lorelei checks once more to make sure the rope is tied correctly into her harness and double-checks the other end anchored around the ladder rung. All appears secure to Prewitt. If she does lose her balance, at least she won't go completely off the roof. She gives Prewitt a thumbs-up and hauls the tool case up the rickety ladder and through the roof hatch.

While Lorelei does her work, Prewitt takes a quick tour of the other rooms. Servants' quarters. They are noticeably small and mostly empty. He finds a few beds with naked mattresses and dusty dressers. It seems no one has been up here in ages. Times have changed from when the aristocracy required dozens of servants to meet their needs. He thinks about where someone might hide jewels, and decides he needs to get down into the basement of the castle; as good a place as any for a vault. Though there could be a safe in Ranger's office.

Prewitt exits an empty room and is startled to find Pensee leaning against the wall by the stairs. "Madame du Courtemanche, bonjour."

Pensee tosses a coin in the air. She's in 1950s garb: lilac billowy skirt, embroidered top, a large hat, and sunglasses. She tosses the coin again.

"I need to go to the flower market. I have a meeting with the man from Lloyds of London about the insurance," says Pensee.

"I see. Why? Something concerning your valuables?"

"Insurance, it's a lot like betting, and I have a long shot for you."

Is that so?

"I'll see you later," Pensee saunters off down the stairs.

Prewitt thinks back to her earlier comment about jewels and wonders why Pensee would now mention insurance. *This sister, too?* How could she possibly know he has taken an interest in the stash of her family's jewels that he hopes exist? Though it makes him wonder if Pensee didn't just confirm they do.

***

Fourteen hours later, stars dot the dark night sky as Lorelei climbs up the green rope from the bushes. Her feet get tangled in the ivy of the chateau wall, but she is able to use her jumars to ascend. Working them with a practiced ease, Lorelei reaches the second floor. Only a few windows of the chateau glow with light.

Lorelei leans back on the rope, looks to her right, and counts the windows. There are four from the corner. She is just to the left of a chimney where it juts out several feet. She looks to her left—window number five then window number six. The sixth is her target. Lorelei kicks out from the chimney and swings back in. She kicks again and builds momentum so her swings arch sideways. As she passes in front of the sixth window, she slaps on a suction cup.

Secured to the window by a tether on her harness, Lorelei uses both hands to apply a plastic film to the window's glass around the suction cup. Next, she takes out a small mallet and shatters the window.

Lorelei, the window glass, and the suction cup still holding it all fly free. Lorelei prepares for impact with the chimney and uses her legs to absorb the shock. She looks back at the window. All is quiet. She looks down at the broken window glass neatly caught against the plastic coating. Its jagged edges hang a meter below her waist. She cuts the tether free from her harness, and the glass and suction cup fall into the bushes.

Back on the jumars, Lorelei climbs up to the roof. She refastens the rope to her harness by running it through a metal device, then swiftly rappels down to the ground. One strong yank and the whole rope slithers free, whipping down into a messy heap. She finds one end, then coils the rope over her shoulders and walks off into the night.

18

"It's about damn time," says Ranger.

"I'm sorry, I didn't get your voicemail until I was awake this morning. Are you sure it was a break-in?" Prewitt, led by a visibly shaken Bertrand, arrives at the top of the main staircase. Ranger is standing in the upstairs hallway.

"Yes, I'm sure."

"Can you show me where?"

Bertrand heads back downstairs as Prewitt follows Ranger into an empty room.

"Right here. Look. The window glass is missing."

"Interesting. Do you think they were in the chateau?" Prewitt says.

"How the fuck should I know?"

Prewitt walks over to the window. It's barely big enough for a child to fit through.

"Anyone could have passed through this." He takes a pen from his pocket and runs it along the inside edge of the window. Small chips of glass flake off. "If they were careful."

Ranger looks at the edges. "But where is the rest of the glass? How do you break a window and leave no glass on the floor?"

"No one heard anything?"

"No."

"Has anything been stolen?"

"I don't know. I don't think so."

Prewitt feigns thought. "You should check. If you have cash or valuables, they would be targeted."

"There really is nothing of value here."

Certainly a lie. Ranger has lied already.

"Nothing belonging to your sisters is missing?"

"You'd have to ask them."

"I will," says Prewitt, knowing he won't. "Let's see what we can learn from outside."

Ranger leads Prewitt from the room and down the central stairs to the first floor, then Bertrand opens the front door, and they walk to the east side of the chateau. A path leads through trees and along the chateau where bushes grow wildly, and ivy climbs the walls.

"What are we looking for?" Ranger is staring up as they walk through the grass below the imposing stone wall of the chateau, his hand tented to shield his eyes from the late morning sunshine. He glances around, then spots the broken window in the overgrown juniper shrubs. "There!"

Prewitt reaches out his hand to stop Ranger from plunging into the bushes. "Allow me to take photos."

Prewitt moves forward, taking pictures with his cell phone of the glass, the bushes, the chateau wall, and the window above. Finally, he beckons Ranger forward.

"This doesn't surprise me at all, not with the report I just received," Prewitt says.

"You plan on sharing it with me?"

"In the last twenty-four hours, since the cyber shield has been activated, the Santa Alleanza detected two pings from Paris. One is from a residence we believe is a Knights Templar safe house, and one is from a police station."

"Was it the police station in Blois? Did I tip them off?"

"Yes, to the first question. I don't know, to the second. But we should also move forward with the anti-hacking software later."

Prewitt lifts the broken window glass adhered to the plastic film out of the grass. He takes more photos.

"What is that on the glass?" Ranger tries to get a closer look.

"The Templar use military level technology and equipment. It's not just robes and swords anymore."

"Well, how did they get to the window, a ladder? We could have been murdered in our beds. They seem to be much more of a threat than you said they would be."

"No, this was just meant to intimidate. And distract from their real goal, your money."

Prewitt carefully works the window glass into the plastic evidence bag he brought with him and ties it off. He pulls out a Sharpie and writes the date on the bag. "I will send this to the Vatican for analysis."

Prewitt starts walking across the grounds and around the side of the chateau. He heads to the Peugeot parked out front. Ranger follows him.

"I am not comfortable sleeping another night in this chateau knowing the Knights Templar can come in any window they like. I want security."

"I've already . . ."

"Around-the-clock guards."

"That will take a couple of days. But the security cameras and motion sensors have already been shipped. And I can have them installed by tonight if you want."

Ranger composes himself as he stands in front of his chateau. "Yes. Yes, I want them tonight."

19

Later in the early evening, after Lorelei parks her white work van in the castle drive, she begins to install the security system. Using a tall ladder, she mounts boxes the size of bread loaves along the exterior roof line. They have battery packs inside that run a series of green blinking lights mounted next to fake camera lenses. Lorelei films a few minutes of footage with her cell phone from each camera position and sends it to Prewitt in case he should need it later.

In Ranger's office, Prewitt sits across from Ranger at the desk, following through on the promise to install the cyber shield software. "First, login to your laptop and email."

Ranger types. "I'm logged in."

"Next find an email from pmarcellus@vatican.org. Open that and click on the software download."

"I haven't done this before. Amelie always does my computer business. Should we get her in here too?"

Definitely no. She's the only part of the con making Prewitt nervous. *Let's keep her at bay until I know what she's up to and how to deal with it.*

"No need. I'll help you."

Two clicks later and Prewitt's spying software is downloaded onto Ranger's laptop. He will now get notifications of all of Ranger's site visits. If he can get keystroke recordings, he might even get the logins.

But that's where the software is hit or miss. *Fingers crossed.* He could be looking at Ranger's bank accounts in less than twenty-four hours.

Prewitt pretends to read a text. "Earl du Courtemanche, it's the technician. The cyber shield is armed."

"Well, that's good. I'm pleased you set that up so quickly."

"I said I would. Anything else I can do for you today?"

"You tell me."

"No. I think for now, we've done all we can."

"Okay." Ranger waits a moment, then adds, "Thank you."

Prewitt knows the "thank you" means Ranger is swimming toward the rod now. Easier for the fish than to pull against the line.

"Call me if anything else comes up. I'm going to go now. There are still calls to make to secure guards for you."

Prewitt closes Ranger's office door behind him, and when he turns toward the stairs, Bertrand is right there.

"Bonsoir, Bertrand."

"Bonsoir." Bertrand can't hide his worry or that he was listening in.

"Is everything alright?"

"You're asking me?" says Bertrand, looking confused.

"I mean, with you, is everything alright with you?" Prewitt has been wondering what makes this squirmy butler tick.

"Oh, yes. Can I get you anything?"

"No, thank you."

Bertrand looks at his shoes, then back up at Prewitt. "Monsieur, forgive me. Um, sometimes I, by the nature of my position, hear words that are being said, though I let them drift from my mind and get on with my work."

"I understand."

"But recently, well, since you arrived, the words are not drifting from my mind as easily."

Prewitt waits. *Never interrupt a confession.*

"I've worked here for many years and seen the Courtemanches treated unfairly for most of them. These are decent people. I have devoted my life to this family, and I would just like to know they are . . . that whatever is happening, it's going to be okay."

It's an unexpected openness from Bertrand, and Prewitt can see how uncomfortable he was crossing this line. A form of bravery. He chooses a tone to make Bertrand more comfortable.

"It will all be fine. No need to worry."

"No need?"

"No. That's why I am here. But we can talk more if you ever need to."

"Okay." Bertrand takes a moment, then straightens. "Are you sure there is nothing else you need, monsieur?"

"Quite sure. Thank you, Bertrand."

Bertrand turns and hurries off.

Back in his hotel room, and having taken the last of Duke's pain pills, Prewitt opens his laptop and goes straight for the piracy software. It's done its job. He has a backdoor into Ranger's laptop. And the keystroke recordings show Prewitt the password to unlock Ranger's email account. He scans through the emails and finds one from a bank. Prewitt would love to go to the bank homepage and get into Ranger's online dashboard to see how much money is there. But the software hasn't provided Ranger's password. This simply means Ranger hasn't logged into the banking site manually since Prewitt installed the software. Prewitt can't get in yet. But he can fish around on Ranger's computer to look for statements from this bank. He locates a folder of recent downloads. There he finds a statement Ranger downloaded on the second of the month. There is a checking account, two savings accounts, and an investment portfolio. He reads carefully. It's not at all what Prewitt expected. The accounts are low. Way low.

He adds up all the holdings and balances twice. "Hmm," he whispers to himself while resting his head on his hand like The Thinker.

Altogether they have €61,000. Prewitt calculates it at about $85,000 in American dollars. There is no safe deposit box listed. Prewitt checks Ranger's email for any other possible locations of money. Nothing. Okay, maybe Ranger still feels more comfortable doing things non-electronically. Prewitt will try some old-fashioned digging in Ranger's office for mail and other paperwork. There could be other banks. The major investments might be somewhere else, too. Ranger may keep the bulk of his money hidden in Switzerland or the Isle of Mann, two places Prewitt knows are favored by Europeans hiding cash.

Prewitt reminds himself the spyware never was a high probability of finding where Ranger kept all his assets. There are other ways to do that. Each con is a chess game, with the attacking strategy planned before the first move is made. Prewitt simply brought the queen out fast. But the bishop was always going to fianchetto.

Prewitt's mind returns to the jewels. He's still thinking about da Vinci's secretary Melzi and his lover. He needs to find out if their affair might really have anything to do with the Courtemanche jewels.

He decides he'll track down any surviving correspondence from Melzi and the girl. If he can find their letters, there might be a clue that would tell him if he's right about the jewels. Again, he considers how extraordinary a treasure the jewels would be if they were connected to da Vinci. The most famous artifact Prewitt had ever held was at Standish's estate outside Philadelphia. A Japanese sword owned by Japan's first shogun, Tokugawa Ieyasu, that went missing when American soldiers occupied Japan after World War II. It was made by Honjo Masamune, Japan's greatest sword maker. Prewitt had learned what he was holding when Standish casually asked him to help unwrap it and hang it in his office. Right over his desk. And later that night, Prewitt read all he could find on Masamune and the sword. He knew it was the real thing. How Standish got it and how much it was worth, Prewitt had never asked. But he'd known it was a lot. These jewels, if they came from da Vinci, wouldn't be quite on that level. But they'd be valuable enough.

Prewitt gets a text from Benny. He and Kat are at an address just up the street from his hotel. It reads:

Something to show you.

Prewitt decides he'll have a drink with them.

Prewitt walks down the sidewalk to a small bar with tables outside. He finds Benny and Kat are already there. Kat is sitting on Benny's lap. They are rubbing their noses together.

"Bonjour."

"Bonjour, Prewitt," Kat says, hopping to her feet. She grabs Prewitt by both hands and pulls him forward so she can wrap him in a full hug. It surprises him, and he can't help but smile.

"You will like the work I've done. Come sit."

Prewitt takes a chair, and Kat finds one for herself and opens a laptop on the small marble-topped table. Benny signals for a server to bring more wine.

Kat pivots the laptop screen so Prewitt can see it. "Here is the Vatican banking page I've built for you. It has a masked URL. When you look, you see a secure page in the vatican.org domain, but really it is not. It is on my server at home. It will appear that bank funds entered here will go to an account at the Vatican," Kat points with her scarlet painted fingernail, "but they will actually be sent to you."

Prewitt knows what she's done is not simple.

"Straight into my account?" Prewitt says.

"Whatever account you want, oui. It took me a while to perfect. There are several confirmation steps put in place by both banks involved in the transfer. They are all done invisibly by my code. This one page collects all the information required."

"And you can change the graphics and the masked URL to look like any site you want?"

"Oui," Kat beams.

Benny leans over and kisses her on the cheek. "She is brilliant."

"Merci, Kat."

"And the way she looked in that police uniform. I mean . . . wow, right?" says Benny.

Kat reaches over and pushes the laptop closed.

Kat and Benny look at each other like there's no one else in the world. They kiss.

Seeing it, Prewitt notices a twinge of jealousy. But he makes himself feel happy for them. They kiss again. And keep kissing. Benny runs a hand up Kat's long bare leg. Prewitt gets up and leaves, wondering if they even notice.

Prewitt is up with the sunrise to a not-hurting back. *Nice.* He showers, texts Boniface about meeting up later, then opens his computer and starts digging. Last night, he had gotten tired and closed the laptop as soon as he'd opened it. He fell asleep to a rerun of *Fantasy Island* in French with English subtitles.

For an hour, he follows leads down rabbit holes and back up again. Then, after finding the image of the Courtemanche family tree again, he pinpoints the most likely mademoiselle du Courtemanche to have caught Francesco Melzi's eye. Lisette. But Lisette is a dead end online. Other than her thin limb on the family tree, there are no records of her life. Prewitt goes back to da Vinci as a starting point and tries to work down from that angle to find out more about Melzi.

And he does.

There is a university thesis on da Vinci's relationships that contains a few quotes from Melzi. The bibliography cites letters belonging to the Melzi family, written from Francesco to his sister Martine. They date from the year of da Vinci's death. Prewitt searches for the Melzi family letters. They are in a university library collection in Milan. *Perfect.*

Prewitt's phone rings. It's Ranger.

Prewitt answers in Italian. “Ciao. Marcellus here.”

“Marcellus?” Ranger asks.

“Ah yes, Earl du Courtemanche,” Prewitt switches back to French.

“Amelie insisted I call you.”

“About what?”

“She would like you to come and help Pensee.”

Okay.

“How?” says Prewitt.

“Amelie told me Pensee is behaving strangely, and you need to help.”

“Did she describe anything specific?” Prewitt wonders what he’s being set up for.

“No. Amelie asked that I get you to come to the chateau. I don’t argue with Amelie, so you shouldn’t argue with me.”

“Right.”

“Come now, please.”

“Sure,” says Prewitt. He hears Ranger hang up.

Amelie.

He checks his watch. He can get there before nine. *Acting on behalf of Pensee. Okay, so they’re working together?* Again, he wonders to what end. If he knew, he could plan something, but he will have to go in blind. It’s just not even remotely anything Prewitt had expected.

20

Prewitt walks to the tiny cafe by the hotel for a coffee and a pastry, then he heads for his car. Driving to the castle, Prewitt ponders Amelie and what is coming. His gut tells him this is some kind of test. But if she's on to him, why not just call him out? If this was another grifter he was dealing with, he'd have a better read. But Amelie is no grifter. She's a hippie rich girl who doesn't seem to give a shit about anything. *Or so I thought.* Prewitt glances at the car's clock as he parks the Peugeot in front of the castle. 9:00 a.m.

Just before Prewitt knocks, Amelie opens the door.

"Bonjour, Madame du Courtemanche."

"Bonjour. Could you come with me?"

Prewitt follows as Amelie walks from the front hall to the main staircase. She's wearing a summer dress that swishes behind her with each confident step. Amelie goes up the stairs, turns left on the second floor, and walks down the hall. "I've come to help your sister, right?"

"She's up here."

Prewitt follows Amelie up the stairs to the third floor, down the servants' hallway and into the last room. He sees the trap door is open. Amelie climbs up, and Prewitt, worrying they've inspected the cyber shield, goes up after her.

Amelie steps off the ladder onto a small platform on the roof, but it's only a few feet wide. Beyond that, the pitch is steep, and the tiles are old. He stands next to her on the platform, ready to grab hold of her arm.

"There's my sister." Amelie points east across the roofline.

Prewitt squints into the morning sun and makes out a black-clad figure perched like a gargoyle twenty yards away.

"Pensee said she needed in on the action. Next thing I know, she has climbed out onto the roof," Amelie says.

"What action?"

"Well, you're the one with all of the goings-on."

"Do you want me to talk to her?"

"No, I brought you up here so we could stare at the clouds."

"Okay. Wait here."

Prewitt takes off his shoes and socks. He puts a foot out onto the warm tile. It feels rough enough to give him some grip. He carefully makes his way toward Pensee.

As he gets closer, Prewitt sees Pensee looking out over the back of the property toward the river. He doesn't want to startle her.

"Pensee," he says softly. "Can I call you Pensee?"

She doesn't move.

Prewitt continues creeping toward her until he is less than ten feet away. He stops.

Pensee turns her face up toward him. In addition to her black clothing, Pensee is wearing a black knit hat with all her hair tucked away and a sparkling diamond necklace over a turtleneck sweater.

"Here, you can see the most fascinating sights." Pensee brings her hand to the jewels at her neck. "I was talking about the river."

"Yes, it's a nice view," Prewitt says, glancing at the necklace before turning his gaze to the scene below.

"The way you were looking at my necklace, I didn't know."

She's on to me. The two of them are onto me and just fucking with me.

"Could you come inside with me, so I can admire your necklace in better lighting?"

"I think the Sanfords should be our next job."

"Are they neighbors? Do the Sanfords need the Vatican's protection?" says Prewitt, playing along but not breaking character.

"All right, Le Chat. We'll study the layout, draw the plans, work out the timetable, put on our black clothes and our crepe-soled shoes and we're over the roofs in the darkness," says Pensee, her smile growing. "The cat has a new kitten. When do we start?"

"Forgive me if I don't understand. Perhaps we can talk inside. This doesn't seem like the safest place for us."

Pensee stands. She wobbles. Prewitt reaches out and grabs her arm.

"You have a very strong grip. The kind a burglar needs."

Yeah, yeah. Alright already, so what's the Ask?

Pensee lets Prewitt help her across the roof to Amelie.

But there was no Ask. After they got back indoors, Pensee sped off, leaving Prewitt alone with Amelie.

"Well, thank you for that. She wouldn't listen to me. Something about talking to you seemed to do the job."

"I suppose," Prewitt says, waiting for more. Amelie simply stares at him.

Ranger comes through the door. "Bertrand told me Marcellus had arrived. Why are you two up here?

"He talked Pensee off the roof."

"Why was Pensee on the roof?"

"Not sure. What did she say to you, Marcellus?"

"Nothing of substance," Prewitt says, staring back at Amelie. "But I'm bringing in a security expert to guard the chateau as we discussed, Earl du Courtemanche," says Prewitt. "He will be here twenty-four hours a day, so if you could find him a room . . ."

"I think we should insist Monsieur Marcellus himself moves in, too," says Amelie. "I would certainly sleep better knowing someone with his extensive knowledge of the Knights Templar is on hand to protect us."

Strong move, Prewitt notes curiously, as he also realizes the gift she's handing him. If he's here, he can more easily snoop around, both for the finances and for the location of the jewels. And he can still leave when he needs to.

"Yes, that sounds like a smart idea," says Ranger.

"Works for me," says Prewitt.

"Great," says Amelie.

"And perhaps you can keep Pensee off the roof," says Ranger as he turns to go.

Ok, fine, Amelie. You wanna play? I'll play.

Amelie takes Prewitt down the hall of the abandoned servant's wing. Walking beside her, he smells something floral with a hint of patchouli.

"You can stay in this room." She opens the door to a sparsely furnished bedroom halfway down the hall from where Lorelei accessed the roof. "There is a bathroom down here. I'll show you."

"Thank you, Madame du Courtemanche. This will make things easier for me."

"Least we can do."

Neither gives anything away.

Amelie looks into a few of the adjacent rooms they pass as if she hasn't been up here in a long time.

They both look into the bathroom as Amelie opens the door. There is a clear plastic shower curtain and a quartz countertop. Amelie flips the light switch, and two of four globe lights come on.

"I'll have some towels and sheets left for you. Hope this will work."

"It will be fine."

Amelie looks into Prewitt's eyes. Then she steps closer, just on the border of his personal space. He watches what seems like several emotions or thoughts pass. He can't decipher any of them. He tries to look only at her eyes but the lines of her jaw, her hair, her lips. *One thing I do know, she's really pretty.*

"It's a job for you, right?"

"How do you mean?" says Prewitt.

"If the Knights Templar weren't running around scaring people, you wouldn't be here working. That's what I mean."

"If that's what you mean, then in that case, yes, that's right."

Amelie seems to be waiting for Prewitt to say more. He doesn't. She takes a step back.

"Can we expect you to move in tomorrow?"

"Yes."

She smiles. "See you then." Amelie turns and heads toward the stairs.

Prewitt watches her go. *What the hell is she waiting for?* He stands there a moment, considering why she hasn't busted him open. Prewitt doesn't like not knowing. But he doesn't feel the con is at risk. *No, this is something different.* He resolves to wait and see. Let it be a challenge. He's safe. Either that or he's blinded by her beauty, which would be pathetic and a disaster. It's a fleeting thought he doesn't entertain. Time to pack a bag.

21

On his drive back into Paris, Prewitt rethinks his next steps. He also decides to devote some time to his research into the history of the jewels. His buddy convinced him they are still in the family, and his instinct is telling him they are in the castle. Where else would they be that would feel secure to a guy like Ranger? A bank? It doesn't seem like his style. Besides, there was no record of a safety deposit box at his bank or in his emails. And he wouldn't send them across Europe. *No. For Ranger to feel his jewels are secure, they'd be somewhere in those old walls.*

Prewitt gets into Paris, makes plans to check out of his hotel the next morning, and texts Boniface:

Meet me at the bar at
Lorelei's restaurant.

Prewitt arrives at Chez Jeannette, takes a seat at the bar, and orders lunch. As he waits for his food, he watches Lorelei happily restock bottles.

She stops in front of him. "Do you want a real drink?"

"Just a water, thanks."

"Why?"

"Because I like water."

"You are a drunky?" she says in English.

"Are you asking if I'm an alcoholic?"

"Oui."

"No, I'm not."

"So, you just don't like to have fun then?"

"I'm a professional."

"Bullshit. You are a broken-hearted man. So broken is your heart, I can hear it clinking around in your chest. I saw you when I installed the cameras yesterday. You thought no one was looking, and your face was so sad."

Damn. "Seriously?"

"Yes."

"I was concentrating."

"Don't bullshit me, Prewitt. I can always see through a man's bullshit."

Austrian psychology from a whip-smart wiseass French chick who happens to be right on the money.

"Would love to get back to my work now."

"What, I am a bother to you? You don't want to talk with me. Fine, be that way, assface. Drink your water."

Prewitt opens his laptop and checks in on his hacking software. Ranger hasn't been to any new bank or investment sites. Prewitt's still going to have to break into Ranger's office and go through his real paperwork. He'll check for a safe while he's there too.

Lorelei drops off a shallow bowl of white beans, duck sausage and a single sprig of basil in front of Prewitt. He stirs some of the steam out and takes a bite. *Delicious cassoulet.* Realizing just how hungry he is, he quickly finishes the meal and pushes the dish aside. Boniface still hasn't shown up. Okay, time to get back to the jewels.

Prewitt looks up the phone number for the university library in Milan that holds the letters Francesco Melzi wrote to his sister Martine. He takes out his cell phone and calls.

"Ciao, Universitá degli Studi di Milano Biblioteca del Polo di Lingue e Letterature Straniere," says the woman who answers.

Prewitt responds in Italian, "Hello, signora, I am looking for some letters in your collection. In reference to research I'm doing on Leonardo da Vinci."

"Si, what letters?"

"Francesco Melzi."

"Si, we have the Melzi letters. Are you a student here?"

"No, I am a screenplay writer, American, working on something for Hollywood in France. Would I still be allowed access?" Prewitt has made sure his Italian isn't perfect.

She's quiet for a few seconds.

"I think there's a story there. It could be a great movie."

"Okay, yes, that is no problem. They're in our special collection. You will need to look at them here at the library."

"Great, I am happy to visit the university. Thank you."

"A story with Melzi?"

"I hope so. My name is Prewitt Pearson. Whom do I have the pleasure of speaking with?"

"Gianna Conté."

"Well, Signora Conté, I can come to the university in the next few days. Will you be working?"

"Si, Signore Pearson. I will be here tomorrow and the next day, but then I'm off for the rest of the week. The library is open from 10:00 a.m. to 10:00 p.m. I'll give you my office number so you can tell me when you're coming. I can have the materials ready."

"Fantástico," Prewitt takes down Gianna's number then hangs up. *Not tomorrow, but the next day. And I'm gonna find something.*

Somehow, he knows it. Prewitt doesn't believe in fate, or magic, or bullshit that's not logical. But he believes in winning streaks. Doesn't understand them but believes in them. Because he's seen it happen. Luck too. And so far, he's got a good feeling about the libraries.

***

A few minutes later, Boniface sits down next to Prewitt at the bar. Lorelei comes over and gives him the up-nod hello.

"Lorelei, I'd like a bottle of the Domaine Thibault Liger-Belair Richeborg Grand Cru," Boniface says.

"You know I can't give you that bottle."

"Fine, the Domaine De La Romanee Conti '89."

"You wish," says Lorelei.

"I've changed my mind. The Louis Jadot."

"You'll pay your bill?" says Lorelei with a sideways stare.

"Of course."

"Two glasses then," Lorelei says.

"No, thank you," Prewitt says.

Lorelei walks off.

"Talk to me, my friend. What do you need?" Boniface says.

"Security for the chateau. Specifically, you, as an onsite security specialist so the Earl feels safe. Maybe Duke can get some guard dogs."

"Yes, Duke can do the dogs. But I refuse to do security."

"Refuse?"

"Refuse."

"Why?"

"I don't like to handle firearms."

"I'm sure we can work around that."

"I worry it won't be convincing."

"You could be a Vatican specialist who doesn't need—"

"I like it!" Boniface interrupts.

"And who always—"

"Yes, yes. Very clever."

"That way—"

"Of course, of course, say no more," says Boniface, nodding. "Good thinking, thanks."

"No problem," says Prewitt.

"Now tell me, why will I really be there?"

"To make sure Amelie and Pensee du Courtemanche don't blow the con."

"They have made you already?"

"No. Yes. I'm not sure. They're up to something."

Lorelei comes back with a bottle of wine and sets it in front of Boniface. She reaches under the bar and places a wine glass in front of each of them, then removes the cork and pours into both glasses. Then she picks up Prewitt's glass and drinks. "Acid's a bit high. Not enough rain."

Boniface takes a mouthful and sloshes it around like mouthwash. He parts his lips and sucks air across the wine. He swallows. "You may be right. I like it anyway."

Lorelei smiles and heads down to the bar with her glass.

"They don't know what I'm doing. But they aren't straight either," says Prewitt. "Pensee was on the roof talking about jewels and being a cat burglar this morning, and Amelie laughs everything off like she's not buying the approach. I'm trying to figure out Amelie."

"Sounds like they're on to you."

"Maybe."

"Maybe not?"

"There's just something about it . . . I don't know. And they haven't made any moves yet, either. Keep an eye on them, okay? And let me know what you think."

"Say no more," says Boniface as he lifts his glass for a sip.

"The one on the roof . . ."

"Pensee," says Prewitt.

"Older or younger?"

"Older."

"Tall or short?"

"Medium."

"Loud or quiet?"

"Both."

Boniface thinks a moment.

"So, what's she like?"

"I have no idea," says Prewitt, shaking his head.

The next day Prewitt checks out of his hotel, grabs some breakfast of cinnamon rolls and coffee at a small bistro called Baguett's Café, then starts his drive to the castle. He's in a good mood from the Paris vibe, the Paris food, and a good night's sleep. Very little back pain the night before and none that woke him. Only Lorelei and her annoying truth treatment bothered him a bit. But he resolved to drop it. *Why focus on the negative shit?* The con is flowing. Boniface will help with the sisters. The jewel hunt is heating up.

When Prewitt arrives at the castle, he turns into the driveway but is blocked by the handsome kid and his mower.

"Hang on!" the boy yells. He pulls the mower into the grass and cuts the engine. "You'll want to park on the East side of the chateau, by our cars."

"Merci," Prewitt says. He steers the Peugeot between the castle and a side yard that slopes down quickly into thick trees. There are three cars nosed in at an angle to the side of the castle, a Renault, an old Citroën, and an even older Citroën. He adds the Peugeot to the line and pops the trunk. He feels excited to be moving in. Tonight, he will get down into the basement for an overdue reconnaissance mission.

Prewitt pulls his suitcases from the trunk and looks up to see the lawnmower kid coming his way. He has a slight limp.

"Bonjour."

"Bonjour, I'm Prewitt."

"I'm Henri. Here, give me a bag. I'll help you take it up."

Prewitt looks down and sees Henri's lower right leg and foot are prosthetic. "If you have more mowing to do, I can manage the bags . . ."

"Why? Because of my leg?

"Oh, no. I didn't mean . . ."

"It's okay. But I can take a bag. No problem."

"Okay, thank you, Henri."

Henri picks up one of the suitcases, then he and Prewitt head in through the kitchen door and up the narrow stone steps to the third floor. Henri puts down the bag outside Prewitt's room.

"Again, I'm sorry," says Prewitt, still feeling bad about the prosthetic. "It was my gut reaction."

"It's no problem, Prewitt. Many people think this. But even though I was born with one leg, it hasn't stopped me from doing anything. I have a special prosthetic for running. Perhaps we race some time?"

"No need. You'd probably win."

Henri's cell phone chirps. He checks it. "Gotta go. Madame Farine needs me in the kitchen."

"Madame Farine is the cook?"

"Oui. Madame Farine. See you later."

"See you."

Nice kid.

Prewitt heads into the bedroom Amelie pointed out to him yesterday. Nothing has changed. No sheets, no blankets.

Prewitt checks the bathroom. No towels. No soap. He'll ask Bertrand the next time he sees him.

Prewitt comes down the stairs and walks to Ranger's office. The door is closed. He knocks.

"What?" snaps Ranger.

"Earl du Courtemanche, it's Prewitt Marcellus."

"Come in."

Prewitt enters and sits in the chair that has remained in front of Ranger's desk. Ranger has his laptop open.

"I'd like to go through some additional security measures the Santa Alleanza recommends," Prewitt says. "But I can come back."

"Sure, okay. I mean, that's fine. I'm working on some bullshit, but I need a break."

"The security specialist will be arriving tomorrow. He can also help with Madame Pensee. She needn't be up on the roof."

"She's being dramatic to get attention. There's no logic to anything she says."

"Well, it won't hurt to keep her happy. He'll bring guard dogs too. I'd like to discuss the additional . . ."

"Before we go any further, Marcellus, I have to tell you I am not going to pay for any of this. If I get a bill, I won't pay it. The Vatican is to blame for this landing at my doorstep. You should have handled the Knights Templar long ago."

"I have already spoken with my supervisors. The costs will be covered fully. Your family has been generous with their charity in the past, so it's the least we can do."

"Yes. Right. Exactly."

"I'm going to have floodlights installed on the roof. Floodlights doing sweeps of the grounds at night should deter intruders. Also, I'd like to install sensors inside the chateau."

"Sounds complicated."

"Not at all. And we'll know immediately if someone were to get in, especially at night, after everyone is in bed. This should make you feel safer, yes?"

"Yes. Good."

"They only record the date and time motion is detected. It won't show video, so privacy is maintained. I can show you where we'll put them now if that's okay."

"Not really. I must gather documents for this lawsuit I told you about with my neighbor. I can't spend the day walking around the chateau."

Prewitt stays quiet.

"Fine, let's do it now," says Ranger.

Prewitt walks Ranger out into the second-floor hall.

"Motion sensors will be in all of the second-floor hallways."

"That's fine."

"Let's head down to the first floor." Ranger follows Prewitt to the stairs and down until Prewitt stops on a landing and points to a large skylight with an even larger painting on the wall below it. "The skylight should have a sensor. Is that painting of high value?"

"Hardly."

Prewitt moves to go but sees Ranger has paused to examine it. Prewitt takes the moment to look, as well. There is a family depicted, a couple with one son and one daughter.

"If I can ask, who is in this picture?" says Prewitt, not caring but employing casual conversation to build trust.

Ranger waits a moment before answering.

"The boy is me. The girl is Pensee. And my parents. It was before Amelie was born." He continues to stare. "My father looks happier than he was. I think my mother asked the artist to do that."

Prewitt and Ranger walk from the base of the stairs down the main hallway. "We will use window sensors on the first floor instead of motion sensors."

"There are a lot of windows," Ranger says as they arrive at the intersecting back hallway. It goes in both directions. "We don't use the east wing of the first floor." He turns right, the same way Bertrand took Prewitt his first time in the castle.

"And we'll install sensors on all the exterior doors," Prewitt says as they pass the doors leading to the terrace. He has Kat to thank for an app on his phone that will monitor all the sensors.

Ranger leads Prewitt to the end of the hall and into the kitchen. Seeing it for the first time, Prewitt takes in the long stainless-steel island, an older stove with two ovens and six burners, a refrigerator, and two large sinks. A small wooden dining table with chairs sits under the window, and he counts eight doors leading off the large room. "What's behind all these doors?"

Ranger points to one nearby. "That's the only one that goes outside.

The rest are pantries, storage, and things like that. And the swinging door leads out to the dining room."

Ranger looks around the kitchen. "And that one goes to the cellars."

"Any exterior doors down there?"

"Yes. It's bolted shut."

"Let's look."

Ranger flips on a light switch and leads Prewitt down the stairwell into a vast cellar of old stone walls, thick supporting arches, and dusty flagstone floors. Continuing, they pass aisle after aisle of empty wine racks. There are discarded barrels along the walls, too, their lids lying on the ground.

"Is there no wine?"

"No. I sold the last vineyard decades ago."

They continue until finally coming upon what is clearly a newer wall blocking what would have been more cellar.

"Behind here was the ramp and large doors to load the wine, but it's been closed off." Ranger leads Prewitt away from the new wall to a small but solid-looking wooden door with two metal rods bolted into the stone on each side. "As you can see, there is no way in now."

"Yes, quite secure. Is there another wine cellar?"

"No. That was torn out when we closed off the ramp."

"I would have thought there'd still be wine. There's nothing left?" Prewitt doesn't need to know the answer, but he wants to keep Ranger talking, hoping the conversation will lead him on to other assets.

Ranger turns to Prewitt in the dim light. "My father auctioned most of the best bottles when he inherited the estate from my grandfather. Then he drank his way through as much of the remaining wine as he could."

"He was an alcoholic?"

"Is every detail of my family history your business as well?"

"Forgive me. I didn't mean to pry. I was just curious."

Ranger stares at Prewitt. "No, I'm sorry. That was rude of me," he says with an unexpected self-awareness. "The stress . . ." Ranger hesitates. "My father was a decent man, but he was . . . he spent his life drinking away the family shame. I might have headed down the same path, but alcohol never took hold of me. I've done my best to shoulder that weight while I 'preserve the family name.' And it's been more difficult than I thought. I don't judge him."

Ranger rests his hand on an empty shelf, almost caressing it. He looks off, thinking.

"The vineyards were nice. I miss them. I grew up wandering the vineyards with Pensee. Row after row. They were endless. Tasting ripe grapes before harvest. My grandmother did that with me. It was our secret."

Ranger smiles, then looks again at the empty shelves. "The wine was excellent. It's been thirty years since a bottle of Courtemanche sat here. Now, if Amelie wants a glass, the staff has to buy her a bottle at the grocery store."

Ranger turns slowly, scanning the cellar.

"Well, I hope this tour was helpful. I have to get back to my office and my unkind neighbor, Duran."

"It was," says Prewitt, deciding not to press further into other valuables since Ranger got sentimental, which is not what Prewitt normally sees from Ranger's type. He'll suggest another time for more conversation.

Ranger and Prewitt start back. They round the last empty rack, heading toward the kitchen stairs when Prewitt hears Ranger say something, as if he'd forgotten for a moment Prewitt was a stranger.

"Lily loved our whites best, the dryer, the better." Then, after a moment, "I'm sorry . . . Lily was my wife."

22

Prewitt and Ranger get to the top of the stairs and re-enter the kitchen. Madame Farine is there cooking.

"Do you have any Scotch?" Prewitt says to Ranger. "Sometimes I have a Scotch in the evening."

"Bertrand can bring it to you."

"Would you join me? Drinking alone is not my preference."

"I haven't had anyone to drink with in quite a while. I suppose that could be a good idea. Why not?"

Not surprising to Prewitt. Ranger's type usually doesn't have friends. Prewitt will play the friend. And a mark loosened up by a few drinks talks and trusts even more.

Prewitt lingers as Ranger exits the kitchen, leaving him alone with Madame Farine. She is stirring things in four pots on the stove. Without looking at Prewitt, she turns and picks up a huge chef's knife from the cutting board on the island and violently but expertly chops a bunch of carrots.

"You like French cooking?" she says.

"I do, yes."

"Because I can make you some nice Italian pasta dishes too, make you feel at home. I heard you'll be staying with us."

"You don't have to worry about me. I can bring groceries in."

"Don't be stupid. I'll feed you too. You think I can't handle one more mouth?"

"It's not that."

"Then what is it? You're a guest."

It's an odd quirk he has, but the random Scotch aside, Prewitt never eats the food of a mark. Sure, he is aware he's attempting to con them. And for quite a bit more than the cost of some carrots. But to Prewitt, there's no honor in it. Any schmuck can mooch grub. What con artist with any self-respect would take advantage of the mark by feeding himself along the path to the prize? Earn it first. Finish the job. Then you can raid the fridge as a farewell fuck you. But until then, have some class.

"You will eat." Madame Farine scoops the mound of julienned carrots into a pan of oil. The smells coming from the stove make Prewitt's stomach grumble.

"Thank you, but not now. And by the way, don't worry about anything. I am doing my best to keep you all safe."

"Me? Worry? Anyone comes through that door I don't like the look of, and I'll hit them with a pot."

Prewitt wonders how long Madame Farine has been working for Ranger. Probably a long time. And he doesn't doubt she'd defend this castle from attack, or at least her kitchen. *I'll leave plenty in the kitty to keep her in service. And Bertrand too.*

When Prewitt leaves the kitchen, he finds Bertrand coming through the dining room.

"Bertrand, can I ask you about sheets and towels?"

"Taken care of by Madame du Courtemanche."

Upstairs, Prewitt enters his room to find the bed made and curtains installed. He grabs his toiletry kit and makes his way down the hall to the bathroom. Walking along the creaky wood floor, he feels like he's in a college dorm again.

Prewitt sees a stack of towels has been added to the bathroom. He undresses and takes a long shower. Once done, he reaches out for a towel. Unfolding the top one on the stack, he realizes it is a washcloth. So is the next. And the next. Then there are three hand towels. The last towel in the stack is only slightly bigger than the hand towels. It's heavy. A floormat.

Prewitt dries himself hastily with a hand towel. He looks to the crumpled wet pile of his dirty clothes sitting next to the shower, then wraps the floor mat around his hips as best he can and heads into the hall.

Amelie steps out of his room.

Prewitt stops in the middle of the hallway. He tightens his grip on his pathetic towel and sucks in his gut.

She walks toward him, showing no guilt.

"Was there something you needed from my room?"

Barefoot, Amelie wears loose cotton pajama bottoms with light blue pinstripes that fall off her hips. She also has on a simple white tank top. Form-fitting. No bra. At all. Whatsoever.

"Just checking to make sure you got everything you need. I think, though, we didn't leave you adequate towels."

"It's fine. Larger would be nice."

"I'll see what I can find." She stops a few feet in front of him, "How are your plans with Ranger coming?"

Yeah, yeah. "Well, so far. There is still more to do."

"To protect against the Knights Templar."

"Yes, the Knights Templar. A very real organization and a very real threat."

She takes a step closer. Her hair is brushed aside so Prewitt can see her bare shoulder. He can't help but admire her, and she smiles, knowing it.

Prewitt stands straighter, tightening his grip as the towel thinks to dive for the floor.

"Would you be happier with a big fluffy robe?"

"Right now, at this moment, I would. In general, no. I'm not really a robe guy."

"Well, come to think of it, we don't have any extra. And mine would be too small for you, I think."

"We tried."

"What is a robe guy then?"

"Pampered."

"Oh, I see. Soft?"

"I suppose."

"You're not soft, you're . . ."

She takes another step closer and pokes at his chest. Nothing subtle about this come-on.

"Did you need something?" Prewitt says, shutting it down and hoping to finally get the Ask.

She takes a step back.

"Just curious, how long do you see this threat existing? I'd like to know if you're going to be here for a while."

That was the moment to show her cards, and she didn't take it. She seemed almost disappointed he didn't flirt back. *Hmm.* He offers his most boring answer.

"Hard to say for sure. Hopefully not long. As long as it takes to stop this threat and keep your family safe."

"Okay. Well, goodnight, then," says Amelie.

Amelie walks past Prewitt and heads for the stairs. He stands there a moment and considers again. More flirting. Serious flirting. And she approached when she knew he'd be arousable. But why try seduction? Heading into his room, he feels like his undergrad now has an attractive female RA who knows he's sneaking beer into the dorm but doesn't bust him. Does she want some for herself? Or does she have something completely different in mind? Or does she want *him*? Prewitt heads into his room and closes the door. No way he's risking treasure hunting tonight.

23

Prewitt is up at 5:00 a.m. It was a restless first night in the castle, and he misses the city sounds. No sirens, or growling motorcycles, or drunk girls screaming on the sidewalk. Not even a voice praising their lover for hitting the spot. What he would have done for some singing nightingales and sauced raccoons to feel more at home.

Prewitt has booked a TGV train that will get him from Paris to Milan in six and a half hours. One night in a hotel, then back on the high-speed train to Paris the next day. That will give him several hours with Gianna and the Melzi letters.

As Prewitt turns the corner to head to his car, he sees a figure carrying a large postal package disappear into the bushes that separate the main drive from the various outbuildings. Maybe it's Henri getting a jump on the day's work. But there is no limp. *Who the hell?*

Prewitt slips into the Peugeot and silently closes the door. He has a view of the drive and the hedge and some time to wait unnoticed.

The figure climbs back through the hedge. Pensee, clad again in an all-black outfit, speed-walks out of view toward the front of the castle. Then she's back, carrying a garment bag.

Pensee crosses the drive with the garment bag and maneuvers it through the hedge before disappearing. Just a few minutes later, she crosses back to the castle. *What's she up to?*

Prewitt looks at the clock. He's got to catch a train.

***

Prewitt is already well on his way to Milan when he places a call to Ranger's cell phone. "This is Ranger."

"Earl du Courtemanche, this is Prewitt Marcellus."

"Oui."

"I must travel to Milan for a day to follow up on a possible lead. I will be back tomorrow night."

"What kind of lead?"

"We have an informant who may have intelligence about your case. I want to interview him. Also, the floodlights have arrived, so you shall have them and the inside sensors the day after tomorrow."

"Good, that's good."

"Call if you have any questions."

"Okay. Thank you."

As Prewitt hangs up, he decides to try and doze off. He closes his eyes and thinks of the Courtemanche jewels. Just before falling asleep, he imagines opening a safe and seeing a pile of diamonds and rubies shining out.

The University at Milan is composed of old buildings, all made from local stone and worn down by centuries of the humid Mediterranean seasons. Prewitt regards the map on his phone and winds his way under porticoes until he locates the Universitá degli Studi di Milano Biblioteca del Polo di Lingue e Letterature Straniere. The façade of the building is composed of columns, arches, and flying buttresses sprouting from the upper reaches. Prewitt walks among the students who come and go and imagines Josh laughing with friends, out of class and heading to the library. He pictures them, all smiles, chatting, then quieting down as they head into the stacks to tuck away into study carols. He wonders what classes Josh will be taking in the fall. Has he thought about a major yet? Prewitt decides to call Josh as soon as he's finished here.

Prewitt approaches the main circulation desk and sees a woman he hopes is Gianna Conté. "Signora Conté?"

"Si."

"Buongiorno, I'm Prewitt Pearson."

Gianna comes out from behind the desk. "Of course. Ciao. Your Italian is good for an American, Signor Pearson."

"I have a knack for languages."

Gianna hands Prewitt a box. It's dark heathered gray, ten by twelve inches, and from his experience with historical artifacts, Prewitt assumes it's lined in acid-free paper to preserve its contents. "Here are the Melzi letters. Good you speak Italian. They have not been translated." Gianna leads Prewitt into the main room of the library with its vaulted ceiling and two-story stacks of books. "Melzi was da Vinci's secretary, but they were very close, like father and son. Melzi devoted his life to da Vinci," says Gianna.

"These are the originals?"

"Yes, you are welcome to read them at a table here if you'd like. Please wear these." She hands him a pair of white cotton gloves. "I'll be in my office if you have any questions. Just call."

Prewitt watches Gianna cross the room. She uses her badge to go through a door at the far end.

The late afternoon light slants golden and dusty through the tall lead-paned window and across the table as Prewitt sits and opens the box. Inside is a protective sleeve holding a decent size stack of pages. Prewitt withdraws the letters. He reads the date on the first one from Melzi to his sister. It's from the beginning of the period Melzi and da Vinci were in France. There is nothing there about a Courtemanche. Prewitt skims through several more letters, searching for a name.

He spots it after six pages and starts reading . . .

Martine, she stops my heart. This girl from the family Master da Vinci dined with, she is the prettiest I've ever seen. Her hair at first seems brown, but when the candles dance, it glows with its own fire. I know I shouldn't stare from my place against the wall. I tried to look at my feet, Martine, but it was impossible. I learned her name from the staff at their chateau. Lisette.

Da Vinci had nothing but disappointment from the dinner. The beautiful girl's father is not an agreeable conversationalist. His wife tried several times to comment to Master da Vinci on his work, and the man shouted over her. I saw the beautiful girl flinch at his voice like it was a whip.

She looked so unhappy. Her eyes were sad, and the Master would have captured it with a few strokes of his brush. But that is not to be the case. The master will not paint her. Her father is too much of an ass.

Then in the next letter. . .

Martine, I spoke to Lisette in the market. She looked up from a cart where she was agonizing over the choices of pears, and our eyes met. There was recognition, and such warmth came into her cheeks. I swear she blushed as I stepped up beside her and introduced myself. Perhaps I disregarded society's rules, where I should have known my place, but I did not think to halt in that moment. I had only the thought of speaking to her and knowing her. I hope the blush was not one of offense.

The letters continued from Melzi to Martine, mostly concerning the work da Vinci was doing in France. But there were a few more times he confessed to his sister he couldn't stop thinking about Lisette.

Da Vinci never named Melzi's lover in his journal. Prewitt first found the name Lisette on the Courtemanche family tree. But here,

Melzi has named his lover. Lisette. Is it Lisette du Courtemanche? It must be. Da Vinci gave the jewels to Melzi, but there isn't a record connecting them from Melzi to Lisette, at least that Prewitt has uncovered.

Prewitt skims through the rest of the letters. Melzi worries openly to Martine about da Vinci's failing health and his feelings for what he is going through. So why isn't he telling Martine more about Lisette? Their affair would have been happening exactly at this time in Melzi's life. Did he keep the affair a secret from his family?

Prewitt remembers da Vinci's journal recording a possible pregnancy. He wonders if Melzi and Lisette had a child. Prewitt turns to the last pages. There is one more letter to Martine.

> Martine, my Master, has succumbed. He has died. His body was too weak. His heart and his soul were too big to continue living on in such a sad frame he has flown away to our Lord. I have not even begun to grieve, Martine. I must do everything I can to keep myself a steadfast servant. I must put my Master's household into order for the return to Milan. All his most personal items as well as the paintings he brought with him. They are priceless now that he is gone.
>
> Martine, there is so much I will have to tell you when I am finally back home. Remember the beautiful girl with the cruel father. Just writing this to you now causes my hands to

Then the letter stops. Prewitt looks through all the pages in the box, but he already knows none are out of order. *Come on.* Were some of Melzi's letters lost? Prewitt wonders if the rest of this letter is gone for good.

Prewitt goes to the last page again. He notices the afternoon light has dimmed. Students around him are turning on the table lamps.

Prewitt gets out his phone. It's 7:14 p.m.

He calls Gianna. She tells him to meet her at the office door.

Prewitt closes the box, and by the time he has crossed the library,

Gianna is waiting. She leads him down a quiet hallway to an office at the end. "Here we are."

Prewitt hands the box of letters back to Giana and takes a seat on a tiny yellow sofa.

Gianna sits at the desk. "So, how else can I help? Did you find the story you were hoping for?"

"Maybe. Are there any other letters? Is this everything that is available?"

"We have the complete collection. Every Melzi letter is there."

"The last one. It ends in the middle of a sentence."

Gianna seems puzzled. She opens the box, pulls on her own pair of gloves, and looks. "Wait." She gets up and leaves the office.

After a minute, Gianna comes back with a page in her hand. It is inside a clear protective sleeve.

"It was left in the special collections room. I'm sorry. Would you like me to do the translation for you?"

"Please."

Gianna takes her office chair and begins to read in English:

> . . . shake. I've loved a beautiful girl, Martine,
> and I've lost her. How can a heart break twice?
> I loved the Master like a father . . .

Prewitt listens as Gianna finishes off the letter. Melzi doesn't speak of Lisette again. He tells Martine he'll see her soon back home in Milan with the Master's things.

"Are there response letters from Martine back to Melzi?"

"No. And scholars don't concern themselves with Melzi beyond his connection to da Vinci. "But about your love story, it sounds like it ended in heartbreak. He said he lost her, the girl he called Lisette."

"There aren't many details."

"I think you will have to make up a lot of the story if you want it to be a good movie. Let me check in case for any other information in the university's database."

Gianna clicks her computer mouse a few times. "There are a few more things about Melzi and da Vinci. But nothing about Lisette. If we had a time machine, maybe we could find out if it ended in love. That's the movie I'd want to see. You can always write a happy ending for Francesco and Lisette."

Prewitt emerges from the library into a cityscape lit by the rich, fading light of dusk. But he is still lost in the story. Did Lisette and Francesco ever see each other again? Did they live out the rest of their lives alone? Was there a child? Melzi had to have given Lisette the Courtemanche jewels. How else could they have made their way into the family? Prewitt feels a pang of hunger and decides to calm his mind with a call to Josh then some authentic Italian pasta. He pulls his phone out and dials.

"Hey, Dad! How's France?"

"It's good. How are you? Getting excited for the crimson?"

"I am, yeah. Mom and I got a list of stuff to buy for my dorm room. Grandmother took us shopping and bought all of it."

"That was nice of her."

"I'm still waiting to get a roommate assignment. I got an email yesterday; they put me in a quad. I'll have a roommate and share a bathroom and living room with two other guys. That's what I was hoping for."

"Sounds perfect."

Prewitt wanders down a narrow side street off the university campus.

"I've been looking at the course catalog; it lists all the majors and minors. I have some time to decide. Mom said I can start the first semester with some required classes and see where my heart takes me next semester."

Her words. Prewitt has always loved the way Honey Hair raised Josh.

"But I also want to take a poetry writing class. You don't mind if I do that, do you?" Josh says.

"I don't mind at all. That's the point of college."

"I am thinking about jobs too, you know, for after I graduate."

"Don't worry about that now. It's too early to worry about that stuff. You're smart. You can do anything you want to do."

"I'm smart like you."

"Smarter."

Prewitt crosses an intersection, and the narrow street dumps out into a modest piazza. He walks over to a bubbling fountain and sits on its lip.

"I'll try to be back in time to help get you moved into your dorm room."

"Oh, okay, Mom didn't know if you'd be around for that or not."

"I'm gonna try my best. I gotta go now. I love you, Josh."

"Love you too, Dad. Bye."

Prewitt ends the call with his heart warmed. Then he has the urge to call Johnny. He wants to talk to his friend. Besides, Johnny will be wondering where he is.

Johnny picks up after the first ring. "Where the fuck are you?"

"I'm in Milan."

"What's in Milan?"

"Museums, gardens."

"You're into some shit."

"Is it not possible I'm taking a vacation?"

"No, it's not possible."

"Why?"

"'Cause you would have told me about it, you dumbass."

"It was last minute."

"I can't help you if you end up in jail in Italy."

"It would more likely be France, and I don't plan on ending up in jail."

Johnny stays silent.

"I gotta pay for Josh's college Johnny. Kid got into Harvard. I have a responsibility. And his grandfather offered to pay it and everything else but only if I cut ties. He's trying to push me out of their lives."

"Their lives?"

"Josh's life."

"Well, your son will be a grown man in four years. He can do what he wants then."

"Yeah, but he'll know who paid for his college."

"So you found a way."

"I do what I know."

"Well, I hope you're not rusty. Because if that kid has to spend his Thanksgiving break flying eight hours to visit your sorry mug behind bars in a country filled with cheese and assholes, I doubt you'll see much of him after that."

"I'm not rusty."

"That's what we all think. Every crook who ever made a mistake. Boxers ain't the only ones who get ring rust."

"I'll be fine."

"I sure hope so. It would be nice to see you again in New York."

"You will."

After a few more minutes of chatting about Johnny's dance class squeeze, Prewitt hangs up the call and looks around the piazza. It's brimming with people. Prewitt gets up and walks toward a nearby restaurant. The wait staff are lighting candles on each of the tables.

The host seats Prewitt at a little table off to the side of the group of maybe a dozen others. A server arrives, and Prewitt asks for a glass of wine and osso buco alla Milanese.

He looks out across the piazza. Lights have come up on the fountain. Children run in circles shrieking, high on gelato. He watches parents conferring in pairs. A man his age scoops up a kid who looks six years old and carts him off. Toward home? Perhaps a bath and a bedtime story? The rest of the family is right behind them, the mom holding a little girl's hand. After the children are asleep, will the two of them drift to opposite sides of the house, or will they have a glass of wine on the balcony together, even get a little tipsy and fool around quietly in their room while their children are sleeping? Prewitt hopes it's the latter. They're working hard at life. Let them enjoy it on a night like tonight.

24

After getting in from Milan late and slipping off to his room unseen, Prewitt rises before 9:00 a.m. and tests his back with a little forward and backward stretch. It's some kind of miracle. Prewitt feels no pain anywhere. The sciatica has come and gone in the past, but not as quickly. *I'll take it.* He gets showered and dressed, then eats an energy bar from the stash he bought at a drugstore in Milan as he makes his way down through the castle. It's quiet. He walks out the front door into the fresh country air and finds two white work vans. One has both rear doors open, and he can make out Lorelei in her coveralls stacking crates of sensors onto the ground. Henri emerges shirtless from the dark interior of the van. Smiling at Lorelei, he hands a box out to her. She is smiling back. Lorelei will install sensors inside the chateau hallways, windows, and doors. She sees Prewitt and gives him a happy wave, then turns back to smiling at Henri.

In the other white van, large flood lights are visible through the open side door. Michel climbs out of the passenger side. In a white painter's bib and white T-shirt, he's dressed to look the part of a laborer, but his big blond, stylish hair doesn't quite fit the role. It stands even higher than it did the night they met. Approaching the van, Prewitt can tell Michel is not pleased about something. Louis comes around from the driver's side.

"All ready to go, boss!"

"I'll take you up to the roof access. From there, you can walk to an empty bell tower in the center of the chateau. There isn't electricity there, so you'll use the extension cords."

"Just as long as there aren't spiders," says Michel.

"Of course there will be spiders," Louis says.

Michel punches Louis in the arm. "That's not a funny joke."

"Who's joking?"

A cold panicked sweat seems to come over Michel.

"Relax, will ya?" says Prewitt.

"I'm relaxed," says Michel, now counting his breaths.

An hour later, Prewitt goes to the second floor to check on Lorelei in the long hallway at the back of the castle. When he steps off the landing, he sees she's halfway down the hall, setting up an aluminum ladder. Prewitt walks toward Lorelei, then movement through a window catches his eye. Prewitt stops and looks out. Below in the garden where the rose bushes were cut, Prewitt sees Ranger bending over. He has gloves on, and his hands are reaching carefully among the empty stems. Ranger peers closely at one, then moves on to inspect another. *He's looking for fresh growth*, Prewitt realizes. Ranger reaches into a bag he has hung across his chest, pulls out a handful of powder, crouches, and spreads the fertilizer on the soil at the base of the plants.

Prewitt continues on from the window. He walks up to Lorelei, who is nose-deep in a box of motion sensors. She has heavy-duty scissors sticking out of her back pocket and a large spool of double-sided tape hanging from her work belt.

"How's it going?" he asks.

"Easy. I climb up the ladder, tape up a sensor, climb down the ladder, move the ladder. Really giving the ass a great workout." Lorelei climbs up the ladder and positions a piece of tape on the wall.

A door opens. Amelie comes out into the hallway. "Bonjour." She's wearing snug yoga pants and a loose white sweater. Her hair is held back from her face with a floral scarf. A yoga mat is rolled up under her arm.

"Bonjour, Madame du Courtemanche," Lorelei says.

"I apologize if we disturbed you, Amelie," Prewitt says. "This is Lorelei. She's installing motion detectors."

"Thank you," Amelie says. "I did hear you out here, and I wanted to see what was going on. It's nice to meet you, Lorelei." She walks over to the box of sensors and looks in. "These will tell you when anyone is walking around in this hallway?"

"Yes."

"Hmm. Well, I have a tendency to be up in the middle of the night. But for now, you've encouraged me to take my yoga outside. Fresh air and sunshine. I'll let you get back to it." She smiles at Prewitt, then brushes past and saunters down the hall before turning out of view.

Lorelei stares at Prewitt.

"What?"

Lorelei rolls her eyes accusingly, then climbs back up her ladder with a sensor in hand.

Prewitt heads up to the third floor. He walks into the room at the end of the servant's hallway to find Michel sweating and peering up the ladder to the trap door.

"Shit, shit, shit, shit," Prewitt hears Michel whisper to himself.

"What's wrong?"

Michel walks away from the ladder, holds back his sweep of blond bangs, and wipes his forehead with a handkerchief. "I usually do the hot guy jobs. You know, distractions, light seduction work. I don't do old cobwebby chateaux."

Muscular legs pop into view on the ladder as Louis climbs down from the roof. He climbs off. "Hey boss, the floodlights are ready to be bolted in. Just give me a second to talk this big baby into coming out there to hold them in place."

Louis stands in front of Prewitt, coverall rolled down to the waist, bare arms glistening with sweat from the summer sun. Prewitt takes a moment to look over the tattoos that make up two full sleeves. They are all large and colorful with bold black outlines. There's a pair of bluebirds, some roses, a dagger, a skull, a snake wrapping its way around a large bicep, a moth with human eyes in its wings, and a heart with a banner across it that reads: Grandma. Prewitt thinks it makes Louis look both tough and beautiful.

"That ladder was covered in cobwebs. The roof will be crawling with spiders," Michel says.

Louis turns to Michel. "I wiped away all the cobwebs. There are zero cobwebs."

"You lie. You always fucking lie," says Michel, now in a legit panic.

"There are no spiders on the roof. I promise. They're scared of heights."

Prewitt interrupts, "I'll come help with the lights. Michel can prep the extension cords."

"Okay, yes. Thank you," says Michel.

"You're lucky he's nice, you big baby. Do the cords. Then plug them into the outlet."

"Which outlet?"

"The one over there on the wall, below the window. I swear you're like an idiot."

"Shut up."

Prewitt follows Michel's eyes as they find the outlet. The window is filled with cobwebs.

"Just use a broom," says Prewitt.

Michel says nothing.

"Are you going to be alright?"

"I'll be fine," says Michel, finding courage.

Prewitt grabs the end of an extension cord and lets it uncoil as he heads up the stairs after Louis.

***

Prewitt holds the last floodlight in place as Louis tightens the bolts. Then Louis plugs it into a weatherproof power strip with the other floodlights.

"Ready?" Prewitt flips the power switch on and plugs the power strip into the extension cord. No power.

"Fucking Michel! Plug it in, you baby!" Louis yells toward the trap door.

They wait a moment. Still nothing.

"I'll go back and check. You secure the cord to the roof, so it doesn't shift around in the wind," says Prewitt.

Louis produces a bundle of white plastic ties. "Okay, boss."

Prewitt traces the extension cord back along the roofline. He gets to the first join. Picks it up and checks it. No issues. He keeps going, hits another join. Picks it up, checks it, fine. He's now almost to the trap door.

Just at the top of the stairs, there is one more join. Prewitt reaches down to pick it up, but it's snagged on something below, and there is no slack. He sees it's not connected all the way. He gives a gentle pull on the cord to try to get enough slack to connect it properly. It won't budge.

"Michel, give me some slack!" he yells down the trap door.

There is no answer.

Prewitt sticks his head down through the trap door and discovers Michel passed out under the window. The extension cord is plugged in, but Michel fainted on top of it.

Prewitt climbs down the ladder. Halfway down the rungs, Prewitt's left leg gets tangled up in the bundle of extension cord. He reaches with one hand to free his leg but can't reach. Prewitt presses his shoulder against the ladder to brace himself and grasps the extension cord with both hands to pull his leg out of the loop of cord.

He gives it a little yank down.

Prewitt feels the extension cord pull up. *Shit.* It must be Louis securing the cord to the roof. It's enough to make Prewitt lose his balance. He reaches out for the ladder, but it's too late. He crashes four feet to the floor.

A moment later, Louis sticks his head through, "Boss?" Then he sees Michel. "Michel? Michel! No!"

Louis clambers down the ladder and past Prewitt, who sits on the floor with his hands grasping his right ankle.

"Michel!" Louis grabs Michel by the arms and shakes him.

Prewitt turns around as best he can.

"Michel, you're okay. You fainted," says Louis.

Michel comes to.

"Spiders!" he screams.

"It's okay. It's okay. I've got you," says Louis, cradling Michel's head like an infant, his blond hair all dirty with dust.

Michel flings Louis's hands away, springs up off the floor, and retreats to the doorway. There, gripping the door frame, he stops and turns around to look at them. He rubs the back of his head and regains his composure.

"Uh. Yes. Okay." Michel brushes the dust off his pants. "Got the cord plugged in. Should be all set now." He looks over at Prewitt. "What happened to you?"

Prewitt stands, using the ladder for support. He tries putting weight on his right foot and winces in pain. "Fucked up my ankle when I fell down the ladder, that's what."

Amelie comes into the room. "Who fell?"

Prewitt notices she's changed into linen trousers and a blouse, and her hair is damp.

"Not me. It was Marcellus," says Michel.

"Sorry if we disturbed you again," says Prewitt.

"Hard to stay Zen when you think someone is coming through the ceiling."

"We have installed the floodlights," says Michel.

"You should feel safer now, madame." Louis beams. "Okay, boss, we're out." Louis hands Prewitt the remote control to the floodlights, and he and Michel leave.

Prewitt steps toward the door. The pain forces an involuntary wince.

"You hurt yourself?"

"I'm fine."

"I can see your ankle swelling from here."

Prewitt looks at his ankle. It has ballooned. *Fuck.*

"Would you like some ice?"

"Oh, no, no. I'm fine."

"You don't look fine. Go to your room."

"Excuse me?"

"I'll bring you ice. Don't argue."

Amelie leaves, and Prewitt hops down the hall and into his room. He sits on his bed and flexes his foot as far as it will go to the right and the left, up and down, assessing the damage. He grabs the back pain pills and takes the last one.

Amelie enters and hands him a plastic bag with ice cubes and a white dish towel.

"Thank you."

As Prewitt wraps the ice into the towel, he feels Amelie's gaze still on him. He looks back at her, intending to stay professional while she flirts again but instead sees her caring look. It's real.

"Keep that on for a few minutes. No more accidents, okay?" Amelie heads out the door.

25

After ten minutes of icing, Prewitt gives walking a try. The sprain is bad enough to stay off for a couple of days. But he can't. He'll have to suck it up. And he can get some more pain meds. Duke's pharmacy in Paris. Yes.

He texts Lorelei and asks her to meet him at the stairs to help him down to his car. Driving the Peugeot will be sketchy.

"What the hell happened to you?" Lorelei says when she meets him at the top of the staircase.

"Don't ask."

"Sit."

"Lorelei, I need to get out to the car."

"Sit, or I will smack your face."

Prewitt eases down on the narrow stairs. Lorelei checks out his ankle.

"This is pretty swollen. You need to put ice on it."

"I did."

"And elevate it."

"I'll do that when I get back."

Lorelei pauses, then her eyes light up. "This is part of the job. You got hurt on purpose."

Prewitt stands back up and starts down a step.

"No."

"You get injured, and Madame du Courtemanche will take care of you, and that's your in with her. The old guy will think you're feeble and not so much a master criminal."

"None of that is right, Lorelei. What are Boniface and Duke teaching you?"

"Things. We're working on it. I show promise. Lean on me."

Prewitt gratefully leans against her, and they make their way down to the front door.

"But Madame du Courtemanche, you're definitely going to fall for her."

'Huh?"

"The clanky pieces of your broken heart, I don't hear them so much today. Were you talking to her?"

"There is nothing happening with Amelie."

"You're a terrible liar."

"Well, I saw Henri helping you this morning. Is that part of *your* act?"

"Not an act. He's cute."

"You're on a job."

"And so are you, you hypocritical shit."

"It won't work out."

"You think I am only interested in sex?"

"I didn't say that."

"Yes, you did if you think I think it can't work."

"You think it can?"

"I don't worry about it."

They take a few more stairs.

"You should worry about getting hurt. That's something Duke and Boniface forgot to tell you," says Prewitt.

"Like you've been hurt? I don't worry about that shit."

"No?"

"If love fails, I wipe my tears and open my eyes and look around. I can always love again. There are so many people to love."

"Is that right?"

"Yes."

"Sounds dangerous."

"Only to someone who is afraid."

"I'm afraid now?"

"I didn't say that. *You're* saying it."

"Okay, I'm done talking."

They reach the front door, and Lorelei helps Prewitt outside and to the Peugeot.

Then Lorelei heads to her van. She comes back with two more rolls of double-sided tape.

"Lots more sensors to install on the first floor, Marcellus. Four more hours of work, I'd guess." She strolls toward the chateau. Prewitt reaches into his pocket for his car keys.

"Shouldn't you be resting that?" Prewitt hears.

Amelie has come outside.

"I thought I might head into town and pick up some painkillers, maybe a wrap."

"You aren't planning to drive yourself, are you?"

"Yes, I am."

"I don't think so."

Prewitt limps toward the driver's side door and takes the keys from his pocket. "I'm fine."

"Let me drive you," says Amelie, walking over and lightly touching his forearm. Prewitt looks over to Lorelei, who is watching and smirking at him.

"It's a rental car, so . . ."

"I'm not going to crash."

Prewitt doesn't trust Amelie. But this caring still feels real. Besides, there isn't a way to say no that won't sound like bullshit. He'll use the time to figure out her game.

"Actually, would you mind if we went all the way to Paris? I have a doctor friend there."

Amelie's smile widens. "I haven't been to Paris in forever. Hand me the keys."

"Do you have a license?"

"It's expired."

"When's the last time you drove a car?"

"So long I can't remember. Give me."

She reaches out again, peels open his fingers, and plucks out the keys. She meets his eyes, her smile even wider. And maybe it's the pain, but he can't help what he's feeling, so he smiles back, admittedly charmed by this woman.

"See if you can get in, Limpy," says Amelie as she opens the driver's side door, sits, and starts the engine. Prewitt hobbles around to the passenger side.

Prewitt fears for his life a couple of times during the first half hour of the drive as he learns Amelie has a thing for high speeds on empty country roads. But soon they calm down enough he can text Duke Wellington about his ankle and needing more pain meds.

Prewitt hears a text alert and looks at his phone. Duke Wellington's response is a thumbs up emoji, an address, and a time.

Then a text comes in from Honey Hair:

We have to discuss Harvard.

Prewitt starts to type:

Sure, give me . . .

But before he can finish typing, she sends another:

The first payment is due
a week from today.

He deletes his words then waits because his phone indicates she's still typing. Then she isn't typing. He waits. There isn't a new text. She's gone. Prewitt clicks his phone off.

Later, as he looks out the window, farmland passes by and slowly gives way to the suburbs. Soon they are driving through Paris. Under the blue sky, the streets seem carnival-like. People everywhere.

Prewitt feels the energy of all the moving pieces, moving people, and messy lives. He sees a young couple on what looks like a date and wonders if they will fall in love today. It's a little game he always played with himself in Manhattan, trying to pick the winners and losers. Though he stopped playing it when he found himself only picking losers.

Prewitt looks at Amelie, one casual hand holding the top of the steering wheel. Her left arm is draped along the open window, and her fingers drum lightly against the frame. Amelie is calm and seems to be enjoying herself, lost in her thoughts. *And what thoughts are they?*

Prewitt pulls up the map app on his phone so he can give her the directions.

"What did you do?" says a kneeling Duke Wellington as he pokes at Prewitt's ankle. They're backstage at a very small theater around the corner from the pharmacy where he last met Duke.

"I fell off a ladder. Why are you wearing a doublet?" says Prewitt since Duke Wellington is, and it's tight and red with puffy sleeves.

"We're rehearsing. It's not a dress rehearsal, but I prefer to be in costume through the entire rehearsal process."

"When is the play?"

"In three months." Duke Wellington hands Prewitt a small bag. "Take two, every four hours. No more. And keep icing tonight. Then wrap."

"How much did you give me?"

"Enough."

"The back is better."

"That's probably temporary."

Duke Wellington pokes at the ankle again. "Swollen, but not a break."

"Please stop poking me."

"It reminds me of the time I played Hamlet on a broken foot. Did that curtain rise each night? It did."

"Thank you again."

"No problem." Duke looks off. "A performance no one else could have given. Not Mr. Olivier. Not anyone. I channeled my pain. The entire audience was on their feet."

Prewitt waits a moment. "I should go, Duke."

Duke returns to the present.

"I'm working on the dogs."

"Good. Thanks, Duke."

"You're welcome. Remember to ice tonight."

Prewitt comes out of a theater with his paper bag and gets back in the car.

"Your friend is a doctor?"

"He does theater as a hobby."

"I found a chocolate shop I want to go to," says Amelie as she puts the car in drive.

Prewitt opens the bag. There's an elastic bandage and a pill bottle.

He swallows two of the pills dry.

"It's in another part of the city, though. I hope you don't mind."

"I don't mind."

Amelie whips the Peugeot out into traffic. A man on a bike rides up onto the sidewalk to avoid getting hit, then screams "Fuck you!" and flips them the bird. "*Oups! Pardone*," says Amelie as she waves an apology and drives on. Soon they are a few blocks away.

Prewitt decides to wade in. "I'd like to know if you are concerned, Madame du Courtemanche, about what is happening with the Knights Templar?"

"Why?"

"Well, you don't seem to be. Are you?"

"Not at all. You're protecting us, right?"

"Yes."

"Then what's there to be concerned about?"

She doesn't look at Prewitt when she says it. Prewitt considers how blasé Amelie has been about things, playing like she doesn't have a care in the world. Maybe when you're as rich as she is, this kind of stuff doesn't bother you. But challenging him had to have been part of a plan. Or was being doubtful of the con simply her way to get his attention? He looks at her soft, elegant profile. There is the slightest smile on her lips.

Prewitt ponders the flirting again. Perhaps it's not a game? Perhaps she likes him? She seems to enjoy pressing his buttons. *And why?* He watches her mouth and sees the smile flatten. And as it does, her lips tremble for a second, almost imperceptibly. Then she smiles again. It's the slightest self-consciousness. And now, alone with her, Prewitt knows why. He knows it's real. He's been reading people his entire life. And Amelie du Courtemanche is no con artist. No. She's sweet. And she's lonely. And in this moment, driving through Paris, she's enjoying herself, perhaps more than she has in a long time.

Prewitt is more curious than relieved. Sure, this will be easier to deal with, *but what is Pensee up to?* He has no idea.

Amelie pulls into a spot across the street from À La Mère De Famille. "This is Paris's oldest chocolate shop. I used to come here with Pensee and my mother . . . a thousand years ago." Amelie gazes at the storefront. "My mother passed away from cancer when I was young. In my twenties.

"I didn't know that."

"Well, how would you? Being here makes me miss her," Amelie says with a warm smile.

"Ranger and I have been talking about your family a bit."

"Then he must have told you about my father drinking himself to death."

"Those aren't the words he used."

"And about losing *his* family?"

"Yes."

"It's just us now. The fabulous du Courtemanches."

She gives Prewitt a "shall we?" look as she opens her door. Prewitt gets out. He gives the foot some weight and takes a step. It hurts.

They cross the street, and he holds the door open for her. À La Mère De Famille is a corner shop with a green, painted exterior. Inside, the floor is tiled in a pattern of stars and diamonds. Counters and display cases are made from dark wood that shines with a polish imparted from centuries of use and care. Shelves everywhere are covered in baskets and boxes of confections trimmed out in a signature orange ribbon. It all gives Prewitt a feeling that generations have run this shop, and it makes him feel like he's being welcomed into someone's home.

Amelie, delighted, floats from one case to another, peering in at the florentines, orangettes, and chocolates like a bee collecting pollen. Soon a shop person has a large confection box and is filing it as directed. Amelie buzzes back to Prewitt.

"What would you like? I'll add some to my box."

"Oh, no, thank you. I'm fine."

Prewitt hobbles toward a case with mendiants, truffles, and chocolate-covered marshmallows. She walks over to him. "These look good," she says, pointing to a marshmallow dipped in dark chocolate and sprinkled with pistachio.

Into the box, they go.

Prewitt remembers Josh loves marshmallows. He wonders if he should mail Josh a graduation present since he missed the ceremony and party. Not something from this shop. Maybe some cool Paris clothes or something. Yes, he absolutely will. He wishes he had thought of it sooner.

After Amelie has finished making her purchase, she lingers in the store, seeming reluctant to hop back in the car and return to the castle.

Eventually, she returns to Prewitt's side near the exit. "I bet there is somewhere nearby to get a drink."

Prewitt considers how a beer might dull the pain of his ankle even more. *Done.*

A few storefronts down the sidewalk, they come to a vintage shop. Amelie's eyes go to a set of four matching bracelets, dark green and marbly, set on a scarf in the display window. "Look at these. A bit pricey for some plastic."

Prewitt looks at the price tag. €600 for all four. "That's a bargain. If they're Chanel Bakelite, they're worth five times that."

"To a fool," says Amelie with a chuckle. "Come on, let's go in."

It's a perfect place to find something for Josh, so Prewitt agrees.

Amelie disappears into a section of women's clothing. Prewitt starts to flip through a wooden crate of old records. He looks around and ponders what Josh might want. A European concert tour t-shirt, a pair of coveted old basketball shoes? He walks past some shelves with cut glass decanters and a hodgepodge of antique barware. *Not yet. Still a kid.*

Prewitt comes to a dining room table. It's round, set on a pedestal. The top is covered in books and candle holders. Underneath are heaps of leather shoes and boots. That's where the bag catches Prewitt's eye. He pulls it out and sets it on the table. The deep brown leather is worn in places, but its quality has held up over the years. There are two pockets on the front with heavy metal clasps. And a long leather strap to wear across your body.

Prewitt unzips the main compartment. The interior is sectioned with beige canvas trimmed with leather detail. The workmanship is high quality.

"Is there a designer stamp?" Amelie is standing next to him and looking into the bag too.

Prewitt turns the bag over and around. They both look but find nothing.

The shopkeeper has come over now. "I was hoping to place it as Dior or Balenciaga, but I can't find a mark on it anywhere," he says.

"Are you looking for yourself?" Amelie asks.

"For my son. He just graduated *liceo*."

"That's a perfect gift for that. Send him out into the world."

"I agree too," the shopkeeper chimes in.

Prewitt winces as he adjusts his weight off the bad ankle.

"How much is it?" Prewitt says.

"€140," says the shopkeeper.

"Oh, that's too much," says Amelie. "You must be able to lower the price."

"Well, I could perhaps . . ."

Amelie and the shopkeeper's voices fade from Prewitt's attention as he eyes the bag more closely, imagining Josh wearing it over his shoulder, walking with a girl, sitting next to her at a coffee shop late at night, both using studying as an excuse to flirt with each other. As he pictures his son, he feels pressure building up from his heart and tears forming in his eyes as he realizes the Josh he is imagining is looking older, a young man with his own life. And Prewitt feels in his gut a sick knowledge that he missed it. He missed his chance to spend those last happy years with Josh as a boy. Missed it all. His and Josh's last years have been stained with the muck of the damn divorce, and the pain of Prewitt's very being sprinkled over every memory they both share. And now, for some reason, Prewitt feels all he's lost, and he feels how it's over. *Damn it. This is not the way I wanted it to be. For Honey Hair, for me, for our child.*

Prewitt turns and looks out the window, wondering how the hell he got to this day, in this shop, in this city, confused by it. He watches the cars pass outside. Then no longer letting himself have this moment, he pushes the thoughts away and stops the tears from filling his eyes any further.

"It's not worth any more than €100," Prewitt hears Amelie say.

"I can go no less than €130 and normally would not lower the price."

"Are you the owner?" says Amelie.

"I am the owner."

"Then, of course you can."

"I'll take it," Prewitt says, turning to them both. "The original price is fine. I'll take it. Thank you. Please wrap it."

"I'll give it to you for €130."

"€140 is fine," says Prewitt, not wanting to cheapen anything about the bag or the transaction or anything about buying this gift for his son.

Amelie and Prewitt sit next to each other at the bar of the first place they come to, an English pub named Nigel's with Liverpool FC soccer posters and jerseys everywhere. Their shopping bags are at their feet. Prewitt is finally feeling better from the combo of painkillers and two fresh pints. Much better. And the strange catharsis of tapping into some well of emotion not usually accessible has loosened him up. He finds himself curious to learn more about Amelie.

After Prewitt shares he is divorced, Amelie probes and learns the ex-wife felt alienated by Prewitt's work. Tell the truth when you can.

"I never married," says Amelie.

"Why is that?"

"I didn't meet good men."

"Ever?"

She hesitates, thinking. "No," she says with noticeable pain, which Prewitt takes to mean that when she trusted her heart to life, life stomped on it and left it staring out of a castle window. "And I don't meet men anymore. I don't really meet *anyone* anymore."

"Surely there must be society events or . . ."

"I don't belong with those people. I never have."

Amelie continues to share bits and bites of her past over the next hour, including the years in her thirties she thought about having a child on her own, though she never did. And as Prewitt finishes one more pint, he learns Amelie has had a sheltered and rather boring life. She doesn't venture out much, she doesn't have any friends other than a few from high school and college, and those aren't nearby. She does yoga at home. She reads a lot at home. She's learning guitar at home. She's kinda stuck at home.

She cares about Pensee, that's clear, though she's offered nothing about Pensee's behavior. Prewitt notices the flirting has stopped too. Amelie is acting much more genuine. He decides he's certain. She's no femme fatale. No, she's a bright, unique woman who is not enjoying her life all that much. It's either that, or she is a genius con artist who plays her role better than he ever could.

On the drive back from Paris, Prewitt, buzzed, slumps comfortably lower in the passenger seat, his arm resting on the open window. The warm wind and the late afternoon glow have relaxed him even more. The silence in the car too. It's like he's driving with someone he's known for years and doesn't need to speak with to feel at ease. The pills and alcohol could account for this trance, but Prewitt knows it's Amelie. Her being here with him. It's nice. A companionship sort of nice. And he hasn't felt that feeling in so long he's surprised by how comforting it is. He's been operating in a sad, oxygen-less state without realizing how crappy he's felt, and now suddenly, he can breathe. He looks out the window, past an old wooden fence, and down into a shallow green valley where a farm and a small farmhouse sit. Then he looks forward at the dark gray road winding out in front of them; its white line faded to nothing. Prewitt's eyes feel heavy, and he thinks about how this is something he shouldn't indulge. But it's too easy to ignore the warning. He'll allow himself this little moment.

26

Prewitt wakes to the alarm on his phone at 1:00 a.m. He flexes his ankle. Not too bad. He gets out of bed, grabs a small headlamp and a lock pick kit, and throws on pants and a shirt, no shoes. Time to check out the basement. Prewitt makes his way down the steps to the first floor, walking along the left edge of each to avoid loose planks. There are a few creaks, but nothing loud enough to wake anyone or worry him. Getting to the first floor, he pictures the walled-off area of the basement where there used to be an entrance to the wine cellar. There should have been more space than what he saw when Ranger showed it to him. *Something is behind that wall.* It's a good place for a hidden room, which is a good place for a safe. Prewitt could have looked during the day, but if there is a hidden room Ranger is keeping from him, he would rather not be seen searching for it.

Light on his bare feet, Prewitt slips noiselessly through the dining room toward the kitchen. Through the windows, he sees strong beams of light from the floodlights installed earlier. *Perfect.* Prewitt peeks through the swinging kitchen door. Lights off. Empty. He eases through and walks toward the door to the basement. Prewitt opens the door and closes it behind him. The stairwell is pitch black, so he pulls the headlamp from his pocket and slips it on. The low beam casts a warm, narrow light.

Prewitt reaches the bottom of the stairs and heads in the direction he walked with Ranger. He continues until he gets to the walled-off part of the cellar that used to be the old wine ramp. Prewitt pans his headlamp over the floor and follows the worn gouges in the stones where heavy wine barrels were rolled in and out centuries ago. They disappear right into the new wall. Then he takes a close look at the wall. A skim coat of plaster over cement block, made to look old.

Prewitt looks more closely at the floor and sees sweep marks. The dust is disturbed where a door would swing open. There are shoe marks too. Someone has definitely been here recently. *It feels good to be right.*

Taking his time, he examines the wall and finds the seam. He also looks for a camera. Sensors. Wires. Anything that might detect his presence. It seems clean.

Prewitt searches for a handle but can't find one. It must be a solid door. He pushes against the edge, hoping it will cause the door to swing out from a magnetic latch. The door moves in then comes out a few inches, revealing a hollowed-out handle on its side he uses to pull the door the rest of the way open.

The hidden room is twelve feet by twelve feet, and there's a safe sitting right in the middle. Prewitt takes it in. No other exit. One wall has two pairs of bunk beds shoved against it, and each bed has an empty mattress and a sleeping bag in its case, store tags still hanging from their drawstrings. Another wall is solid shelving filled with what looks like emergency food and supplies. *So, Ranger has kitted out a panic room.* Prewitt turns back to the door. Sure enough, it has two huge deadbolts that can be flipped from this side to keep someone out.

Prewitt takes a good look at the safe. Much older than the panic room. And it's a beauty. About four feet tall, sitting on heavy-duty wheel casters. It's black with a solid gold border painted around the door and an ornate gold scroll added in each of the four corners. Two-inch-high letters spell out RIALTO. Prewitt crouches to see what he's up against. There is no combination dial. Just one big keyhole and a lever. He can't pick this lock. His tools are too small, and though they work in every kind of modern lock, they'd be useless on this guy.

Prewitt stands and gives the panic room another look. Not a chance the key is in here. Ranger would keep it on him or near him. Unless he's willing to blow the safe open, Prewitt will have to find the key. He knows the jewels could be sitting right in there. *Damn. That was almost perfect.*

Prewitt exits and closes the door. He makes his way back to the stairwell and climbs up, thinking about where he'll start looking for the key. Ranger's office is the first place. He puts the headlamp back in his pocket, enters the kitchen, and pulls the basement door quietly closed.

Prewitt listens for the ambient sound of nighttime in the castle but hears footsteps. They're coming through the dining room toward him. He beelines for the refrigerator.

The kitchen door swings open. It's Amelie. She turns on the light but doesn't look surprised to see him.

Prewitt acts startled. "Merde! You scared me."

"Sorry, I didn't know you were here. Sneaking around?" says Amelie.

Prewitt opens the freezer and removes some ice cubes.

"For my ankle."

"I'll get you a towel," says Amelie.

"I can do it."

"Let me help you."

What's she doing up?

"I hope I didn't wake you," says Prewitt.

"No. I don't sleep well. Sit."

Prewitt sits at the head of the wooden antique kitchen table.

After his day trip with Amelie today, he feels okay sitting here with her. *She wanted a little attention. Fine.* Amelie can do what she wants moving forward, and Prewitt will stay completely professional. Just play your role. Sometimes that role includes giving the mark space to interact with the persona. If needing attention is the test, then make sure to pass. Never give up your authority. Amelie is harmless. The con is safe. No threat here.

Amelie grabs a clean dishcloth from a drawer, takes some ice from the freezer, and wraps it into the towel.

She walks to Prewitt, who props his bare foot up on a chair. She takes the ice from his hand and adds it to the towel. Instead of handing him the towel, she gently settles it onto his ankle. She crouches to do it, like a shoe saleswoman helping a customer. It's purposefully submissive. And very sexy. *Okay, so the flirting has returned.*

"Most nights, I read myself back to sleep, but tonight, I decided to come make a cup of tea. Lucky timing."

Sure.

"As long as it wasn't my noisy limping around that woke you," says Prewitt.

Amelie takes Prewitt's hand and puts it on the towel so he can hold it in place, then heads to the stove and picks up a kettle. She fills it at the sink.

"I enjoyed our trip today," Amelie says. She places the kettle on the stove and turns it on.

"A quick reprieve. All the lights and sensors they installed today are working," says Prewitt.

"And I enjoyed our talking," says Amelie. "There are layers to you." Amelie looks over at Prewitt. "And a lot of pain," she says. "Even though you try to hide that part of yourself."

"I try to be professional."

"I know you do."

She sounds sincere to Prewitt. And the slight mischievousness about the way Amelie is acting tells him she couldn't care less about the con. The way she's looking at him too.

The kettle whistles, and Prewitt watches as Amelie pours the hot water into a mug. She grabs a tea bag from the cupboard and adds it.

"Do you want a cup?"

"No, thank you."

Standing at the counter, Amelie waits a bit, then takes a sip of tea, her large brown eyes looking at Prewitt over the cup.

"Very hot."

Amelie walks toward Prewitt and sets the teacup down on the table. She touches her mouth with one hand. With the other, she reaches down to where she sat the towel of ice on Prewitt's ankle and plucks out an ice cube. She sits in the chair next to his foot and applies the ice cube to her lips.

Then Amelie runs the cube slowly back and forth on her lips. The ice wets them. Prewitt stares.

Now she looks at him as she does it. She stops moving the cube and holds it on her lips, puckering them. Prewitt imagines pulling Amelie to her feet and kissing her. He can feel her kissing him back.

As the ice melts against her lips, a bit of water runs over her fingers and down her wrist. She is still looking at him. Prewitt allows his eyes to hold her stare in a clear message: *I'm as up for it as you are.*

Then Amelie plops the ice cube into her mug, stands, and walks toward the door. "Goodnight, monsieur."

Prewitt watches the door swing after she has passed through it. His eyes focus there for more than a moment as he feels his quickened pulse pumping in his body. He keeps staring at the door as if looking away would mean he has to return to the empty kitchen table where his self-disgust has spilled over like the water from the ice and is now dripping onto his lap. He finally does, shaking his head and sighing at his weakness.

Some professional you are.

27

The next day, Prewitt walks out the front door in time to see a sleek red Sunbeam Tiger pull to a stop. The humming engine shuts off, the door opens, and Boniface gets out wearing a beige linen suit and dark lens aviator sunglasses. *Where do these cars come from?* Boniface runs a hand lightly over his slicked-back hair and twirls the car keys around his finger before slipping them into his pants pocket.

Prewitt walks over to Boniface, and the two shake hands, then Boniface pulls him in for a hug and a few kisses on the cheeks. *Oh yeah, we're playing Italians.*

Bertrand opens the door and, as Ranger steps outside, announces, "The Earl du Courtemanche, Viscount of—"

"Yeah, yeah, yeah," Boniface interrupts. "He's not the Pope, so we can skip the rest."

Prewitt so far likes the character Boniface is playing. And the more attitude, the better. When you're obnoxious, people are less likely to question whether you're real. Boniface saunters past Ranger into the castle. "Take me to my office."

Bertrand follows Boniface through the entryway hall and into the dining room. Boniface turns to Bertrand. "I will use this room as my office.

I will also need a ten-meter extension cord and a chair; any chair, wood is fine. Preferred, actually."

Prewitt and Ranger enter the dining room, and Prewitt sees Madame Farine come in through the swinging kitchen door with a chafing dish to stock the lunch buffet. Amelie and Pensee soon enter the dining room as well.

Prewitt fixes on Amelie. She wears a pair of charcoal gray linen shorts tied off with a bow at the waist and a white t-shirt tucked in with a loose blazer over it. The leather sandals on her feet are all sexy and strappy, and her muscled tan calves pull at his eyes. He keeps himself from staring.

Madame Farine hands Pensee a Diet Coke from her apron pocket. Pensee cracks it open. The noise echoes through the room. "Madames du Courtemanche," Boniface executes a low bow. "I am Robere Redmayne of the Vatican. The Pope's most distinguished security officer."

"What's the model year of your car?" Pensee asks. She steps forward, the voluminous skirt of her white wrap dress swishing around her feet.

"Sunbeam Tiger 1965."

"Very nice."

"You like this car?"

"Yes."

"Then perhaps you can show me how to drive it sometime."

Pensee smiles coyly at Boniface.

Prewitt notices Amelie smiling and pictures last night in the kitchen.

Ranger steps forward, "Monsieur . . ."

"Redmayne. Of the Vatican."

"Monsieur Redmayne . . ."

"Oui."

"Where is your gun? I said I wanted armed guards," says Ranger.

Boniface smooths the lapels of his jacket. "I am armed. But my weapons are concealed. Besides, Courtemanche, you do not need an armed guard when you have a specialist. A specialist knows how to persuade."

"With fists, you mean? Martial arts?"

"If needed. But it never is. Not if you are a specialist. A specialist is a negotiator. I use the power of my mind and my words. And I am effective."

"I see," says Ranger.

"You will not see. And that is my other specialty. Stealth. And observation. I disappear. But I am always here." Boniface spins around, taking in the room and the people. "Yes, you're in good hands now, Courtemanche. Rest assured. There will be no surprises on my watch."

Prewitt's phone rings. "Oui?" He hears barking coming through the phone. "I'll be right there," Prewitt says and ends the call. "Earl du Courtemanche, the security dogs have arrived."

Prewitt returns to the front drive of the castle. Duke Wellington is standing outside the driver's side door of a light blue minivan. High-pitched barking comes from the inside.

Duke wears military fatigues and wading boots. A multi-zippered fanny pack secured around his middle and his khaki pith helmet are straight out of a jungle safari. He has several leashes clutched in one fist.

"Ah, Monsieur Marcellus. I am here with the security dogs."

"Good. Let's see them."

Duke shamefully tilts his head down. "I'm just going to say; this is the best the Vatican could arrange on such short notice."

Duke slides open the side door on the van a few inches, and the barking intensifies. He reaches in and manages to clip two leashes before the pack of dogs bursts out into the driveway.

Prewitt sees two chunky golden bread loaves tear off into the bushes. The other two dogs on the leashes are yanking and crying as they attempt to follow their companions.

He looks at the dogs, then back at Duke Wellington. "Corgis?" Prewitt says.

"I'm sorry, Prewitt, they're my sister-in-law's dogs," Duke says. Then he looks past Prewitt to the front door. Ranger comes marching down the stairs.

"Earl du Courtemanche, this is Monsieur Wellington, our canine specialist," Prewitt says.

Ranger gawks at the chaos at Duke's feet.

"Are you joking?"

"Meet your canine guards," says Duke, fully committed.

"Where are the security dogs? The German Shepherds, Belgian Tervurens, hounds even?"

"The queen," Duke says.

"I beg your pardon?"

"The queen."

"The queen what?"

"The Queen of England. She was always surrounded by a pack of them. It was no mistake."

"I don't follow, Wellington."

"The Pembroke Welsh are the best at what they do."

Prewitt looks at the two dogs. One is chewing on its leash and whining. The other is licking its privates.

Duke reaches down and pats the one that's whining. It nips his hand. He unclips both dogs, and they disappear into the bushes.

"They are expert sniffers. Can smell an incendiary device a mile off."

"I thought corgis are a herding breed."

"That's what they want you to think."

"Who?

"The dogs."

All four dogs burst out of the bushes and tear across the driveway, barking and biting at each other. They circle Bertrand, who retreats up the steps as they swarm his ankles.

"Oh, quit being so afraid, Bertrand," Ranger says.

"These dogs are not harmless," Duke says. "They can be killers if need be. Killers."

Soon the dogs lose interest in Bertrand. They race off across the driveway then disappear around the castle.

"Your killers are now loose on my grounds."

"They're scouting, and surveilling. Come with me. I will tell you all about all their abilities. And their exploits," Duke says, rushing off into the backyard. "Come on, Courtemanche," he yells.

Ranger looks to Prewitt, who nods reassurance. Then Ranger begrudgingly marches off after Duke.

"Robere, the Sanfords are having a masquerade ball next week," says Pensee.

"That sounds enjoyable. And who are the Sanfords?" says Boniface.

"As if you don't know. They own the biggest chalet in Nice."

Boniface and Pensee are standing on the back terrace. He holds a plate of fruit and cheese from the buffet.

Pensee is barely visible beneath her giant hat and sunglasses. She grabs a handful of fabric from her dress, blowing around her legs, and holds it to the side. "I hope the night of the ball is less breezy. I hear there will be fireworks. It would be terrible if they were canceled," she says.

Boniface eyes Pensee, seeming to take a few seconds to consider what she has said. Then a small, satisfied smile comes to his lips. "Are you in need of an escort for the ball, Madame du Courtemanche?" says Boniface. "White is such a nice color on you, by the way. Here. Have a strawberry."

Pensee blushes and eats a strawberry, then another. They both look into the yard where Duke and Ranger are trying to corral the corgis.

Prewitt is walking through the backyard toward the back terrace when he hears the hum of a small engine coming closer and sees Henri round the castle on the lawn mower. Henri wears only a Speedo and large headphones and appears to be bopping along to music only he can hear. Prewitt watches as Henri mows a curving line that follows a previous curving line into the back lawn. Henri stops the mower, gets off and moves a thick branch, then hops back on and continues toward the water and . . . *Lorelei?* Lorelei is climbing out of the river in a red bikini. When Henri gets to the river's edge, he stops the mower, steps off, gives her a kiss. Then after he takes off his headphones and prosthetic, the two of them jump into the river. Henri climbs out, puts his leg and headphones back on, gets on the mower, and continues his cutting route. Lorelei stays in the water. *This is definitely not on her list of tasks.* Prewitt watches as Henri, wet and smiling, bops along to his music while steering up the lawn. And he feels a bit of envy. The good looks, the great attitude, the carefree morning. The youth, too. Soon Henri is passing Duke and Ranger walking along together, the dogs zooming around them.

"They are searching for any explosives that might be here. Allow me to demonstrate some of their skills, Courtemanche." Duke hands a wooden tube to Ranger. "Blow into this."

Ranger takes it. "Is this a duck call?"

"No, it mimics the cry of a sheep in distress. The pack will come straight away."

Ranger blows. All four of the little golden dogs streak toward him.

"Sit!" Duke says.

All four dogs sit.

"Down," Duke commands.

All four dogs ease down onto their bellies, their tongues lolling from exertion.

"Bang," Duke says.

One of the four dogs rolls onto its back, legs in the air.

"Is that part of their security training?" Ranger says.

"No. That one just knows a few tricks." Duke reaches out his hand to Ranger for the whistle. "All done," Duke says to the dogs, and they go streaking off toward the terrace.

"Oh my, look at these darling dogs!" Pensee gathers a handful of cheese from the plate and tosses it down over the railing. The corgis sprint for it.

"I don't eat cheese, Robere."

"An allergy?"

"No, it's too fatty."

"Well, I love it. Could you be accompanied to a ball by a man who eats cheese?"

"All depends on the man, I'd say."

"How about this man?"

"Well, aren't you a forward one."

"Can't get ahead in life being backward."

Pensee gives Boniface a quick once-over. "I'll tell you, Robere. I make it a rule to be on guard when a man is this clever."

"And I make it a rule to be this clever when a woman is on guard."

A smile grows on Pensee's face. "My, my," she says, all coy and turning her chin to her shoulder. "The dogs may still be hungry." Pensee gathers up the rest of the cheese and flings it into the bushes.

"How will we know if they sense anything dangerous?" says Ranger.

"They have specific barks . . ." says Duke.

Loud snarling barks ring out in the bushes under the terrace as the dogs spazz.

"They are alerting now!" Ranger points to the shaking bushes. "Look!"

"Leave it! Leave it!" Duke yells. He runs toward the dogs.

Ranger notices Pensee and Boniface standing on the terrace above the bushes. "Pensee! Run!" Ranger screams as he follows Duke.

***

"Well, this is exciting!" Pensee says to Boniface. "Can you hear what my brother is yelling about?"

"I can't quite make it out, dear. I say we head down there."

Pensee and Boniface start toward the yard as Duke enters the bushes.

"No. No. They're heading for a bomb," Ranger says when he sees Pensee coming down the terrace steps.

"It's not an alert! No danger. I repeat, no danger!" Duke yells from inside the bushes. "Get out, you assholes," he yells at the dogs.

The dogs waddle out onto the grass. Duke follows. Pensee and Boniface join them there. Prewitt too.

"Sorry if that scared anyone," Duke says. "They got into something under the bushes."

Ranger gets to them, winded.

"They're always alert and will never tire. I'll put them through a thorough training run tomorrow," says Duke.

"Earl du Courtemanche," Bertrand calls, coming out onto the terrace. "You have a phone call."

"Who?"

"The lawyer. He insists on talking to you."

"Again? Damn it. Pensee, the lawyers are going to cost me more than the land," Ranger says, starting toward the terrace steps.

"Oh, my dear brother. I'm glad you're the one who handles the business affairs."

Pensee, Boniface, and Prewitt all stand there for a few seconds watching the dogs as Duke places their leashes on them.

"Wellington," Boniface finally says to Duke. "Could I borrow your hat?"

"Of course," says Duke, taking it from his head.

Duke hands over the pith helmet, and Boniface puts it on. "What do you think?" he says to Pensee.

"I think you look adventurous," she says.

"Well, I am certainly ready for anything that may happen here," says Boniface as he starts toward the chateau. "Shall we?"

Pensee joins him.

Duke unzips his fanny pack, pulls out an army green baseball hat and puts it on, then leads the dogs away.

Bertrand has come a few hesitant steps into the yard. He approaches Prewitt. "Monsieur Marcellus, do you have a moment?"

"Yes, Bertrand."

"You said we could talk if I need to," says Bertrand.

"Yes."

"I need to."

"Okay."

"Are things getting better or getting worse? I can't tell."

"Better."

Bertrand looks sideways at Prewitt. "They don't seem better."

"Well, they're getting better because we are safer now."

"With this extra help and the lights?"

"That's right."

"I see," Bertrand says, half satisfied. "But you don't know when this will all be ending."

"Well, I think soon."

"You think?"

"I told you before, don't worry."

"Okay." But Bertrand doesn't look reassured. "May I speak candidly?"

"Have you not been?"

Bertrand appears to find a more authoritative version of himself. "More candidly."

"Please."

Bertrand studies Prewitt for a moment. "Can I trust you?"

"Yes. Of course."

"Can I? Really?"

"Yes, you can. Why do you ask?"

"Because I am the butler," Bertrand says, raising his voice. He calms himself before continuing. "And I am responsible for the well-being of this family." Bertrand takes a deep breath. "I've worked here since I was twelve years old, monsieur. My father worked for Earl du Courtemanche's father and grandfather. And I have seen many people fail the Courtemanches. These are people who, like you, were supposed to help with one problem or another. But in the end, they didn't really care. Some even seemed to relish in failing this family. For years my employers have lived quietly, but they've been continually shunned and mistreated by people who seem to hate them. The earl, he is good, deep down. People don't see that."

Prewitt knows those working for the wealthy over generations come to see them in a shiny light, even the rotten ones, becoming what's known in the trade as "Stockholm-ed." *But Bertrand is also pretty damn decent.*

"So again, I ask, can I trust you? To do what you say you will do? To really protect this family?"

"Yes, you can trust me," says Prewitt in a lie that, because it's directed at Bertrand, feels slightly crappy.

"I will take you at your word." Bertrand straightens. "And do you need anything at this time, monsieur?" he says, all proper again.

"I'm fine, thank you."

Bertrand heads back inside.

Prewitt walks across the lawn and turns into the formal gardens. He pulls out his phone as he begins through the beheaded roses and plantings. *Let her pick up.* He hits dial.

"Hello, Prewitt," says Honey Hair.

"Hey."

"Are you going to have it?"

"Yes."

"How?"

"I'm working something out. How are you?"

There is a moment of silence. In it, Prewitt pictures Honey Hair standing by the window in the apartment they'd shared. She'd always looked out of the large bay windows when she talked on the phone. Prewitt would watch her raise one foot and point her toe to the floor, then turn her leg and extend it out. Always lifting a leg, or pointing a foot, leftovers from childhood dance training. And sitting across the room at the little table he liked to work from, Prewitt would gaze at her back and her long hair and marvel at how beautiful he found her. *This is love*, he'd thought to himself. And the sound of her voice, soft and caring, had soothed him to be there with it, lightly filling the space. *I miss that.*

Imagining her now, Prewitt sees her face as if he is outside the window looking in.

"I'm fine," she says.

"I wanted to ask if Josh has a move-in date. Maybe I can be back in time to go with you guys, help him into the dorm."

"My father hired movers."

"Oh, okay. Maybe I can still come."

"If you want."

"Great."

"Just make the payment on time, Prewitt. If you don't come through on this, you'll never be able to make it right."

"I know."

"I'm going to go."

"Okay, bye."

Prewitt hears the phone hang up. He walks a few more paces, then looks up from his feet, realizing he's not in the roses anymore. He's passed through hedges and is near the pool. The sun is blazing down in the early afternoon, and Prewitt feels the heat of it on his face as he steps closer and looks toward the water. Near the deep end, Amelie is lying on her stomach on a chaise lounge naked, her head covered by a sun hat. Prewitt is close enough to see a sheen of sweat on her skin. Aroused by the sight of her glistening body, he wonders if she might have heard him talking to Sharon in English. No, too far away. *Relax.* Amelie turns her head to face the opposite direction on the lounge and adjusts her hat. Prewitt can see headphones in her ears. She swats at a fly on her back, and his eyes move down along the side of her breast, pressed firmly beneath her rib cage, then to her hips and past them to her muscled legs. Then he turns away.

Prewitt walks back in the direction he came and out of the roses. He keeps walking into the yard and past the terrace toward the path to the front of the castle. But the attraction stays with him. He can still see her in his mind. He purposely focuses on the trees lining the Loire to change the image. He doesn't like the feeling of being turned on by Amelie. And it's because he knows it's not only her body that gets him. It's all of her. He wonders how he is so easily enticed. This is not why he's here, and in the light of day, it feels foolish and reckless. Prewitt thinks about last night in the kitchen. It wasn't only teasing. It was an overture. *Wasn't it?* The way she looked at him when he finally locked eyes with her. *It was.* Prewitt walks until he gets to the driveway. He's never been attracted to a mark. He never would allow himself to consider it. Prewitt thinks back to Johnny's comment about being rusty and realizes he's not on his game as much as he thought. A part of him is still that sad sack moping around Manhattan. The persona couldn't keep that hidden for even two weeks. Prewitt gets to the front of the castle and slows. He suddenly feels silly. He knows people sometimes jump into the sack. But even as a kid living in a horny dorm at CMU, he knew it's not always without feelings. They are people, after all. *Someone could get hurt. But will it be her or me?*

28

"Duke insisted on sleeping in the van with the dogs." It's dusk, and Boniface is packing a week's worth of clothes into the tiny closet and chest of drawers in his room on the third floor. "And his understudy will take over rehearsals until he is finished here. I walked the chateau three times. The earl was occupied with angry phone calls whenever I passed his office. He's involved in a lawsuit, you know."

"I'm aware. So Pensee, any thoughts?" says Prewitt.

"Ah, Pensee. Lovely girl."

"And?"

"Might be a cuckoo."

"You think she's cuckoo?"

"No. I think it's something else."

"That she is onto us?"

"Nothing indicates this."

"She was wise on the roof."

"She has said nothing about the job to me."

"Why?"

"Don't know."

"What did you talk about?"

"Sheer nonsense."

"The entire day?"

"We improvised. Like in an acting class."

"She didn't talk about being a thief?"

"No. She talked about masquerade balls and eating cheese, like a character from an old movie."

"No thief talk."

"Not a word."

"And what did you do?"

"I played along."

Prewitt thinks for a second. "Why do you think she's doing that?"

"Perhaps she's cuckoo."

"You think she's cuckoo?"

"No, I do not."

Prewitt takes a pause. "Okay. Good work."

"Thank you."

Boniface reaches into his suitcase and pulls out a fluffy bathrobe. "Fear not, Prewitt. We are still in business. Whatever is afoot is now under the watchful eye of Robere Redmayne of the Vatican. And he will keep that eye on this Courtemanche sister. Right now, I bathe."

"There are only small towels."

"Which is why I always bring a robe."

Prewitt checks the time. It's 1:40 a.m. He wants to find the key to the safe in the basement and knows Ranger's office is the most likely place. His office door will be locked, but Prewitt can spring that easy. He grabs his headlamp, pockets what he needs from his lock pick kit then leaves his room. When he gets to the second floor, he treads barefoot down the hallway, sticking to the outer edge. Amelie admitted to having insomnia, and she's been in the right place at the wrong time before, so Prewitt has an excuse ready in case she shows up again.

His chest feels tight, and his breathing shallow. It's because he wants to find these Courtemanche jewels so badly. The idea of touching something da Vinci touched . . . he takes a deep breath to settle his nerves and slows his steps. Maybe there will be more there than the jewels. Maybe there will be something that tells him what happened to Francesco and Lisette. He's been thinking about them too, wondering if they ever saw each other again.

Prewitt arrives at Ranger's office door and checks his phone. Only his motion was detected on the second floor. *Good.*

Prewitt kneels at the door lock and works it with his tools. Once in, he closes the door behind him and clicks on his headlamp. The beam cuts through the room. Prewitt travels the perimeter looking for a wall safe. He checks paintings and seams and shelves. Nothing. *That means any valuables Ranger has are more likely to be in the basement.*

Prewitt opens the top drawer of Ranger's desk. There's the cheat sheet of what looks like passwords. He snaps a photo with his phone. Nothing else but pens and a stapler and about a thousand rubber bands. And no key.

The second drawer is hanging folders. Prewitt reads the handwritten tabs: Manuals. That folder is jammed with instruction books for the coffee maker, toaster oven, and TVs. There's a folder labeled Receipts and a few more useless ones. The last folder in the desk has a tab that says "Important." Prewitt pulls it out. Inside is a sealed envelope, one of those big brown mailer jobs. The front of the envelope has a printed label that reads: "In the event of the death of Ranger du Courtemanche, this should be opened by Pensee du Courtemanche and/or Amelie du Courtemanche." There is a return address in the corner. It's an attorney's office. Prewitt guesses the envelope contains Ranger's will, which would include a list of all his assets. So tempting, but for now, he can't risk opening the envelope. Prewitt snaps a pic with his phone then puts it and the folder back. He doesn't see the key in this drawer either.

Prewitt's ankle is starting to ache from crouching in front of the desk drawer. He didn't take any of Duke's pain meds tonight. He wanted to get a feel for where he was at with the healing. *Still in the woods.* Prewitt sits on the floor and leans back against the desk drawers. He's looking straight into the mouth of the fireplace. He clicks his headlamp off. Prewitt wonders where else the key could be hidden. He hopes it isn't something Ranger carries around. The last thing he wants to do is go through Ranger's clothes while he's in the shower.

Moonlight comes through the tall windows, and soon, Prewitt's eyes adjust to the low light. He lays down to look under the desk . . . and that's when he sees the glint of metal. Prewitt clicks on his headlamp. On the underside of the desk, hanging from a nail on a gold ribbon tied in a bow, is a very old key that looks to Prewitt the exact size of the safe's keyhole.

The key goes into Prewitt's pocket. He clicks off his headlamp, gets up, and opens Ranger's desk drawer enough to be noticed. Then he heads for the door, impatient to get to the safe in the basement. He stops at the door and listens. No sounds from the hallway. Prewitt eases it open and steps out. He closes it behind him but purposely doesn't lock it.

He's almost to the stairs when he hears the creak of a footstep and turns. Someone rounds the corner at the other end of the hall. The feminine figure is a silhouette in the moonlight streaming through the window behind it. *I know that body.* She gets closer, and as Amelie steps out from a shadow, her face is illuminated by the light coming in from the window by the stairs.

"Madame du Courtemanche?"

"Why are you up?" Amelie takes another step forward into his personal space.

"My phone had an alert from the motion sensors."

"That really takes the fun out of sneaking up on a guy."

Not the response Prewitt was expecting. Does she know he was in Ranger's office? Amelie runs her hand up Prewitt's chest.

Oh.

His heart pounds, and he knows she can feel it. Prewitt looks down at what Amelie is wearing. Hardly a robe, and the front is slipping open.

"Come with me." Amelie turns, her hand lingering on his chest and sliding down his arm as she starts back down the hallway.

Prewitt wants to go with her. He can't go to the basement now that she's seen him, and, though he should, he doesn't want to go back to his room. Maybe he can go with her and sit and talk. Or not speak and just kiss. There might not be harm in that. Turning her down might raise suspicion. *Would it?* He doesn't trust his thoughts but can't seem to refute them.

Prewitt follows Amelie down the hallway, and when he gets to her room, he stops outside the open door as she goes in. He can hear Amelie's footsteps on the wood floor in the room. Then he hears her weight on the bed. He knows he is going to go in but hesitates as if standing there, he might find the will to change his mind.

"Come in," Amelie says, and now Prewitt feels as if he's caught in floodwater pulling at his body. The step toward her door frees him to take the next one. When Prewitt enters, he sees Amelie sitting on the bed. He walks to her. She stands and drops the robe to the floor. Seeing her shapely breasts, Prewitt feels a wave of arousal. His eyes move up along her bare chest, to the gentle ridge of her collarbone, then to her neck. *This woman is stunning.* Then he meets her inviting gaze, her lips slightly parted. Prewitt pulls his shirt over his head. He undoes his pants. Amelie touches his chest. He puts his fingers into the waves of her hair and runs his thumb over her cheekbone. She kisses his palm. Then Amelie pulls him to her and kisses him deeply. He kisses back, her tongue moving on his, then she's kissing along his jaw, reaching down to get his boxer shorts off.

"Are you sure?"

"Yes. Yes, please . . ."

It has been so long since Prewitt felt wanted. He kisses her mouth again, feels how soft her lips are, how erotic the weight of her breast feels in his hand. They fall back onto the bed. He caresses her nipple with his thumb. He can feel how she's aroused by his touch. Amelie kisses him harder. She reaches her hand down and grips him, taking his breath. Prewitt thinks to stop, but then Amelie moves him inside of her and presses her hips into him, and he presses into her, and he is with her completely.

Amelie lays next to Prewitt, her cheek resting on his chest. He looks to his hand buried in her hair, then up at the ceiling, trying to understand his feelings. He's had sex with a French heiress in her giant castle while trying to con her brother. And the key to her family safe is sitting in his pants pocket on the floor. So why does he feel calm?

"Prewitt?"

"Yes?"

"Are you alright?"

"Better than alright."

"Good." Amelie pushes herself up onto her elbows and looks at him.

Hair tousled, lips swollen from kissing, her face flush, she glows. Prewitt notices the few candles flickering here and there in the room. One window has the curtain drawn back over the arm of a chair, so the wedge of moonlight falls onto the bed. There has been music playing the whole time. *She was planning to bring me here.*

He looks her way.

She smiles. "Just catching up, are you?"

29

"How was it?"

Boniface has barged into Prewitt's room. It's early, and soft light leaks from behind the curtains onto Prewitt, tangled in his sheet.

"How was what?"

"Last night. Was it nice?"

Prewitt looks up at Boniface, then at the 6:12 a.m. on his watch, and, realizing it would be useless to lie, lets his face fall back into the pillow.

"None of your business."

"Don't be soft. You're here to get the money."

"I don't know how it happened."

"I do. She's beautiful, and you couldn't say no."

"I could have said no. I chose not to."

"So, this is you in control, using good judgment, carefully sleeping with a member of the family you are trying to swindle?"

"Something like that."

"Then I'm relieved," says Boniface. "And I'm also not concerned now that she has manipulated you completely, you might not see how she could blow it all up."

Prewitt sits up. "She's not a risk. I'm certain."

"You can't be."

"I am."

"You've been seduced."

"I see your point. But I don't think that's what's happening."

"Ah, you're here for love then."

"Please get out of my room."

Boniface turns and walks out.

Prewitt takes a shower. But he can feel the shaky lack of sleep in his senses. He left Amelie's room in the middle of the night and crept down the moonlit hallway as quietly as possible. He made a stealthy stop to put the key back in its hiding place under Ranger's desk, left the office door unlocked, then went to his room and passed out within five minutes. *But those few hours of sleep . . . not enough z's.* He's meeting Benny in the village of Blois this morning. He'll find a cup of strong coffee and a good breakfast there. He turns off the water and steps out.

Prewitt pops two of Duke's pain pills, heads down to the first floor, out the kitchen door, and into his car. Aside from the ankle, his body feels good. The sex was amazing. Slow and strong, and intense. After any other night like last night, he'd be in a good mood. But he has a sick feeling because he knows he's complicated things.

Or have I? Have I? It's only complicated if he cares. *Wait, do I have love feelings for this woman?* He looks at himself in the rearview mirror. "You idiot," he mutters, deciding it will never happen again. *You got one free pass. Fun time is over.* Then he thinks about the jewels. How the hell is he supposed to get to the safe with her sleepless and roaming the castle halls at night looking for a potential rendezvous? He mentally shelves this for now.

Prewitt parks on a main street in Blois. Emerald ivy climbs the building walls, and a copper topped spire, green with age, sits atop a stone church like a wizard's hat rising above the fog-ringed hills. Being here makes Prewitt feel like he's in a different century, a feeling he loves. If only he were in a different life. Maybe he could stay. *But Josh.*

He dials Mace. Just to check-in.

"Prew! Gimme the good news?"

"Nothing to report yet."

"Well, how about a figure? What's the take?"

"Don't know yet."

"Best guess."

Over the last ten years working together, Prewitt and Mace have been more off with best guesses than he thought possible. Like some strange karma-type losing streak. The laundromat guy in New York was only one in a long line of jobs that fell short of the cleanup Mace had hoped for.

"Come on, Prew. It's got to be a fortune." The way Mace says it, all sunny and green, gives Prewitt a surge of sympathy. He won't set her up for disappointment.

"Just don't know yet. Careful getting ahead of it."

"Yeah, yeah. I'm excited, that's all."

"I know. We're moving forward, okay? Hang tight."

"Let me know what you know when you know," Mace sings, "And I'll start planning your welcome home bash." Mace barks out a chunky laugh. "We deserve this one, Prew. Call me when the cupboard is open."

"I will. Soon."

"Bye, Prew."

Mace hangs up.

Prewitt heads into Boulangerie Marlau and comes out with a coffee and a slab of quiche Lorraine. There are a few metal tables on the sidewalk out front. He takes a seat next to a young couple and their dog, opens his laptop, and sips his coffee as he hooks up to the café's Wi-Fi. He bites into the quiche and, in his sleep-deprived, senses-heightened state, tastes every flavor. *Wow, that's amazing.*

Prewitt sifts through his personal email. Honey Hair has forwarded a couple from the Harvard admissions office: health form "sign and return" and finance office "fill out your annual income numbers, sign and return." Prewitt doesn't open the attached files.

A chair scrapes loudly. The couple with the dog is leaving. Prewitt sees an email from the Bibliothèque Kandinsky. *The library in Paris?* Curious, he opens it.

Monsieur,

I hope this note finds you well. I'm the librarian who assisted you with locating the image of *A Lady Without Her Jewels,* by Boucher. You said you were researching historical members of the Courtemanche family. We have updated to a new database, and I looked for Courtemanche and found a result. I can show you what I've found any time you'd like to stop by the Bibliothèque Kandinsky. I'm available Wednesday through Sunday. Just let me know.

Sincerely,
Mitta Cleremart

What has Mitta turned up? He might have to make a trip to Paris this weekend. But today is about getting to Ranger's money.

Then there's tonight. Tonight is about using the key to the safe and discovering what's waiting there. Prewitt looks at his watch then checks his phone. There is a text from Benny:

New location,
1 Pl. du Château,
41000 Blois.

When Prewitt arrives at the three-story brick building on the small plaza, he sees six life-size dragons poking their heads out of the windows and looking around as if to eat someone. *Uh, okay.* He walks toward the front door and soon observes they are mechanical, though no less impressive. *What is this place?* Prewitt heads in and, looking around, realizes he's in some sort of magic museum. A sign says just that, Maison de la Magie, and as he wanders around, he notes various optical illusions and magic memorabilia, no Benny. Prewitt makes his way into a hall where a magic show is going on and decides to watch for a minute while he waits. The magician, clad in a tuxedo and top hat, passes a hoop over and around a floating woman in a pink dress. Then he covers her in a blanket. From his angle, Prewitt can't see how the woman might slip away unnoticed, though he's certain she'll be gone soon enough.

Watching, Prewitt is reminded of another top-hatted illusionist, Standish, who'd worn tails every chance he got and had certainly pulled the wool over many eyes. But Standish knew a fair share of actual parlor magic too, and he would entertain guests with it at the dinner parties he threw at his Shady Side mansion on Fifth Avenue, near campus. Graduate students, university higher-ups, and local famous folk, they were all drawn to the outsized personality. Just like Prewitt had been. It annoys Prewitt that by watching some magic, he's now thinking of Standish again, picturing the smug smile that hid a truly sinister soul if ever Prewitt has known one. But there seem to be ghosts around every corner lately. *Why not here, too?*

As Prewitt brings his attention back to the illusion in progress, the magician lifts the blanket off the woman. She is still there, floating. Then she drops her feet to the floor, stands up straight, grabs the blanket, and, as a cloud of smoke explodes out from her feet, throws it toward the audience, where it floats on its own. But Prewitt keeps his eyes on the woman as she sinks into the floor and is replaced by a large man in a pink dress rising up. As the blanket floats back to the front and the audience notices what's different, they all clap. *But how'd she go from floating to standing without the trick being revealed?* Prewitt wonders, glad he doesn't know.

Prewitt feels a tap on the shoulder and turns to see Benny and Kat. Both have lollipops in their mouths. He follows them to a corridor beneath a winding staircase.

"So why here?"

"Oh, we wanted to see this place," says Kat, her red ponytail bouncing out of the back of a plain white baseball cap.

"And once we got here, we thought you might like to see it. Pretty cool, huh?" says Benny as he motions to the display case beside them. A set of old handcuffs and a chain with padlocks sit inside on a red satin cushion conjuring images of Houdini in his underwear.

Benny takes a sheet of letter-sized paper from his pocket and shows it to Prewitt. Its letterhead says "BNP Paribas."

"Good," Prewitt says as he hands Benny a slip of paper. "The account numbers."

Benny slides the paper into the front pant pocket of his faded jeans. "No problem. It will be in the mail at their chateau on Monday," says Benny. Then he hands Prewitt a lollipop.

Back at the castle, Prewitt is almost to the kitchen door when Duke comes jogging up with all four of the dogs on leashes.

"I need to give a corgi back."

"Back?"

The dogs are pulling Duke toward the yard.

"Heel, you relentless creatures." Duke turns back to Prewitt.

"My sister-in-law's kids didn't sleep last night. They love these dogs. She said she needs at least one at home so the kids will go to bed."

"Okay."

"I can explain it easily. I have it all worked out."

"I'm not too concerned."

"We never know what will raise suspicion."

"I don't think it's that big of a deal, Duke."

"Details, my friend. The ruse lives and dies by them."

Duke and the corgis head off toward the distant tree line.

Prewitt enters the kitchen as Ranger pushes through the dining room door.

"Marcellus," he yells. "There you are. They broke into my office."

"No one was in the chateau." Prewitt takes out his phone and scrolls through a screen. "I have the report from the motion sensors last night in this hallway. There was one instance of movement, which we checked the moment it was triggered. It was your sister Amelie walking around. She was the only one in the hall last night. And none of the window or door sensors went off," says Prewitt.

"Well, *someone* has broken in."

"Why do you think so?"

"The door was open."

"Show me."

Ranger's mobile rings. He picks up, "What is it?"

Prewitt follows Ranger through the dining room as Ranger listens to the person on the other end of the call. Then he says, "City Hall has records from when the road was put in. They have to. No. It was a forced easement. The land on the other side of the road is mine. The whole section inside the stone walls. Just get the city to give you the records. Sue them if they won't give them to you, damnit!" Ranger hangs up.

"This fucking town. They won't release records I need for this lawsuit."

They finally reach the hallway outside Ranger's office.

"By the way, what did you find out in Italy?" says Ranger.

"Oh, it was a dead end."

"Hmm," Ranger says as he reaches for the door and opens it.

"I always lock this door, Marcellus. Always."

"Why?"

"Habit. There used to be many more people in and out of this chateau. It makes me comfortable."

Prewitt bends down and peers at the lock he picked last night. "What was stolen?"

"Nothing."

"Do you keep valuables in your office?

"No. But there are passwords to bank accounts in my desk drawer. It was opened. I've checked my accounts five times today. My banker thinks I'm mad."

"If someone got those and learned where you bank, they could try to access your funds. But that didn't happen."

"How can you be sure?"

"Because no one was in the chateau. My security systems work. Perhaps you thought you locked the door but didn't."

Ranger sighs in frustration. "It's possible, I suppose."

"I'm certain that's what occurred. It happens to me all the time."

"What was Amelie doing?"

"A bit of insomnia, she said."

"Perhaps we should have some armed guards outside, in addition to this security man you brought in."

"Not necessary. Earl du Courtemanche, you're under some stress. And you're understandably concerned about someone breaking in and stealing your money. But that's not what happened here."

Ranger sighs again.

"Okay. It's true; I am under stress. And I am concerned. Yes, I must have left it unlocked."

"Of course," says Prewitt, satisfied this little episode had the intended effect of alerting Ranger to the possibility of someone hacking his bank accounts. But there is more Prewitt wants to talk about.

"Earl du Courtemanche," Bertrand stands in the doorway. "Sorry for my intrusion, but the dog man is insisting everyone gather in the dining room right away."

30

When Ranger and Prewitt arrive in the dining room, they find Amelie, Pensee, and Boniface sitting in a semicircle of folding chairs facing the fireplace, where Duke stands solemnly, one hand folded over the other at his belt. Madame Farine and Bertrand are poised beside Amelie, completing the arc. Amelie sees Prewitt then turns her attention back to Duke.

"Thank you. Thank you for joining," says Duke, as Ranger, looking perplexed, stands beside Amelie.

Prewitt goes and leans on the wall by the window off to the side of the group. *What are you up to, Duke?*

Duke scans their faces. "I'm sorry to take up your time like this. I would not have asked if it wasn't important. Josephine has died, you see."

"One of the dogs?" says Pensee.

"Yes, dear. She passed away last night."

Pensee's posture melts into a hunch as she puts a hand to her chest. Duke takes a small step forward.

"Don't worry. It was not poison or some sort of device intended to harm any of you. Though she would gladly have given her life to protect us, that I promise. Josephine, my faithful Pembroke Welsh Corgi, gave selflessly. No, it was heart failure. A sudden, unexpected coronary event, congenital, the veterinarian said. Turns out Josephine was destined . . . ," Duke pauses with a sad inhale. " . . . to shine bright but leave us young."

Though the words should sound silly to Prewitt, Duke speaks them like a military man trained from youth to avoid feelings, someone whose formality protects from emotional vulnerability. But that vulnerability is showing. It's subtle and human. *And it's darn good acting.*

Pensee looks to Boniface, who shares a comforting nod. Amelie leans in.

"I asked you to join me because, as is tradition when a soldier on duty perishes, we must hold a eulogy. Josephine died guarding this chateau. So, of course it is to be here. Her last place of service. But beyond the rituals we use to make sense of the cruel winds of nature, that sting of impermanence, I sensed from you decent people a desire to be a part of this moment to also say goodbye."

The strength in his posture weakens. "Perhaps I am imagining this; perhaps it is because . . ." Duke chokes up, ". . . I needed you to be here with me."

Duke collects himself, but now a tear is running down his face as he looks at the ground, his lip quivering. "Well, I thank you. For her and for me," he says, the formalness of his speaking almost gone.

Duke lifts his head, and his eyes meet those of the group. "You see, I raised Josephine from the litter," he says, a tear now running down the other cheek of his reddening face. "And she was very . . . she was my child." Duke pauses as the transformation completes, and a wave of sadness moves him to sobs. The crying is soft but made of deep guttural grief that echoes and carves a hole in the air of the room. And it's so quiet now it's as if the ceilings and walls of the entire castle have stopped to listen.

Watching Duke shake, Prewitt feels a warmth, then stiffness in his chest as he instinctively suppresses his own wave of sorrow. He remains sad for another moment but then remembers the corgi isn't dead. Prewitt's relief is followed by a sudden annoyance with himself. *Why the hell am I sad?* But then Prewitt recalls Honey Hair and Josh, then a toddler, strolling along Hudson River Park in Greenwich Village. Then Honey Hair, alone, sitting at an outdoor table at Esca, on 43rd Street, looking up at him when he arrives to join her, smiling and deeply in love.

When Prewitt pulls himself back to the present and scans the faces of the others, he sees they are just as sad, more. Pensee is crying, and Amelie dabs away tears with the sleeve of her top. Madame Farine looks ready to gather Duke into a hug, and Bertrand has covered his mouth with his hand. Even Boniface looks mushy. *They're all buying this shit.* Prewitt looks to Duke. *And why shouldn't they? I bought this shit.* Duke, as the lingo goes, in acting as well as conning, is slaying them.

"And I cared for her deeply," Duke says, his voice quavering. "This soul who lived and walked on this earth among us."

Duke sobs again as he looks to the floor. Shaking, he wraps his arms around himself in a desperate hug. "Noooooooooo," Duke weeps as he holds himself.

Prewitt feels the pull of regret again. His eyes water. But he doesn't fight it. Prewitt doesn't care anymore that it's a performance. Now that he's there, he decides he'll stay. Because somehow, here with these people, it all feels safe and comforting. For a full minute, the weeping continues, the room watching, silent but for Duke and Madame Farine's sniffles.

Then Duke's sobs subside, and he lifts his head and again scans the room. When Duke gets to Ranger, he holds there. And Prewitt, following Duke's eyes, stops on Ranger, too. Ranger is crying. Though he stands still and tall, pretending not to be, both eyes are leaking tears. Ranger seems moved more than anyone.

Staring at Ranger, Duke continues. "And is it not in the joy and the play of an animal we cared for that perhaps we see more clearly who we are? In their running, in their resting, in their sleeping on a sofa beside us, their little chest moving with every breath. Because who are we? We are, all of us, souls who want nothing more than to be happy, to love, and to be loved."

Then Prewitt watches as Duke directs to Ranger the warmest, kindest smile. Ranger doesn't look away.

Seeing this, Prewitt wonders when the last time Ranger cried was. And knowing the answer, he feels a deep compassion for him.

Duke looks down again.

"Thank you, Josephine, for reminding me of that. For showing me how much love I have in my own heart. It is broken now and will remain that way. I miss you. I love you. Goodbye."

Lifting his head, Duke shows a grateful, sad half-smile to the group.

"Thank you all for being a part of this ceremony. I think Josephine knows you were here."

Prewitt almost expects clapping. But here, in this aging castle, with its aging occupants, there is simply the delicate fog of compassion floating out over everyone in the room.

Madame Farine goes after Duke first, but soon Pensee and Amelie are also giving him long hugs.

As Prewitt watches, he smiles to himself and wonders if he's ever seen a performance on stage like the one he just witnessed. Not even close. *Well done, Duke Wellington.* Slowly, the people begin to drift out from under the edges of Duke's spell.

Prewitt heads outside and stands in the drive. He's glowing with introspection and comfortable with the quiet, with everything. He notices a warmth in his chest, and he wonders when last he felt this at peace. It's an odd feeling to have since his life is objectively a disaster. *What is this place doing to me?* He looks up at the blue sky and, noting how wide open it is, thinks about how he would never look up in Manhattan. What is there to see beyond the buildings? "This color is so beautiful," he whispers to himself, welcoming the change in his perception. He feels like he's in a trance.

Then Prewitt pictures Honey Hair at Esca again. It was their favorite spot. And after dinner, they'd stroll the two blocks to Times Square and keep going through on their way to Bryant Park behind the library, where they would always walk right into the middle of the grass, take each other's hands, then kiss. Prewitt looks down at the grass at his feet. Behind him, Prewitt hears the front door open. He turns and sees Pensee and Boniface come down the stone steps. Pensee has on a huge hat with a scarf tied over it and looped around her throat, and her hand rests in the bend of Boniface's elbow.

"Perhaps I should drive, Robere. You aren't even from France, and I've lived here all my life."

They don't see Prewitt.

"Madame, have you lately driven a car?"

Pensee laughs. "On second thought, I will be a better tour guide as the passenger."

Boniface opens the door of the Tiger and guides Pensee into the passenger seat. As Boniface walks around to the driver's side, Pensee puts on a pair of huge sunglasses. Soon they are heading down the driveway.

Prewitt suddenly remembers Pensee sneaking around earlier with packages and feels a pull to find out what is going on behind the hedge. As the engine noise from the car fades in the distance, he heads toward the bushes and finds only enough of an opening for a bony little body. Prewitt squeezes through anyway and gets scratched up by some branches.

On the other side of the hedge, there is a path leading to the outbuildings that line the drive. The grass is beaten down, leading to the nearest door. He knows during the castle's early days it would have housed livestock and agricultural equipment. *What's she got in here now?*

Prewitt tries the door. Locked. He crouches, pulls out his small lock pick set, and gets to work. In a moment, it's open, and he is in. It's dark, and there are no windows to let in light. Prewitt feels along the wall for a switch. Nothing. He takes out his phone and turns on the flashlight. To his right, a human form enters the beam. Prewitt jumps back. But it's a mannequin in a gold evening gown and a blond bob wig.

Prewitt raises his phone to the ceiling and scans until he sees a pull chain dangling in the center of the room. He moves toward it. When he pulls the string, the room lights up with a soft yellow glow.

The walls are papered in a large green tropical leaf print. The overhead light is a wide crystal chandelier. There is a yellow velvet couch decorated with throw pillows, and there are several more mannequins decked out in costume pieces, each with a hand-numbered tag. One mannequin is wearing a black cocktail dress. Another looks like a flamenco dancer fresh from the stage at the Copa. An antique dresser is centered on the back wall. Opposite the couch is a huge full-length mirror. Looking around, Prewitt feels like he is in a vintage boutique tucked away on a side street in Paris.

Prewitt goes to the dresser. Beside it is a giant torchiere with three globes. He snaps it on. On the top of the dresser are a lace doily and a red leather journal. Next to the journal is a pen with an ostrich feather. Prewitt opens the journal and begins to read the entries. Pensee has detailed every item here. The date, the history of the piece, the price she won it for on eBay, and even the number of bids against her before she emerged victorious.

Prewitt thinks back to the first morning at breakfast and realizes she was engaged in an eBay battle. The packages she's been sneaking in here must be her recent winnings.

He opens and closes several drawers. Costume jewelry, each rhinestone and paste gem displayed on a small square of foam in a gift box. There is also a long looping strand of pearls and a cornflower blue pillbox hat carefully nestled in tissue paper. He walks over to the mannequin wearing a black cocktail dress and runs a finger lightly over the embellished shoulder strap, then goes back to the dresser. According to the journal, this was made for Marilyn Monroe when she appeared in the 1962 film *Something's Gotta Give*. But it didn't appear on screen.

Prewitt walks to the first mannequin that caught his attention. Decked out in a full-skirted, strapless dress in pale gold, this mannequin has arms sleeved in long gloves. One glove has a matching golden fan pinned to its hand. He walks back to the dresser and reads about this dress. Then he smiles to himself. *Well, look at you, Pensee Courtemanche.*

Prewitt scans around the room at Pensee's impressive collection of Hollywood memorabilia. He suspects some of these items may be fakes. But it doesn't matter. Every piece is cared for and displayed with love and an appreciation of its value. Prewitt understands that all too well. And the comments about jewels and insurance, he now understands that, too. That was Pensee acting. She was reciting lines. He looks at the mannequin in the gold dress. And Prewitt now knows from which movie.

Back in the castle, Prewitt heads toward Ranger's office. He wants to continue the interrupted conversation with Ranger to dig for more information about his assets. Prewitt knocks.

"Please come in."

Prewitt enters and finds Ranger standing by the window, looking out.

"Earl du Courtemanche, do you have a moment more to talk?"

"I do, yes. What would you like to discuss?" says Ranger, sounding calmer and kinder. *The Duke effect.*

"I thought perhaps we might have that scotch. And continue our conversation from earlier."

"A scotch. That sounds nice, yes. Let's—" Ranger is interrupted by yelling from the hallway.

Both men move to the doorway.

Bertrand comes running toward them. "We're under attack!" He looks first to Prewitt, then to Ranger, then to Prewitt again. "It's them! It's the Knights Templar!"

"Where?" says Ranger.

"The river, they're attacking from the river," says Bertrand. "They're in boats."

"Are you certain?" says Ranger, looking at Prewitt.

"Yes!"

"Being attacked from the river is not likely," says Prewitt. "I'm sure it's a passing boat."

"No. They're attacking. We have to go now. We have to run!"

"No, we don't."

"Yes. We do!"

"Show us," says Ranger.

"We must flee, please, for your safety."

"Bertrand. Show us," says Ranger firmly.

Bertrand hesitates, then turns and scurries toward the stairs with Prewitt and Ranger a step behind him.

Prewitt and Ranger follow Bertrand through the chateau and out to the terrace, then down through the hedge garden and toward the sloping lawn to the wide line of the river. The sun has just set, and its last light reflects weakly off the water. Bertrand, now stopped at the farthest line of hedges, cautiously peers over. Prewitt and Ranger look too. Bertrand isn't wrong. Something is coming.

Lumbering up onto the bank from the Loire is one hell of an armored boat. Muddy river water streams from its underbelly as it rises, the wild shore grasses flattened under its bow. Its engine growls and hums along with the sound of clanking metal.

"It's moving *out* of the river," Bertrand whispers.

The green boat crawls completely out of the water. Prewitt squints and sees tank-like tracks and wheels carrying it forward. The barrel of its long gun catches the light as it starts turning. With a loud squeal, the gun swivels to the right a few feet then back to the left like a blind monster trying to sense prey.

Then the tank boat comes to a stop.

When Prewitt turns to Ranger, he sees Ranger staring angrily back at him.

Madame Farine runs up behind them, holding a cast iron pan like a Valkyrie ready to battle.

Amelie is a few steps behind Madame Farine. "What are we all doing?" she says as she crouches behind the low hedge. Amelie looks at Prewitt with a playful curiosity.

"Madam du Courtemanche, Madame Farine, go back. It's not safe! We're under attack by the Knights Templar!" Bertrand says.

What the fuck is going on here?

The beast moves forward with another loud growl of its engine.

Everyone turns back to it. Then the long gun pivots toward the terrace.

"This is when we perish," whispers Bertrand.

"Quiet," Ranger barks.

Seconds tick by. Its engine shuts off.

"I pray I've served you well," says Bertrand.

"Bertrand!" Ranger hisses.

Then, a hatch on top opens. A tall sweep of blond hair emerges.

It's Michel.

Why the fuck is Michel here in a tank boat?

"It's okay. It's okay. They are part of the security team," Prewitt says as he stands from behind the hedge. He walks down the lawn toward the tank boat as everyone follows.

"Marcellus, bonsoir," Michel yells from cupped hands. The long gun swivels and knocks Michel over, and he falls onto the lawn. "Dammit, Louis!" Michel gets up and brushes freshly cut grass out of his hair. Most of it stays.

"Sorry, monsieur. Where do you want us to park it?" Michel says to Prewitt.

"So, we are safe?" says Bertrand.

"You are safe," Michel says to the whole group.

Bertrand's relief apparently dizzies him, and Amelie grabs an arm to steady him.

"This is an amphibious assault vehicle from the Second World War," says Ranger.

"Yup, it's a DUKW," says Louis as he jumps down from a ladder on the side. "Monsieur Redmayne identified the river as a vulnerability."

"The Vatican sent a DUKW to defend my chateau from the Knights Templar?"

"They did, monsieur," says Louis.

Ranger nods, considering. "Excellent."

Michel smiles proudly at Prewitt as a piece of grass falls onto his nose.

"I've got to finish the ratatouille for dinner," Madame Farine says. She turns and heads back toward the chateau.

"See you later, brother," Amelie says. Her eyes sparkle at Prewitt as if to laud their little secret, and her smile suggests she enjoyed this excitement. Amelie and Bertrand start toward the chateau too. And as she walks away, Prewitt thinks about how Amelie still doesn't seem at all concerned about the Templars. He wonders if it's because she has faith in him. Or maybe she only cares about folk songs and free love. A pang of fear hits him in the stomach. He's conning this woman's brother, and through the lens of having touched and kissed her, it suddenly feels wrong. He knows it's not wrong because of how the Courtemanches got their money and who Ranger is. But will he be taking her money? Or just the old money? There will be plenty left over. He knows that. So it shouldn't affect her. Then what is the problem? It's clear to Prewitt. Her smile, her hair, the way her body sways with every step as she walks away. And how he wants to keep watching her. *The problem is I like her, and it's now giving me the emotional, idiotic thoughts of a rank amateur.*

Prewitt again resolves to stop whatever has started with Amelie, forgiving himself in the same moment.

"Right then. Good. This is what I was talking about, Marcellus, armed men," Ranger says. Then he walks off too, leaving Prewitt alone with the brothers.

"The Vatican sent a DUKW to defend his chateau from the Knights Templar?" says Prewitt. His head is cocked, and his eyes say, "*you shitheads.*"

"This is good, right?" Michel says.

"No, Michel. You scared the crap out of everyone."

"He seemed happy," says Michel. "And now he'll trust you even more."

"I don't like surprises," says Prewitt.

"Wait, you didn't tell Prewitt?" says Louis.

"No. I figured we would tell him when we got here."

"And you didn't think people would notice the damn boat? You idiot," says Louis.

"I'm not an idiot."

"Yes. You are."

"It's fine. But next time we talk first, okay?" says Prewitt. "Where did you even get this thing?"

"It's our grandpa's. He drives it in the Bastille Day parade every year. Won it off a guy in a card game in Normandy," says Michel.

"True story," says Louis

"So, you want us to take it back?" says Michel.

"Oh no, no, no. You've got to leave it here now."

"You can give us a ride home?"

"No."

"You are still mad?"

"No, but you've got to stay with the boat."

Michel and Louis look at each other.

"How does this work if no one is here manning it?" says Prewitt.

"What do you mean?' says Michel.

"It's not a believable defense if the boat is without someone to drive it and shoot it. Did you not consider that?" says Louis.

"Did you?" says Michel.

"I thought we were just delivering it. You idiot," says Louis.

Michel hits himself on the forehead.

"I hope you brought sleeping bags," says Prewitt.

"Merde! Oh man, we didn't even bring any food. Can we have some ratatouille for dinner, do you think?" says Michel.

"If I asked, you could," says Prewitt, walking away.

"Nice going," says Louis.

"Will you ask?" says Michel.

Prewitt remains silent as he continues toward the castle.

31

Back in the castle a few hours later, Prewitt goes in search of Amelie and finds her in the music room, sitting on the floor, holding her guitar. The song "Close To You" by the Carpenters is playing on her phone. He stops in the doorway.

"Amelie," he says, aware he's calling her by her first name.

"Come in." Amelie puts the guitar down on the floor, where pages of music are scattered across the rug, and moves to sit on the couch. "Quite a day so far. What else is going to happen?"

"Nothing else is going to happen."

Amelie pouts playfully.

Prewitt sits on the couch next to her and rests his hands in his lap. Amelie has an arm draped across the back of the couch, and she drums her fingers just behind the beat of the song.

"Regarding what we did . . . I'm here professionally."

"Wait, you do that professionally? Like a gigolo?"

"Amelie."

"No wonder you're so good. You're very good, you know."

"I'm trying to be serious."

The song ends and begins again. Amelie reaches for her phone and pauses the music. "Look, I like you," she says. "I enjoyed being with you. And I wouldn't mind being with you again."

"I don't think that's a good idea."

Amelie smiles at Prewitt. "Just know that I do." Amelie starts the song again, then picks up the guitar and strums along. "And now I'm going to pretend to be Karen Carpenter," she says. "So you need to leave, or I'm going to become self-conscious."

"Of course." Prewitt stands and heads for the door. As he passes through, Amelie begins to sing along to the song. Her voice is sweet. Untrained. *Innocent.*

Prewitt goes up to the second floor and heads toward Ranger's office. He knocks on the door, but no one answers. He heads back down to the first floor. In the hallway, Prewitt sees Bertrand pushing a beverage cart into the blue salon. Prewitt follows him in and finds Duke and Ranger on a couch together. Three different bottles of scotch rest on the low table in front of them. Duke is urging Ranger to try the next glass. Bertrand takes empty glasses from in front of Duke and Ranger and places them on the cart. He hands clean ones to Duke.

"Marcellus," Ranger says, "come have that scotch you wanted."

Okay. Prewitt figures he can wait out the conversations, and after Duke leaves, Ranger, in his intoxication, will be even easier to talk to about the potential hacking of his bank accounts.

"I suggested Wellington join us, and he came back with these," says Ranger, motioning to the bottles

"I have a friend in *Château-Renault*, quite the collector," says Duke.

"Anything else, Earl du Courtemanche?" says Bertrand.

"Not at the moment," says Ranger.

After Bertrand leaves, Duke reaches for one of the bottles. "Balvenie, thirty-year-old, cask strength, single malt. Would anyone like ice?"

"I'll have ice," Prewitt says, thinking he'd better keep himself sober.

"That's a €7,000 bottle," says Duke.

"Then why'd you ask?"

"I was testing you. You've failed," Duke says with a chuckle.

"I'll have mine without the ice," says Ranger.

"Good man."

After taking a sip, Ranger nods at Duke. "Oh yes, that is very nice."

An hour later, after a long conversation about Scottish history and Duke's visits to the famous five ancient Scottish distillers, Ranger takes a last sip of his most recent glass then sets it on the table.

"One more, shall we?" says Duke.

"No, thank you," says Prewitt who is more buzzed than he planned to be.

"Sure, I'll have one more. A very small one," says Ranger, now clearly sauced. Duke pours two glasses and hands one to Ranger.

From the way Duke almost fumbles the handoff, Prewitt can tell he's half in the bag too. Or playing the part perfectly.

"Oops. I almost let that fall to the floor. Bring forth the guillotine! Raise the blade!" blurts Duke with a wet smile.

No, he's drunk.

Duke leans back and sips from his glass. "Mmm," he says, closing his eyes and tilting his head back. "Onto more important things," says Duke. "I noticed, Courtemanche, you were emotional today as I spoke about Josephine. I wonder, were you thinking of a dog of your own?"

Ranger sips his drink as if hesitating to share. But then he puts the glass down and meets Duke's curious stare.

"A horse, actually," says Ranger.

"Oh?"

"Yes. I used to ride horses. From a young age. And as a young man, I played polo."

"A joyous pastime," says Duke.

"I owned many horses. Over time, that changed. Perhaps fifteen years or so ago, I sold my stable," says Ranger.

"So then, a favorite champion that had to be put down? Or a colt you raised as I did Josephine?"

"No," says Ranger. "It was a horse from when I was a boy. An Arabian, smaller, powerful. A jumper. Beautiful horse. This was when I was first learning hunt seat, jumping, and how to ride really. His name was Soleil. My father had sent me off to a riding camp, and I was very lonely, in fact. But I rode Soleil every day and became a good horseman that summer. And I did make a few friends eventually. But, and well, I know this may sound silly, but that horse was my friend, in a way the others weren't. I went back to that camp for four more summers."

"I fear to ask, but did Soleil die that last summer?" says Duke.

"No. It was years later. I was in university, and I received a call from my father, who had received a call from the owner of the camp. He'd remembered my time riding Soleil and wanted to inform me Soleil had died. On a trail ride. No longer the swift and spry leaper from when I rode him, he'd gotten old and had a heart attack on the trail."

Ranger takes another sip.

"I didn't think about it much at the time. Didn't really bother me. In fact, I don't believe I've had a thought of Soleil at all until your eulogy for your dog today."

"Ah, rattled out from the psyche. Life and the mind conspire to remind us of things at interesting times, don't they?"

"I suppose," says Ranger.

"When we need them, I'd say."

There's a quiet moment as the men all seem to ponder. Prewitt hears the ticking of the wall clock.

Duke raises his glass. "Let us toast then, to Soleil. A friend."

Ranger seems uncomfortable with the emotional indulgence, but he raises his glass, as does Prewitt, then follows Duke's lead and takes a sip. Prewitt does too.

"Well, gentleman, the dogs will need some sleep, then up at the crack of dawn, and I with them."

"It's late for me, as well." Ranger stands, but he is a little wobbly.

Prewitt sees he won't be having any more conversations with Ranger tonight. *But this works too.*

Duke takes Ranger by the elbow, "Not a thing wrong with the

excess drink every so often. Let me walk you to your room. I'll tell you about the time I was deployed in the Indian Ocean. There was an island overrun with pigs. They swam in the waters and spent their evenings getting drunk on the fermented milk of coconuts. I too tried it, and I can assure you . . ."

After Duke and Ranger leave, Prewitt looks into his scotch glass. The last drops of the amber liquid roll as he tips it back and forth. He rises and sets the glass with the others on the tray. He listens—just the clock. Bertrand and Madame Farine have gone home. Prewitt takes a deep breath. Time to open the safe.

After going up and taking the key from Ranger's office again, then grabbing the headlamp from his room, Prewitt walks down the main stairs, through the dining room, and enters the kitchen. It's dark except for the little red light coming from the dishwasher in dry mode. Prewitt opens the door to the basement, takes a step down, then closes the door behind him. He pulls his headlamp from his pocket and puts it on, then places his hand back into his pocket to feel the key, its solid weight reassuring him.

Once Prewitt reaches the bottom of the stairs, he pauses and listens again. *The only souls down here are old French ghosts,* and Prewitt feels like they're welcoming his presence. He walks down the hallway past empty wine racks to the area with the new wall and hidden door.

The space around the door feels smaller than it did before. He approaches the wall, places his palm against it, and pushes. There is a click as the door moves in then swings out. He pulls it open with the inset handle. Once inside, Prewitt goes right to the safe. He takes the key from his pocket, his hand feeling shaky. It never goes away, the tightness of anticipation at the moment of discovery. After all this time and all the treasures Prewitt has seen and touched, he still gets it. In his shoulders, in his gut. And the timeless bubble he enters where there is nothing but the eight inches in front of his face, he's in that now, too, because all other thoughts are gone, off somewhere in the dark, way over anywhere other than here. He's not Prewitt Patry in these moments; that's what no one understands. In these moments, his life isn't a scarred mess of shame and failures, it's a field with a thousand armored soldiers or a queen in a distant realm reading a scroll by candlelight. It's a windswept hill overlooking a medieval palace, with dark trees and hungry owls and holes in the brush where the rabbits hide. And it's a gift from a peasant to his noble, oppressed love, given along the banks of an ancient river so they might have a life together. A gift made possible by the kinship between that peasant and an old man who happened to be the greatest artist the world has ever known.

Prewitt slides the key into the lock of the safe. He can feel its uneven edges push the pins upward and free the plug to move. Prewitt turns it. The lock cylinder rotates smoothly. He reaches for the lever handle and turns until he feels a click. The door to the safe opens.

The beam of the headlamp illuminates the inside of the safe: no boxes, no jewelry rolls, nothing but a stack of old papers.

Prewitt reaches in and pulls out the pages to see if anything is under them. Nothing is. He looks at the first paper. A letter. Writing in Latin. Then the second, same. Other letters are in French. One has the seal of the King of France and the name Benedict du Courtemanche. He absently scans and reads everything. It's all from the early 1300s.

Prewitt sighs with disappointment. The con will be over in a couple more days. If he can't find the jewels by then, he will have to move on. He's suddenly angry. *Where else would they be?* Prewitt's mind delivers no answer. And he's tired and feeling the slur of the scotch softening his gaze.

Momentarily curious, Prewitt wonders about these documents that are so precious they must be locked up here. He looks closer as he flips through them again, scanning each but unable to focus and not caring at all about anything he reads.

He puts the letters back. Locks the safe again and slips the key into his pocket.

Prewitt exits the room and closes the door behind him. As he walks past the rows of wine racks and toward the stairs, Prewitt senses the history of the Courtemanche family. And it feels depressing to him, like a rotting color bleeding into all his thoughts. The parcels of land sold off. The wine gone. The barrels empty. The castle, dark and shabby. The family line coming to an end. *Was it worth it?* Prewitt wonders what Benedict Courtemanche would think now if he could see what has come of his deal with the devil. To aspire to wealth and power has felt ugly since Prewitt tangled with Standish. And that was reinforced by Honey Hair's father. Though he'd never considered the thoughts he's having now. *Do they even like this life? How could they?* But instead of the schadenfreude Prewitt would expect to feel, he just feels sad. He wonders if it's self-pity projected onto them because he's so lost. *Of course it is.* And the night spent with Amelie. That didn't help anything. *Never go on the grift when you need a friend more than the money.* Prewitt looks off into nothing. *What a loser you are. What a fucking loser.*

Prewitt continues toward the bottom of the stairs but quickens his pace as, like a child afraid of the dark basement, an urgent need to get out of there rises icy from his belly. He gets to the first step and turns off his headlamp. And leaving those ghosts as he heads up toward the door out of this cellar, Prewitt feels as lonely as he ever has in his life.

Prewitt returns the key to Ranger's office then takes the hallway that leads to Amelie's room. As he walks closer, he can see her door is open, and there is a soft light coming from inside. He could have gone a different way, and considered it since what the hell is he doing thinking about getting comfort from Amelie? Except he's already found comfort in her and feels so alone that not investigating whether she is experiencing a similar pull goes against every instinct he has.

When he nears the door, he hears her voice.

"Prewitt?" Amelie says in a sleepy whisper.

He hears a shifting sheet and, as he steps into the doorway, sees

Amelie sitting up in bed, the sheet held at her breast. Her bare legs stretch down toward the floor.

"Did I wake you?"

"No. I'm glad you came."

As he enters, she stares up at him and reaches her other hand out to his. He takes it, and they come together and kiss. And standing over her, Prewitt feels the sheet fall between them as Amelie reaches for his pants and undoes the buttons. Prewitt can feel his body respond to the moment, his mind now seeing glimpses of the last time.

"Hi," Amelie says.

"Hello."

Prewitt helps remove his pants, pulls his shirt over his head, and lies down next to Amelie. She kisses him hungrily, pressing more of herself against Prewitt's body. As they kiss, they both grow bolder with their touching.

"I love your smell," she whispers.

Amelie's hand drifts down Prewitt's chest and stomach, then onto his thigh, digging in her nails. Prewitt kisses more deeply, and Amelie moves her legs apart, pulling Prewitt between them. She pauses, pushing her forehead into his, then presses her open mouth to Prewitt's and kisses hard as he adjusts his hips forward. She moans and kisses him harder.

They make love with an urgency that surprises Prewitt. He watches as Amelie's face and eyes mirror his lust, her body thrusting up to his. Pulling him closer, she muffles her cries of pleasure in his neck. And as Prewitt loses himself in her, he floats up, free from the weight of his failures and questions. Then he dives back into a dark pool, warm and arousing and electric and safe, and he feels happy and wanted.

"Amelie," he says, his lips on her neck. He kisses there. "Yes," he whispers as he feels her shuddering, her hips shaking as she squeezes. Her hands grip his back, and her moans quicken in surprise.

***

Prewitt wakes with Amelie in his arms. It's early, and Prewitt sees the dim light from beneath the horizon outside the windows. He feels guilt and a sick weight in his gut he couldn't have imagined hours before. It's not that last night felt wrong. It's that he stopped thinking, and now thinking is all he can do. He kisses Amelie's naked shoulder. *This lovely woman.* She stirs and turns to look at him. He runs his fingers lightly across her shoulder.

Amelie stares past Prewitt, then focuses on him again.

He doesn't want to rush out of bed, but the regret is pushing on his brain. Prewitt lets her breath guide his, and after a few, he is calmer.

"May I ask you about your ex-wife?"

It's not something Prewitt wants to talk about now. But he doesn't want her to know how he's feeling. "Sure."

"Were you in love with her?" Amelie asks.

"Yes."

"What was it like?"

"How do you mean?"

"I'm curious. What does it feel like? Was it like this?"

It's the first time Amelie sounds this vulnerable. *Does she not know what it feels like to be in love?*

Prewitt runs his fingers over her back and down her shoulder. "It began like this, yes."

"And then?"

Prewitt hesitates to answer.

"Tell me."

"Then, well . . . then everything begins to feel safe and easy, and one day you wake up surprised at how happy you are in your life, and how much you adore the person you're with. And they bring out things you didn't know were there."

Amelie smiles, but it's forced and distracted. She looks down, thinking.

He watches her, the smile softening into something sad, her hand brushing a curl of hair from her face. And now, to Prewitt, her behavior over the last few days is making more sense. Amelie is not just lonely; she's starving for a connection and wondering about something she's never had.

"Have you been in love?" he says.

She looks up at Prewitt. "I don't know. I was close, I think, when I was at university. I don't believe I appreciated him enough, looking back. He was very kind. And smart. Martin. He was a sculptor studying art. But within two years, it was over, and he was gone from my life. He didn't come from money. Hated the world I lived in. *Hated.* And since I couldn't leave it, he had no choice but to go. We were young. Who knows if it would have worked out had we stayed together? But I think it might have. I remember one night at a party, we'd stepped outside, and he asked me why I had to live this way, the money, this 'society' life. I told him it was all I knew."

Amelie looks away from Prewitt as she gazes back into her past. "Really a very sweet boy." She smiles. "Handsome too. Martin Leandre." Amelie plays with the hair on Prewitt's chest. "I think about him sometimes."

"But you were never in love after that?"

"No."

"Why?"

"I never met anyone. After university, I returned here and assumed my role as a Courtemanche. My world became small again." Amelie shifts her body. "There were flings here and there. But no one I connected with. Then, I don't know, years passed, and I got older. Life went on. I think I gave up on ever having love."

It's a vulnerable room Prewitt sees into now. *I was foolish to think this door wouldn't open.* His is open too. He has a sudden feeling of strong affection for her and responds by brushing a lock of hair from her forehead and placing it behind her ear. He wants to kiss her but hesitates. Then he feels confused. A sobering chill comes over him. As if it's all a bit more than he can take.

Prewitt tries to smile, but he knows he looks distracted. She sees it. The doors softly close.

"It's okay. We don't have to talk like this." Amelie gets out of bed, and when she turns back to him for the slightest moment, he sees that sad smile again.

32

As Prewitt walks back to his room after a shower, disappointment about the empty safe piles on to his guilt about sleeping with Amelie. *How hard was it for the jewels to be in the secret safe in the secret room of the old cellar?* The thought gets Prewitt mad, but then there is curiosity as he wonders why it's so important to him to find *these* jewels. Why does he feel like this is more important than the other prizes from other cons? Why does he care so much? As he wonders, his vision goes fuzzy, and he loses focus on the floor as he's walking. He can't find an answer.

Prewitt shakes his head and looks up. The last pieces of the con fall into place tomorrow. Maybe he can still think his way to a solution. The jewels are somewhere here. *Where?* Prewitt gets to his room and sits on the bed. *I don't know.*

As Prewitt slips on his pants, a sharp pain shoots down his leg and seizes at his back. *Not now, damn it.* He breathes through it, and his back relaxes enough for him to stand. Then the pain recedes a bit. He buttons his pants, puts on his shirt, and sits again.

Prewitt goes over the last steps in his mind. Everything for tomorrow is ready. All he has to do is not be bedridden. Then he remembers the email from Mitta Cleremart, the librarian in Paris, and how she said she found something about a Courtemanche. With the family awake, he can't go on an all-out treasure hunt through the castle to search for the jewels. *What the hell else is there to do today?*

Prewitt puts on his socks and slips on his shoes. *Let's drive to Paris to see what Mitta has turned up. Maybe you'll think of something you haven't thought of.*

After getting down to the first floor, Prewitt walks from the central staircase toward the dining room. There are twinges of pain down his leg, but they don't affect his steps any more than the slight limp his stiff ankle still causes. Nearing the dining room, he stops short when he hears music, then peeks around the corner. In the middle of the room, Boniface and Pensee are waltzing. The music plays from an old wind-up gramophone sitting on a folding chair. He watches them for a few seconds as they gracefully move across the floor, Pensee looking delighted with every step *I almost forgot. The other innocent sister.*

Prewitt heads back down the main hallway and takes the longer route to his car through the back hallway and the gardens off the terrace.

"Mademoiselle Cleremart, nice to see you again," says Prewitt, noting her broad, relaxed smile. "You look happy today."

"I am, monsieur. Nice to see you too," Mitta says as she comes out from behind the reference desk and gestures to a pair of chairs under a nearby window.

They both sit, and Mitta hands Prewitt a piece of paper.

Prewitt looks at the photocopy of an old, weathered parchment the size of a postcard. There are a few sentences written in Latin.

"This letter showed up in the library's new cross-referenced records when I did a search for 'Courtemanche.'"

"This is the Wallace Safe Conduct Letter," says Prewitt. He first learned of the letter when it made global news in 2012. The Wallace Safe Conduct Letter was meant to get the Pope's support for freedom for the people of Scotland. The British had been hiding it away since taking the letter off William Wallace in the Tower of London in 1307.

"The original letter is on loan to National Records of Scotland from the National Archives in London," Mitta says.

"But what is the connection to the Courtemanche family?"

"I'm not sure. There weren't any notes in the system."

Prewitt looks down at the page again. He reads the Latin, translating it out loud:

> Philip by the grace of God, king of the French, to his loyal agent appointed to the Roman Court, greetings and favour. We command you that you ask the Supreme Pontiff to consider with favour our beloved William le Walois of Scotland, Knight, with regard to those things which concern him that he has to expedite. Dated at Pierrefonds on the Monday after the Feast of All Saints in the year 1307.
>
> King Philip IV of France

Prewitt's face gives away his disappointment.

"It doesn't help you with your work, does it?" she asks.

"I'm afraid not."

"I hope I didn't waste your time coming in. The research librarians don't really make mistakes with the cross references. Someone had a reason for linking this to the name Courtemanche."

"Perhaps it will remain lost in history a bit longer. But you didn't waste my time. Thank you for trying."

"Sure."

"Mitta, can you recommend a place nearby to sit outside and have lunch?" says Prewitt.

"Sure. Or I could take you. I have a break now. Would you like to join me?"

***

During lunch, Prewitt learns Mitta is a writer. She tells him about a collection of short stories she's written and the literary agent she signed with. Prewitt says he hopes they find a publisher soon. And as Mitta shares her dreams of working part-time at the library and becoming a published author, his thoughts drift to Amelie and their talk this morning. Then to the jewels again. Prewitt realizes something. *Wouldn't Amelie know about the jewels?* And if she did, wouldn't she know where they are being kept? He wonders if she has ever worn them. Maybe around the castle as a little girl playing dress-up with Pensee. *She must have. Amelie could be my best chance to find them.* The thought is followed by a sick feeling. *I could never ask her. I'd literally be stealing them from her.*

Prewitt pays the bill, thanks Mitta for her help and wishes her all the best with her writing. They say goodbye on the sidewalk, and once he's alone, he heads south toward the Seine River. A stroll along the Parc Rives de Seine leads him to the Musée du Louvre. He considers Amelie again. He wouldn't need to steal the jewels. He could ask about them. And he could ask her if the story is true. Maybe he could see them.

Prewitt pays the admission at the Louvre at the pyramid entrance, takes a map, and walks with the flow of tourists and other wide-eyeds to the Galerie des Antiques and its lifelike sculptures, the subjects frozen in time. For Prewitt, there is always something all-knowing about these gods and mortals. And it calms him to be among them, as if, in their stillness, they are telling him "all ends well." He pauses to look at the armless Venus de Milo; her white marble body incomplete yet seeming so human and fearless.

Prewitt exits the gallery and climbs the Daru staircase to look at the Winged Victory of Samothrace. Awed at the strength it conveys, he imagines it inspiring a small child like the backpack-carrying one here with his school group, except on a Greek island and two thousand years ago.

Prewitt passes through the Salon Carré and the Grande Galerie's collection of Italian paintings before turning into the *Salle des États.* Here, floor to ceiling, the walls are a deep midnight blue, and all hung with paintings, but everyone is moving through two queues toward the Mona Lisa. Prewitt walks with them, but he stops and steps to the side, letting the others push closer. The painting, alone on its wall, behind its railing and protective glass, is admittedly beautiful to Prewitt. Everything about it, even the ornate frame, seems perfect to him. It strikes him this is perhaps one of the greatest gifts ever given to the world. But it's not the painting he came to see. And it's a different gift from da Vinci, one no one here would think to look for, that hides in plain sight on another wall nearby.

Prewitt lingers a moment, watching the people stare and take selfies, then he makes his way out of the Salle des États and into the Grande Galerie's French collection to where *A Lady Without Her Jewels* hangs. He walks to the painting, stops in front of it, and looks at Amarante du Courtemanche. The painting is surprisingly realistic. Some parts look almost like a photograph. And it captures Amarante in what seems like an actual room, and an actual place in time. Prewitt eyes move down the canvas, and he stares at the daubs of paint in the drawer by Amarante's fingertips. He wonders if this is as close as he'll come. *If so, so be it.*

33

Prewitt drives the Peugeot up the driveway to the chateau. There is a horse trailer sitting empty with its back gate open and a ramp slid out and down to the ground. Prewitt parks and heads toward the grounds around back. Walking along a path of dirt and small white pebbles, Prewitt passes through the trees on the side of the castle. There he runs into Lorelei.

"Hello, Romeo."

"Hello, Lorelei." He looks down at an empty picnic basket slung over the crook in her arm.

"I brought food to Michel and Louis." She brushes some pine needles off her pants.

Prewitt reaches forward and plucks one more from her hair.

"Then I bumped into Henri in the woods. He's a good kisser. I like him."

"If he learns what your real job is, it will ruin it," says Prewitt.

"Maybe, maybe not. We'll see."

As Lorelei passes Prewitt, she gives him a squeeze on the bicep. Prewitt continues on the path.

When Prewitt rounds the corner to the backyard, the first thing he sees is Ranger, off in the distance by the water, trotting along on a chestnut brown horse. From the animal's strong, compact body and long neck held high, Prewitt can tell it's an Arabian. The horse is so athletic it looks like it's floating with each step of its boisterous trot. But it's Ranger, with his heels down in the stirrups and his commanding poise in the saddle, who looks even more impressive. Ranger posts up and down with the horse's stride like the riders Prewitt sees on sports channels competing in their tails and black velvet caps. He dips his shoulders a bit as the horse breaks into a bouncing canter and begins to carve a wide, gentle circle on the grass.

Between Ranger and Prewitt is Duke Wellington, a horse's lead rope in one hand, three corgis on their leashes in the other. One hundred yards farther down the riverbank, Michel and Louis are leaning against the tank boat and watching, too.

Prewitt keeps his eyes on Ranger as he approaches Duke.

"Hello, monsieur," says Duke while also watching Ranger. "The man sure knows how to ride a horse."

"Where did it come from?"

"Oh, I brought it for him as a surprise."

Prewitt gives Duke a confused look.

"Well, he doesn't have any of his own, Prewitt," says Duke.

Prewitt watches as Ranger floats along. It's not quite a smile but more a look of wonderment Prewitt sees on Ranger's face.

"And where did you get the horse?"

"From a friend who owns Écurie Montebello. Two Olympians board their horses there, you know."

"No, I didn't know that."

"I obviously don't compete anymore, though I still enjoy a trot around the ring or a nice trail ride."

Of course you do.

"Ranger wasn't lying about his polo days. He's a very good rider," says Duke.

Ranger guides the Arabian as it changes the path of its circle to go in an opposite circle.

"Did you see that, Prewitt?"

"No."

"The way the horse turned."

"To the right?"

"That was a flying lead change. Yes, a very good rider indeed. Do you know what a flying lead change is?" says Duke.

"No," says Prewitt.

"Well, it's when the horse changes which leg leads without changing its gait. So they can shift direction but not break their rhythm."

"Duke, what is going on?"

"One of the most elegant movements in nature."

"Duke."

Duke turns to Prewitt.

"Is this some part of the con we didn't discuss?" says Prewitt.

"No."

"Then what is going on?"

"Ranger du Courtemanche is riding."

"Duke."

"On a beautiful horse on a beautiful day."

"Duke."

"Did you not hear him last night talking about his ponies?" says Duke in his wise, caring tone. "Did you not see him in the dining room, tears flowing from his eyes as the pain of his past came up? I knew it would be good for him, so I brought him a horse. This man needed to ride a horse today. This man has needed to ride a horse for many years."

Duke shows Prewitt his enlightened grin. "There are things that bring each of us joy, Prewitt. We, you and I, have the gift of seeing what *moves* people. We cannot use that gift only to take from them."

What the fuck are you talking about? are the words Prewitt would like to say. But Prewitt knows what Duke is talking about. And he knows why Duke did what he did. Because Duke is Duke. And he knows this doesn't hurt the con. It helps Ranger. And Prewitt is warmed to see Ranger riding a horse on his enchanting grounds along the river. And Prewitt realizes in this moment that despite everything he knows about him, he has come to like Ranger du Courtemanche, or at least feel bad for him or, *well, is there a difference?*

Duke turns his attention back to Ranger. And so does Prewitt. And so do the corgis. And they all watch as Ranger canters a circle on his mount, then turns the horse in an "s" and changes the direction of the circle.

"There it was again," says Duke as the Arabian's outside legs change, in midair, from following to leading the stride. "I'll never tire of watching it."

Prewitt wakes in his bed and sees on his watch it's 11:13 p.m. The nap went much longer than he had planned. Earlier, after watching Ranger ride, he'd come up to his room and laid on the bed to think about where else the jewels might be and whether he could ask Amelie about them. But his eyes had gotten heavy, and he allowed them to close. He hadn't realized how tired he was. And now he's hungry.

Prewitt passes Boniface snoring in his room as he heads down the hall to the stairs. Out in his car, he grabs the container of seafood bisque he'd picked up in Paris for his dinner, then walks back into the castle and heads toward the kitchen. When Prewitt enters the kitchen, a light from the refrigerator is spilling out across a section of the island where there is a whole pie with a fork sticking out of it. *Amelie?*

But the figure who turns to him is Pensee. She's got a tub full of ice cream liberated from the open freezer. Her eyes dart between Prewitt and the pie with a momentary look of guilt.

"Le chat. You were so quiet," she says.

Prewitt holds up his bowl of soup. "Mind if I warm this up?"

Pensee gives Prewitt a long stare then seems to decide something. "Not at all," she says, no longer in character.

Pensee sits on a bar stool. She pries open the ice cream and uses the fork to scrape out a good amount. "I only do this occasionally."

Prewitt takes the lid off the soup container and, realizing it has been in the car for about eight hours, gives it a sniff. He decides it smells okay. Plus, he's starving. He places it in the microwave, then sits at the island with her.

Pensee eats the pie in small bites, occasionally dipping the tines of the fork into the ice cream. She savors each swallow.

"I saw you dancing with Robere," says Prewitt.

"His idea. He's very charming, your security officer. Could have been an actor," says Pensee.

"Why do you think that?"

"He just has it."

The microwave beeps, and Prewitt gets up and takes out the bisque.

"Top drawer on your left," Pensee says.

Prewitt opens the drawer and takes out a spoon. "Thank you." He sits again. "And how about you, Madame. Did you ever want to be an actress?"

"How'd you guess? I chose acting, but it didn't choose me. No one was too disappointed. That sort of thing wasn't really encouraged around here."

"*To Catch a Thief?*"

Pensee rolls her eyes. "I used to look like her, you know, Grace Kelly. The same color hair, the same features, same figure too. I learned how to make up my face like hers and wear clothes that were just as glamorous." Pensee sticks the fork in the pie and puts the lid back on the ice cream.

"La chat, the character from the movie, I didn't get it at first," says Prewitt.

"I didn't give you much to go on. I was having my fun. You were a new audience."

"Your siblings have no idea you've been acting out scenes from movies, do they?"

"No," says Pensee, looking proud of her mischief.

"Well, I think you were very good."

Pensee rises, puts the pie in the refrigerator and the ice cream back into the freezer. Then she sits next to Prewitt. "They filmed that movie here in France. Grace Kelly, Cary Grant, Hitchcock. I auditioned for a film in Nice when I turned eighteen, but I wasn't even cast as an extra. I thought I might have been good. Maybe not as good as her, but . . ."

"But what if you'd been given the chance?"

"I wonder."

"You might have been great."

"Ha. You're kind." Pensee chuckles. "There's probably a good reason they never chose me. But I can still have my fun."

"Sorry I didn't play along."

"Robere has been playing along for two days. We're not even doing a movie. We're improvising. It's like I'm back in acting class."

Pensee pats Prewitt on the arm. "Eat your soup." She gets up but stops at the door and turns back to Prewitt. "*To Catch a Thief*," Pensee says, pausing as if remembering. Prewitt sees the wonder in her smile. "She was great, wasn't she?"

Prewitt walks toward Amelie's room. There is light coming from the opened door. When he gets closer, he slows, wondering if he should turn around. But he knows he can't. He knew he would have to ask Amelie about the jewels the moment he thought about it at lunch with Mitta. Without looking in, he knocks lightly on the door frame.

"Come in."

Prewitt steps into the room. The smell of roses and the river drift in on a warm breeze from the open window. Amelie is in bed, under a sheet, her left foot and calf peeking out. A book is turned face down next to her. She puts a bookmark into the novel and places it on the bedside table.

"Hi." Amelie folds the sheet back. She's wearing pajamas. She sits up in the bed and gestures with her head for him to come to her. "Any intruders tonight?" The way she says it like she's tired but playing along to be a good sport makes Prewitt wonder again about what she believes.

It's not something he'd thought much about since before they slept together, but now that they aren't flowing right into the unspoken romantic questions, there's a space where this question is staring right at them. *I don't think she believes any of it.* But Prewitt isn't sure. And it's because they've slept together, and he can't see anything clear now when it comes to Amelie.

He walks to the bed and sits on the edge. Then there is the problem of how to ask about the jewels. What seemed like a good idea, simply asking about valuables and suggesting the Templar are after some old jewelry, now seems like the most obvious lie. But that's also because he feels guilty about the other lies.

Amelie takes his hand and rubs her thumb along his fingers. The energy is loving but not erotic. She's in her head too.

"I wanted to say hello," he says.

"Instead of kissing me?"

Prewitt now takes over and uses his fingers to rub her hand. He continues for a while until the moment to respond has passed. It feels cowardly, but he's not sure how to answer, and he knows talking locks in positions that might not be certain. Amelie seems okay with not knowing either.

"I was going to ask you about something. But I'm not sure I want to talk about it now," he says.

"Why is that?"

He looks at her, again wondering what she believes. Her face is unreadable. Again, he doesn't answer.

"What did you do before your current line of work?" Amelie says.

"Before I worked for the Santa Alleanza?" Prewitt owes her a response to something. "I started with the Vatican as a historian."

"So, you studied Pleyel pianos, plastic jewelry, and the Knights Templar?"

"I almost finished a *Laurea magistrale* in art and antiquities. But I didn't complete the thesis." Prewitt wants to tell her everything about his tangle with Standish, to connect with her in that way. "I had a close relationship with my mentor. I believed that his passion for rare and interesting artifacts was because of a love for the history of the pieces, who made them, whom they were made for, and what was going on in that small part of the world in that brief moment in time. Turned out, he had an entirely different passion, and it was not motivated by love at all. I made one too many bad choices trusting him, and he burned me. So, yes, I've studied pianos and jewelry and the Knights Templar, but the real lessons have been in the motivations of dark-hearted people. I know them. I know what they want, how they think, and where my place is between them and everybody else."

"You protect the rest of the world from the bad guys?"

Perhaps I do. "In my own way, yes."

"How about I tell you a story, Prewitt." Amelie gets up and walks to the armoire across the room. It's handcrafted, with brass pulls on its timeworn dark wood. Amelie slides open a drawer and lifts out a small wooden box. She walks back to the bed and sits.

Prewitt looks at the box in her hands. Hand-painted, lacquered. Amelie opens it to reveal a bundle of old letters.

"These are love letters."

"How old are they?"

"Very old. They've been passed down through the women in my family, starting with Lisette du Courtemanche. Would you like to hear her story?"

"Yes," Prewitt says, hiding his wonder as he realizes what Amelie is volunteering.

Amelie takes out the bundle, sets the box beside her leg, and pulls the ribbon free from the letters. "It begins around 1516 when a renowned artist came to live in the Loire Valley. The King of France wanted him to design a new capital city right here. The artist brought with him a painting that would one day become very, very famous."

Amelie continues to talk, holding the letters in her hands.

"He continued to work on the painting, as well as others

commissioned by local lords and ladies. He spent three years painting and planning the city and being loved by the king and the nobility of France.

"The artist also had an assistant named Francesco who was like a son to him. Francesco went everywhere with the artist, meeting with the nobles and seeing to all his master's needs. Soon a young woman captured Francesco's heart. And he hers. They began passing letters in secret. Francesco told the artist about the young woman, and a formal inquiry was made. But the young woman's father would not allow the relationship. Francesco was not noble enough for the young woman, my ancestor, Lisette du Courtemanche.

"Francesco and Lisette began to meet in secret. He would sneak from the king's Loire chateau by underground passage then row up the river at night. Lisette would sneak from her rooms right here in the east wing of this chateau and walk down to the water's edge. They would spend hours in the early morning, under the bows of the elms, touching and kissing and making promises.

"Then the first of the tragedies struck. The artist had a stroke, and Francesco couldn't meet Lisette for many nights as he attended to him. During this time, Lisette realized she had become pregnant.

"The artist recovered, and Francesco and Lisette met again under the elms on the riverbank. Lisette told him she was carrying his child. Francesco told her he loved her and now they had to be together. He told her the artist would tell him what they should do.

"But the artist had another stroke. Lisette had to carry on without Francesco while he cared for his master. Then she lost the pregnancy. She didn't trust this information in a letter. She'd have to wait to see him again.

"Then the artist died. Finally, Francesco came to Lisette. He was deeply in grief that night. He clutched Lisette's belly and cried; she couldn't bring herself to tell him about their lost child. Francesco had to get back, but he gave Lisette a parcel and made her promise not to open it until she was alone in a place where she could safely conceal the contents.

"Francesco said he'd come back to the river's edge one more time before he left with his master's body for Italy, so they could make plans to be together. Lisette returned to her room and opened the parcel. She found jewels and a card from the artist. The card was co-signed by his lawyer days before his death, making the jewels a gift to his assistant Francesco Melzi, so he could provide a future for his child and her mother and have the means to marry Lisette. And so they could go their own way in the world as a family, beholden to no one.

"Lisette showed her father the jewels, but he said it made no difference. She could never marry Francesco because he was not nobility. When Francesco returned to Lisette, she told him she had lost their child. Francesco was even more grieved. And she told him they couldn't be together. Even with the jewels, her father would still never accept Francesco or allow a marriage. Francesco tore his clothing and screamed into the darkness. And she wept, too. He begged her to run away with him. But she was too scared to do that. His grief and heartbreak became too much. He left Lisette in tears under the elm trees and returned to Italy. She waited for him her entire life, for even a letter. But he never wrote."

She looks at the letters. "Her final letter was to her niece, telling this story and passing down the jewels, asking that they remain with the women in the family."

Amelie places the letters beside the box. "The artist was Leonardo da Vinci," she says. "And the jewels he gave to Lisette are still here in this chateau."

34

Prewitt wakes up in the bed in his room. After hearing her story, he'd sat next to Amelie for a bit, hiding his excitement as she spoke more about Lisette until she lay down and pulled the sheets to cover herself. He'd kissed her hand, sat a while longer in a room filled with silence and complicated feelings, then left.

As difficult as it is, Prewitt does his best to place last night's revelations on a momentary back burner. He has to. It's Monday. Benny's bank paperwork will show up in the mail at the castle, and Ranger will get the final push he needs from the Knights Templar.

Prewitt opens his computer, navigates to Ranger's bank's website, and makes five incorrect login attempts at Ranger's online bank portal. Then he heads to the bathroom, past Boniface's closed door, and showers. While Prewitt gets dressed, there's a knock at his door.

"Monsieur Marcellus, Earl du Courtemanche needs you to come see him in his office," Bertrand says.

As soon as Prewitt enters the office, Ranger is on him, shaking a letter. "Marcellus, my bank accounts are frozen. What is happening?!"

Prewitt sees the concern on Bertrand's face as he leaves.

"Show me the letter."

"The Knights Templar have gotten to the bank accounts!"

Prewitt reads the letter Benny drafted. "This says the bank has frozen your accounts because of a suspicious deposit. Here's a copy of the slip. Someone tried to make a deposit of €.01 into your primary checking account. Your money is still there."

"Why would they add money? And why such a tiny amount?"

"This is how the fraud is done. The Templar are testing to see if they have the correct account. When the bank freezes, then unlocks, your funds, it gives thieves the routing signature for your specific account inside the bank systems. Then they hack in and take everything," says Prewitt.

"But the cyber shield?"

"Only protects the chateau. The Templar may be attacking your assets through the bank's systems. It's very difficult, but banks can be hacked. We've shut down their other options, so this is how they win. The bank will unlock the accounts after forty-eight hours. And that's when they'll strike."

"Then I can't leave my money in the bank where it's vulnerable. Do I withdraw it? What should I do? Marcellus, tell me."

Prewitt looks into Ranger's eyes with practiced calm. All his research, all his plans, and all the trust he's built have come to this moment. Ranger has been backed up to the cliff edge and can feel the long drop behind him. As he casts about himself in desperation, looking for a lifeline, he will find Marcellus. And he will decide, with all confidence, Marcellus is his solution. And he needs Marcellus's help to move all his money. That's the game. The whole game. And Prewitt will have won.

"The Vatican. Surely the Vatican Bank can't be hacked by the Knights Templar."

"No, it can't."

"I want to move my money into an account at the Vatican," Ranger says.

"That can be arranged, Earl du Courtemanche."

"Then let's do it. What do you need from me?"

"We can simply transfer the money from your bank to the Vatican Bank."

Ranger opens the desk and pulls out his password cheat sheet.

"You only want to protect the funds from the bank in question?"

"There are two other accounts in a bank in Belgium."

Of course there are. "They will strike there next."

"I'll move that money, too."

Ranger goes into his computer and logs on to his bank website. He picks up a pen and writes on the sheet with his passwords. Then he logs into a different bank website from memory and writes more. He finishes and puts the pen down.

"This is all of them, Marcellus. Checking, savings, investments, and the emergency money. Move it all to the Vatican."

Ranger slides the piece of paper over to Prewitt. He has written amounts next to each account. He has also written the total at the bottom of the page. Prewitt looks at the total. He looks at Ranger.

"This is all of your assets?"

"I suppose it's less than what you might have expected."

"There are no other accounts? Nothing offshore? Switzerland? The Templar will find that too."

Prewitt watches Ranger's face for a tell. There is no change at the mention of other accounts. Prewitt would push, but no more pressure is required. The threat of the Knights Templar has been used to its max effect. *There is no more money.*

"Why do you think there would be more?"

"Because you're the Earl of Orleans, Viscount of Blois."

"Sure, of course. And we were given riches by the king. Sorry to disappoint. My debts are ungodly. Out of prudence, I've set things up so we get a monthly annuity payment. It's barely enough to keep us going."

"I didn't realize," says Prewitt, trying to keep from being shocked and rocked right out of character.

"I suppose if the Templar were hoping to seize a treasure from the Courtemanche family, they would be disappointed too. Do you think this will all stop after I move the money to the Vatican Bank?"

“Yes. They will realize your money is out of reach.”

“Ah, that’s good. I’m relieved to hear it.”

Prewitt can feel the malaise coming over him. Ranger sits back in his desk chair and looks up at the ceiling.

“I was born in this chateau. Grandfather, also the Earl of Orleans and Viscount of Blois, taught me about the honor of the family. How I had to be ready to face down my enemy, ‘weather any storm.’ And to always come out on the other side with head held high and the Courtemanche legacy preserved.

“But he died before I could learn what he should have taught me. He never told me the enemy was us, that the dishonor was from my own ancestor, Benedict. He never cautioned me that my father would be the biggest storm in my life. He never warned me that death could take my only joy.”

“Your wife?”

“And children,” says Ranger. He waits, thinking. “Then everyone blamed me.”

Ranger pushes his hair back from his face. “I went to Paris to try and work out a deal with an exporter. To save the vineyards. It was last minute. Lily and I had plans to go boating, you see, and when I couldn’t go, Lily took the kids anyway. And they were lost. My beautiful family, all gone in an instant. I returned from Paris to find empty rooms and silence and . . .”

Ranger wipes his eyes with a handkerchief from his jacket pocket.

“But the deal had been a trap. It was blackmail. The exporter photographed me with a young woman who kept placing herself too close. She touched and kissed me no matter what I tried to get her to stop. Lily and the children were dead, and I was too overcome with grief to pay the blackmail. The exporter published the photos, and the scandal destroyed the value of the wine business. The exporter got what he wanted in the end. And for far less. Since then, I have struggled to keep us from going under completely. And I’ve barely done that.” Ranger waves his arm at the wall and ceiling. “This place is a hellish money pit.” He places his handkerchief on his desk.

“And all the while, the accountants, the bankers, the lawyers, even city hall, they’ve all sneered behind my back. And now this. It never ends. Benedict’s choice is our legacy, I’m afraid.”

“Do your sisters know about the finances?”

“They know we’re not rich. But I won’t put that burden on them. The fear. It’s not fair. Amelie and Pensee are my responsibility, and I will provide. It will be enough. I can do it for a while longer. Then I have life insurance to take care of them.”

He’s just waiting to die.

Prewitt hears himself halfheartedly begin to speak. “We will protect what you have left. That’s what’s important right now. I’ll make a call to the Vatican to help facilitate the transfer of funds. They’ll contact your bank to coordinate the unfreezing of your accounts. You should expect a phone call from your bank manager to verify.”

“Okay. Thank you. Just tell me anything you need me to do.”

35

Prewitt closes the door to Ranger's office. He's dizzy with anxiety as he starts down the hall, thinking about how Ranger is not the aristocratic asshole he was supposed to be. *This is wrong. It's all wrong.* And now Prewitt has waded into deep water with no fat flounder to net.

Prewitt heads down through the castle and out the terrace door. It's cloudy and windy and feels like it might rain. He walks through the hedge gardens, past the swimming pool, then across the yard, and over to where Ranger rode the horse.

In his mind, he can see Ranger's sad little password cheat sheet with its circled amounts. The last one, the emergency money, is only €50,000. Below that, Ranger's liquid assets totaled: €121,000.

Prewitt's on autopilot now, walking and trying to think straight. He crosses a road, and a low stone fence catches his attention. He remembers Ranger yelling into his phone about the easement for the new road and the land bounded by a low stone fence. *This must be parcel sixteen, the land Ranger is suing his neighbor for.* He continues up a slope, noting the majestic view around him. There is a natural rise so all the surrounding land rolls away. And the two trees halfway up are wide and twisted with massive scraggly arms. Further beyond are acres of vineyard. Duran's land. The Loire loops in the distance like the signature of a proud artist. It's not until Prewitt is under the trees that he sees headstones. At once, Prewitt knows why Ranger would fight for this place, why he would scream to his lawyer Duran "can't take my land."

Prewitt approaches a headstone lighter in color than the others.

LILY DU COURTEMANCHE, BELOVED WIFE
AND MOTHER.

The two smaller headstones beside hers belong to Ranger's children. He pauses to study them, the names and dates. Then Prewitt walks among the graves, a dozen or so more. Ranger's parents. His grandparents. And ancestors whose stories are remembered only by the trees.

Prewitt stops at the highest point. Under the bough of an ancient elm, stripped and splintered and long dead, he finds the oldest grave. Benedict du Courtemanche.

Prewitt closes his eyes. Something is nagging like an alert from the back of his mind. His eyes search into his memories, past images and colors, and swords and flames, and paintings and . . . pages. Benedict. Loyal. French. *Agent.*

Then the pages of specific letters drift to the fore. First, the William Wallace letter from the Paris library records. Mitta said it was connected to the Courtemanche family. *Why?* He can hear his brain asking. *Who was the Loyal French Agent that King Philip implored to help Wallace?* It would have been a closely guarded secret. Wallace was captured and executed not long after.

Another letter, this one with a seal from King Philip. *Where?* The safe is in the Courtemanche basement. Who was named in this letter? Prewitt can see it clearly.

> To my loyal agent, Benedict, serving as ambassador in Rome, I implore you to do all in your power to convey our friend Walois safely and with all goodwill established with his Excellency the Pope to present his needs. I will welcome you back with

your due favor, but for safety, conduct this business in strict confidence.

Philip, by the grace of God, King of the French

Prewitt opens his eyes and looks at the name on the grave in front of him. Benedict. "You weren't a betrayer of the Knights Templar," Prewitt says to the grave. "You were the French agent. You helped William Wallace in secret. And King Philip couldn't reward you publicly because that would have put you in danger. People connected your sudden land and titles to the torching of the Templar. To them, it looked like you were the traitor, that it was your doing. But it wasn't. All you did was help William Wallace."

Prewitt lowers himself to the ground and sits in front of the grave. Leaves, high in the distant trees, move with the wind and sound like a wave, and the sound grows louder until it fades into another more powerful wave. Prewitt looks up at the old, broken elm, wondering if it is going to fall over on top of him. He has an instinct to protect Benedict's grave and stares at the tree, waiting. He can see the deep ridges of the hardened bark and the black burn of a lightning strike. *You're so old. And after all that you have seen, would you even want to share it?*

Prewitt pulls out his phone and dials. He gets Mace's voicemail. "Mace, it's me. The con is off."

Prewitt knocks on the door to Amelie's room.

"Come in." Amelie is stretching in a yoga pose on a thin purple mat with tiny white flowers printed on it.

"I need to ask you about something."

"Sure, what?"

"Ranger's lawsuit with your neighbor."

"Okay." Amelie rises from her yoga mat and sits on the edge of the bed.

Prewitt steps into the room and sits in the chair under the window. "He's trying to take your family cemetery, isn't he?"

"Yes, Duran wants those slopes because they have soil for grapes. Ranger's been fighting the lawsuit for almost a year now. Duran is relentless."

"I thought Ranger was suing *him*," he says, hearing the words and knowing there is no importance to what he thought he knew. Prewitt feels foolish sitting here. There is no reason to keep the ruse going, and he knows he should leave this room and leave this castle. But he also feels Amelie is his only real friend in the world right now, and he has an overpowering urge to talk with her. His heart sinks.

"Are you okay?"

"Not really."

"What's going on?"

"I don't work for the Vatican."

"I know."

"You know?"

"Yes."

Prewitt studies her. "Do you know what I actually do?"

Amelie smiles. "Well, it took a few days, but I think I sorted it out."

"No one else did."

"You didn't sleep with anyone else."

Prewitt looks off in self-disgust.

"It was nothing you said. Just things you couldn't hide when your guard was down."

"Which it was. So amateur."

"So now that we're not pretending anymore, how long have you been a con artist?"

Prewitt reflects on his life for a millisecond and finds more of the loathing. "Conning people is all I've ever done."

"Were you going to try and steal the jewels?"

"Yes."

"I figured that was your goal. That's why I took them out of the safe and left the key for you to find in Ranger's office."

It's unexpected, and Prewitt smiles at the cleverness. "I also intended to con money from Ranger. That's what all this was for."

"But now you don't want to?"

"Now I can't."

"Because there is no money to steal."

"And because Ranger isn't who I thought he was. Before I came here, I thought much less of your brother."

"He's a good man."

"I agree. But I don't understand, Amelie. Why did you let me stay here so long? If you knew? Why didn't you say anything?"

"Because I didn't care. Because I was bored, and you are the first thing in a million years that was exciting. Because there is no money to take. And because you're gentle, and you have a kind heart. I don't think you'll steal the jewels now, but if you do, I'll wish you the best and hope they bring you happiness. They've been locked away in this chateau for hundreds of years, Prewitt, it feels like we all have. Maybe we, too, need to be stolen away from here."

Amelie stands and opens the drawer of her bedside table. And just like in the painting, Prewitt sees a drape of black cloth and a flash of color catching the light. She lifts the bundle from the drawer. The jewelry roll is untied, black ribbons hanging down, and Prewitt can see the deep blue of sapphires set in gold. Amelie gently lays the cloth on the bed. "You should look at them."

Prewitt rises and stands beside Amelie. He removes the jewelry from the pockets inside the cloth and sets them on the bed. The largest is a necklace with sapphires in a cabochon cut, ringed with rows of tiny pearls and all of it set in elaborately cast gold. The other pockets contain strings of pearls, sapphire drop earrings, a bracelet with rubies and emeralds, and several gold rings featuring massive gems.

Prewitt marvels at the treasure, though it's not the pure,

history-tinged high he thought he'd feel. And this time, the glow of the gems can't push the present away.

Prewitt places the jewels back in the pockets of the black cloth and rolls them up. "These should be back in the safe." He hands them to her.

"Then we'll put them there."

Prewitt follows Amelie, first to Ranger's office to retrieve the safe key, then through the castle to the kitchen, and down into the hidden room in the basement. She opens the safe. Amelie hands Prewitt the stack of letters to hold while she places the jewels inside.

"Do you know what these are?" Prewitt asks.

"No."

"Amelie, these letters confirm your ancestor, Benedict Du Courtemanche, was the French agent King Philip entrusted to secretly aid William Wallace's fight for the freedom of Scotland."

"I'm not sure I understand."

"These letters explain the Courtemanche family did not get their wealth from betraying the Knights Templar but from helping the Scottish. They would clear your family name."

"Ranger might care about that, but I don't."

Amelie takes the letters from Prewitt and places them back in the safe.

"You should tell him," says Prewitt.

"Maybe you should," she says as she closes the safe door.

Amelie uses the key to turn the lock and tests the handle. "There. Everything is back to the way it was before." She turns to Prewitt. "No, I'll tell Ranger what you said about the letters after you're gone." She takes his hand. "You have to undo the lies you've told him. Then you should leave."

Prewitt sees tears well in Amelie's eyes. She turns toward the doorway and walks through it without looking back.

36

Prewitt sits at the kitchen table. He writes Benny a text:

Call Ranger posing as the
bank manager to let him know
his accounts are unfrozen.

He sends Duke a text:

Canine security no longer
needed. Head out.

He fires off a text to Louis that he and Michel are free to leave. Within minutes, he hears the distant growl of the tank boat engine. Then he feels a light jolt of pain seize his back and shoot down his leg. He stands and straightens up, but it's not going anywhere.

Bertrand comes into the kitchen, "Monsieur Marcellus, the men have started up the tank and are driving away."

"They've been cleared to leave."

"You mean this is over?"

"Yes."

"Completely?"

"Yes."

"Oh, thank you, monsieur!"

Bertrand looks overwhelmed with relief. He smiles widely at Prewitt and leaves.

Prewitt hangs out in the kitchen until he hears confirmation from Benny. Then he takes the main stairs up to Ranger's office.

"Prewitt, come in. The bank called to confirm they have unfrozen my accounts. Let's do the transfer. I want my money in the Vatican bank as soon as possible."

"It's over. Three members of the Knights Templar targeting you have been caught by the Santa Alleanza in Paris. The Vatican technology team traced their hacking attempts to a house and apprehended them there. They've seized all their computers. You're safe."

"It's over?"

"Yes," says Prewitt, forcing a smile and watching as Ranger lets out a big sigh then hangs his head in relief.

"Thank you, Marcellus."

After Prewitt leaves Ranger's office, he goes upstairs and looks into Boniface's room. His things are all there, but no Boniface. He sends him a text:

We need to talk.

Prewitt goes into his own room and closes the door. He lies on his bed fully clothed, opens his phone, and looks at the screensaver photo of Josh. He is going to miss the payment to Harvard.

Hours pass as Prewitt does nothing but stare at the ceiling. His phone rests on his chest under his hand. He's waiting to hear from Mace or Boniface, but everything is quiet.

Prewitt slips in and out of something between consciousness and unconsciousness. He has a vision of Josh drowning in Geoffrey's pool beyond the reach of his hands. Then sleep pulls him all the way down.

***

Prewitt wakes to the sounds of loud knocking and voices. He's still lying clothed on his bed. At first, he thinks he's in his apartment in New York, then, seeing his surroundings and feeling the weight of the yuck in his brain, he quickly gets his bearings. His phone, still on his chest, says 9:41 p.m. He sits up, hurries out of his room, and takes the stairs down. When he gets to the second floor, he sees Amelie in the hallway and Bertrand knocking on Ranger's bedroom door.

"The police are here, Earl du Courtemanche. Come quickly," says Bertrand.

Ranger opens the door. He is putting a dressing gown over his pajamas. "Police?"

"Why are the police here?" says Amelie.

Prewitt studies Amelie. She seems surprised. *It wasn't her.*

Bertrand notices Prewitt and stares at him with a hurt, betrayed look in his eyes. "They claim we are housing a criminal."

They all go down to the front hall, where they find five Paris policemen.

"Why are you in my home?" says Ranger.

"We are here to arrest Prewitt Marcellus, aka Prewitt Patry of New York."

Ranger turns to Prewitt. "You're from New York?"

Prewitt replies in English. "Yes, I am."

"He has a criminal record in America."

"What?"

"Anything he has done here has been in an attempt to steal your money. This man is a con artist."

Ranger pauses to think.

"Is that true?" Ranger says, staring at Prewitt.

"Yes."

"There was no Knights Templar?"

"No."

It takes Ranger a moment to process. Then Ranger looks at Prewitt with a flash of anger that melts into hurt.

"You are under arrest," says one of the officers as two others approach Prewitt. He allows himself to be handcuffed.

The lead officer begins to tell Prewitt his rights.

"Where will you take him?" Amelie says.

"We will interrogate the suspect at the 8th arrondissement in Paris. I'll leave an officer here to explain to you about filing charges."

The officers walk Prewitt out of the front doors.

But how do the Paris police know? Prewitt wonders. *Who spilled?*

It takes a millisecond.

Who isn't here?

Boniface. Prewitt's head sinks toward the ground.

The next thing he sees is the inside of a police van.

37

The officer hands Prewitt a landline telephone through the bars of his holding cell. Prewitt dials Johnny, knowing it's dinnertime in New York, hoping he will answer.

"Who is this?"

"It's me."

The police officer walks away.

"Dammit, Prewitt."

"I'm in jail."

"I know."

"How do you know?"

"I can see where you're calling from on the damn phone. I told you not to get in jail. For such a smart guy, you're pretty stupid, you know that?"

"I had no choice."

"There's always a choice."

"I needed a whole semester of Harvard tuition."

"There are other ways."

"In two weeks."

"Okay, maybe you didn't have a choice. So, what do you want me to do?"

"I need you to bail me out."

"What, none of your cohorts want to help you?"

"There's no one to ask."

"Big surprise."

"I don't . . ."

Prewitt's voice catches in his throat. He looks at the empty holding cell across from him, the blue paint peeling off its walls. *Am I this pathetic?* He looks toward the desk down the hallway where the officer is waiting and listening.

"I thought I still had it, Johnny. I really did."

"We all think that until the ground comes up to smack us in the face, and we learn the hard way we fell down."

"I wanted Josh to go Harvard without having to make a fucking deal with Geoffrey. I didn't want to lose my son."

"You won't lose your son."

"I will now."

"You won't."

"Johnny, everything I try to love turns to shit."

"Oh, fucking hell, will you listen to yourself? If that's not the dumbest crock o' crap. 'Everything I try to love turns to shit?' Could you be more dramatic? You sound like a fucking telenovela."

"It's true."

"Prewitt, you got pinched. You got pinched, and your pockets are empty. And you don't want to let down your kid. So what? Welcome to life."

"But I'm at the bottom."

"There is no bottom, there's just this place we all live, and it's got its hills, and it's got valleys. And sometimes, what happens is just what happens. Out of our hands."

"Even this?"

"No. This is your doing."

"Thanks."

"Okay, even this. It happens."

"You'll come bail me out?"

"That I can't do."

"What do you mean?"

"Can't do it, Prewitt. You're gonna have to face the music on this one. If I bailed you out, you'd try to skip and ruin your life even more. And I'd be out my roll. No, Prewitt, the move here is for you to make your deal, do your time, then come home and pick up the pieces."

"Tell me you're joking."

"I won't tell you that. Because I'm right about this. Take a deal, and at least you can still hide it from the kid. You become an international incident; it won't be so easy."

"You're gonna let me rot here?"

"There's no other way."

"And what am I gonna tell him about Harvard?"

"You tell him you tried. You tell him you love him, and it's not his fault. And you lie about everything else."

"Easy for you to say."

"Yes, it is easy for me to say. And it's the only play you've got left. Sorry, Prew, but you're long past the river. Make your deal. I gotta go.

The call disconnects, and Prewitt hangs up.

The police officer comes back and retrieves the phone. Prewitt sits back on his cot. He adjusts to relieve the ache of his sciatica and thinks about why he is here.

Mace.

Prewitt goes back over the early conversations with her. It was always right there. Ranger was never in Mace's bar. Most old-money Europeans wouldn't make the trip to New York to watch people buy their stuff. Even after meeting Ranger, Prewitt missed it. The Ranger Prewitt knows wouldn't have recently traveled to New York. And Ranger would have never bragged. Not the way Mace described. Was Prewitt so blinded by desperation he missed the tells?

Never go on the grift when you can't walk away from the money.

And how did Prewitt think he'd be the only one to find out about Amarante and the painting? What, Mace wouldn't have spent the time doing the same research and turned up the same jewels? Of course she would have. Which means Mace also would have figured out Ranger was broke. And if Mace knew Ranger was broke, and knew about the jewels, and was working behind his back with Boniface all along, then *the jewels and Boniface are both long gone.*

Boniface warned him not to trust Mace.

So many blind spots. Too many.

The next morning, as Prewitt lays on the cot, he hears footsteps then a buzzing as his cell door unlocks. He sits up to see two officers. "Come with us, Patry."

Prewitt follows the officers out of his cell, down the hall, and into a room where they sit him at a table. Ranger comes through the door. He's in a suit, but his shirt is barely tucked, and his hair is uncombed. He sits in the chair opposite.

"Prewitt Patry of New York."

Prewitt nods.

"Not of the Vatican," Ranger says.

Prewitt can see Ranger's pain at being betrayed. And the fatigue, as if Prewitt is another in the long line of everyone who wants to hurt him. He can barely look Ranger in the eye.

"The only reason I am here is to ask that you return Pensee's and Amelie's jewelry. If there is any remaining decency in you, you will do that."

Prewitt's heart sinks as Ranger confirms his fear about the jewels.

Prewitt can't bring himself to tell Ranger that even though he intended to take the jewels, he doesn't have them because he got conned by his shitty partner, and the guy Prewitt trusted has stolen them.

"There is no decency in me," says Prewitt.

Ranger sits a moment, then, as if accepting the situation, gets up and walks out. As Ranger passes through the doorway, Prewitt sees Amelie staring at him from the hall.

Frozen in the chair, Prewitt watches Amelie enter the room. When she gets to the table, she stays standing.

"I didn't take the jewels," he says.

"Every lie you told before didn't matter because I already knew the truth. But I don't now, so don't lie to me."

"I'm not lying."

"Then where are they?"

"Stolen by Boniface . . . Robere, and someone else I trusted."

"I know what I said before, but I only said it because I thought you wouldn't take them. I need the jewels for Ranger and Pensee."

"Where did you put the key to the safe?"

"In my room, with me."

"Then that's where Boniface found it, or he picked the lock. He's capable. He was working for my partner Mace, who conned me so I could lead her to the jewels. She's known about your family this whole time. She knew about the jewels. She knew your brother was almost out of cash. She knew everything."

"Why didn't she ask you to steal them?"

"Because she knew I could never sell them. And this way, she could take them and pin the whole thing on me."

"So where are they now?"

"Boniface has them. Or he's already handed them off to Mace. But they will sell them on the black market."

Amelie lets the information settle, seeming to accept it.

"Well, I suppose I'm to blame too."

"No, you're not."

Amelie studies Prewitt. She scans from his eyes to his hair, to his mouth, then back to his eyes again. Then she looks down, thinking. Gone is that carefree float he's so used to, and in its place is a seriousness he'd not seen in her. It makes him feel even worse.

"I'm sorry."

"I know," she says without looking up. Amelie turns and walks out.

38

Two hours later, a guard approaches Prewitt's cell and opens the door. "You are free to go."

I am?

Confused, Prewitt follows the guard down the hallway to the booking desk. Standing there watching him approach are Ranger, Amelie, and Pensee. Pensee has a big grin on her face.

"What's happening?" says Prewitt to the three.

"We are not pressing charges," says Ranger.

"But I deserve them," says Prewitt.

"You know who the real cat is," says Pensee.

"Not here, Pensee," says Ranger.

"Sorry," chirps Pensee through the grin.

"Everyone, let's go," says Ranger.

He and Pensee start toward the front doors of the police station.

Amelie lingers with a confused Prewitt. "Come on, we need to talk to you."

Prewitt follows Amelie out to the curb, where Bertrand sits behind the wheel of an old Rolls Royce Silver Shadow. He stares straight ahead to avoid looking at Prewitt. Ranger gets in the front seat next to him. Amelie opens the back door and gets in next to Pensee. Prewitt gets in next to Amelie. *Maybe they're planning to dump me in the river.*

***

Finding himself where he never expected to be again, Prewitt sits on the couch in the blue salon opposite Ranger, Amelie, and Pensee. The ride from Paris was spent in silence, and now all Prewitt can do is wonder even more about what's coming. Ranger looks to the window as if gathering the right words. Amelie watches Prewitt with the same playfulness she had when this whole thing started. Pensee stares with a delighted smile. Finally, Ranger turns to Prewitt.

"We spoke, my sisters and I, for a while in Paris. We haven't been that open with one another in a long time. Haven't had a reason to until now. Foremost, Amelie assured us you didn't steal the jewels. We believe her, which means we believe you. We believed you when you were lying to us. At least I did. But we believe you now, too."

"Okay."

Ranger looks Prewitt up and down. "Amelie not only assured us you didn't take the jewels, but she told us, well, me really, since Pensee had already come to the same conclusion, something else I hadn't considered. And as soon as she told me, I realized it was true. While you were in the process of trying to con us, Marcellus, or Prewitt, something else happened. The isolated, very drab, and stale life we've been living has been, in these last days, filled with excitement. It has been oddly better. My thoughts in the morning, before you came here, were often thoughts of wondering for what reason I should get out of bed. Duty, of course. Which is all I've had in my life, at least the last forty years of it. But this week has been entirely more interesting, at times stressful, I can't deny that. But I also can't deny sitting here now, I would choose what has happened over you never having arrived. Aside from losing the jewelry, that is. Strange, but it's true. Your man Wellington has shown me kindness, and others have been, well, entertaining. The entire show you've put together with all its different pieces has been extraordinary. I feel like I've lived in a clever little survival game. And let me not forget, in the end, you didn't take my money."

"I couldn't."

"Why?"

"Because you're not who I thought you were. I only steal from people who've gotten their riches in an illegal or evil way, who are morally corrupt, or who have harmed others. I steal from people who are bad and continue to do bad. At first, I believed you fit that. But you are none of those things. You are decent. All of you."

"Well, since you didn't steal anything from us, it didn't seem right to let you be imprisoned."

Prewitt is annoyed at being so wrong about Ranger. "See what I mean?"

"But there is another reason we didn't want to see you left in jail. We need you."

"For what?"

"To get the jewels back."

"It seems to me you'd be the right one to come up with a plan to trick your partner and get them back," Amelie says.

Prewitt is struck by the logic of it.

"Surely it's possible," says Ranger.

"Well . . ."

"Possible?" says Amelie.

"I mean, it's possible. It depends."

"And you'd be willing to do this for us?" says Ranger.

"Of course."

"Then it's decided," says Ranger.

"But it might not be so easy."

"You're very good at what you do," says Amelie.

"And you now have us at your disposal," says Pensee.

"There is a lot—wait, what?"

"We will be your accomplices," says Ranger.

Amelie nods at Prewitt's surprised look.

"You want to be part of it?"

"Absolutely," says Pensee, glowing.

The twinkle of a mischievous smile grows on Ranger's face too.

Madame Farine puts a platter down in the center of the kitchen table. It's loaded with slices of ham, tomato, greens, and a loaf of thick-cut bread, freshly baked. Prewitt and the three Courtemanche siblings are seated around the table.

"I can't," Prewitt says.

"Sure, you can," Amelie says.

"No, I can't eat the food of someone I'm conning."

"You're not conning us anymore," says Amelie.

"We're a team now. Eat," says Pensee.

"Or I'll make you eat," says Madame Farine, hands on hips. She stands over him until Prewitt makes a sandwich and takes a bite.

"When was the last time you saw Robere?" Amelie says to Pensee.

"Crafty choice of alias." Pensee points a finger at Prewitt. "Calls himself 'robber' and you don't catch on."

"Good point," says Prewitt.

"So, when was the last time?" says Ranger.

"It was yesterday," Pensee says. "Robere suggested we take a drive along the river. He packed a hamper full of snacks."

"I packed the hamper," Madame Farine says.

"We returned home, and I showed him my collection. I was putting on the hat Ginger Rogers wore in the film *Vivacious Lady,* and he was interested and complimentary, then he said he had a headache and needed to take a nap. Did you see him, Madame Farine?"

"I didn't," says Madame Farine.

"He took the jewels from the safe without anyone knowing," says Prewitt.

"I can call him," says Pensee.

"Let me see if he'll talk to me first," Prewitt says.

Prewitt leaves the kitchen and walks down the long back hallway. His phone is in his hand when Bertrand comes out of a room and nearly bumps into him.

Prewitt slips his phone back into his pocket. "Hello."

"May I get you anything, monsieur?" says Bertrand, visibly glum, his voice betraying a deep hurt. It catches Prewitt off guard, and he searches Bertrand's face for any bit of lightness. There's none.

"Bertrand, I'd like to explain."

But Bertrand stays in butler mode. "If you don't need anything, please excuse me." Then he walks away.

Shit.

Prewitt goes out to the terrace. There are storm clouds, and the trees look dark along the river. He dials. Boniface picks up.

"Oui."

"Do you still have them?"

"I don't know what you are asking about. But no. I do not."

"She's here in France?"

"You know the answer to that."

"Did you and your troupe get the twenty percent?"

"Not yet."

"Well, they're not going to."

"Why?"

"Because there's no money to steal. The con was you getting the jewels."

"No."

"Yes."

"Yes?"

"There was never any money. There is no Courtemanche fortune. That just got me here."

"She . . . no, she wouldn't."

"Of course she would. You're the one who told me not to trust her."

"But that's because she was tricking *you* with the jewels."

"She was tricking you, too. The jewels were the only thing, Boniface. There is no fortune."

"Shit. She used me to get her the jewels, and now I can't pay my crew. I warned you, then I didn't even listen to my own advice. Shit again!"

"When did you hand off the jewels?"

"Just an hour ago. She met me in Paris. She said she didn't have any euros and asked me to pay for lunch. She even hit me for a free meal."

"You're supposed to fence them for her."

"Yes."

"Well, then you're going to get them back."

"How does that make me money?"

"It doesn't. But it keeps you out of jail."

"You wouldn't. You know the code."

"I wouldn't. But they would. And they will. I'd knock you into the street and drop a fancy car on your head because that's what I feel like doing to someone right now."

"I understand completely," says Boniface. "So, you have a plan?"

"Working on it. Meet me at Lorelei's restaurant in two hours. Bring Duke."

39

The crowd at Chez Jeannette is packed in and loud as Prewitt leads Amelie, Pensee, and Ranger through the restaurant. No one spares more than a glance as they glide by tables of Parisians enjoying beers and classic French fare at the end of a workday.

They walk into the back room and find the whole crew. Boniface heads straight to Pensee. Everyone pauses their conversation, and in the quiet, he takes Pensee's hand in his and raises the back of it to his lips.

"Pensee, will you forgive me?"

"Should I?"

"I think you should. But if you give me time, I can prove myself."

"Hard to say no when a fella talks this smooth."

"Then don't say no."

Pensee smiles, and Boniface kisses her hand. Then he pulls out a chair for her. The chatter starts up again.

Boniface approaches Prewitt. "Word got around quickly. They all insisted on coming."

Ranger sees Duke about to sit next to Lorelei and walks to him. "Wellington, hello again."

Duke steps to Ranger and shakes his hand. "Hello, hello. Fine to see you here."

"Nice to see you," says Ranger.

"I am in awe of your choice," says Duke.

"This seems more logical."

"Exactly what I mean. Well, I am at your service."

"And I yours."

Duke smiles. "Welcome to the game."

Prewitt raises a hand to quiet everyone. "We have a new job. Mace, my partner from New York, has the Courtemanche family jewels and is planning to fence them. We need to get them back. Boniface has already informed her he has a top-level buyer here in Paris. She's getting an appraiser from Boucheron or Piaget."

Boniface adds, "As you all now know, she's burnt us on the Courtemanche job."

The troupe grumbles.

Amelie speaks up, "But we're hiring you now, and we will compensate you for this job. I promise."

"We're in," Duke says.

"We're in," say Kat and Benny.

"And we're in too," Louis says.

Michel elbows him. "You didn't even ask me."

"Oh, you're not in? Then leave now, you ungrateful clown. Don't think about staying for dinner."

"I didn't say I wasn't in. I just don't think you should always speak for me like I don't have a say."

"Shut up, Michel," Boniface interrupts. "Prewitt, tell us what you want done."

"As soon as Mace tells Boniface which appraiser she's picked, we'll lock in the details, but for now, here are the parts we need. Oh, and Ranger, Amelie, and Pensee are the faces on this one."

There's a collective "Ahhhhh," as nods and smiles make their way around.

Prewitt pulls a slim stack of papers from his jacket pocket. "Benny, security guard. You and Louis." Prewitt hands off a paper.

"Ranger and Amelie are the buyers. Pensee will be our appraiser.

Boniface will be playing himself. Duke and I will prepare everyone for their roles."

"But you left me out again," Michel says.

"There's more pieces of paper there, you idiot," Louis says.

"Oh. What's my part, Prewitt?"

"Michel. The real appraiser will be encouraged to miss the meeting with Mace."

Michel thinks.

"A distraction."

"Duke will help you choose the method once we know more."

"This is an important role," says Michel.

"Yes. It is."

"Very important indeed," says Duke.

Michel smiles. "Sacrebleu. Thank you, Prewitt."

Michel arrives outside Boucheron as the evening sun bathes the pale stone exterior. While passing through the double glass doors and into the art deco interior of the most famous jewelry salon in Paris, he thinks about all the preparation he did with Duke over the last two days and tells himself not to screw this up. Then he tells himself he won't screw this up. Then he tells himself to use kind self-talk, Duke's other coaching with Michel lately. He imagines Duke saying, "You'll do great," then he says it to himself, and it's enough to settle his nerves.

He smooths his blond bangs back from his forehead and walks from one display case to the next, taking his time. Michel notices the two salespersons conferring behind a desk. Then he sees Eloise Tremblay come out from the back. He browses up to her.

"Bonsoir, monsieur, would you like to see something?" says the jet-black ponytailed Eloise, who Michel knows to be fifty-eight, single, childless, and a talented watercolor landscape painter who sells her work at local art fairs. He also knows she's the appraiser Mace has hired.

"I'm browsing. Taking a little break from the recording studio. Do you play any instruments?"

"I don't. What do you play?"

"I don't play either. I mean, not well. I'm just an assistant to the artist."

"Oh, which artist?"

And that was the question, Duke assured Michel, that would mean his hook had sunk. In their research, they had discovered that Eloise Tremblay, in addition to the other details about her, absolutely adores to no end one musician above all others the world over: Bono.

"Bono," says Michel.

Her eyes widen. "Really?"

'Yes. Do you like U2?"

"Of course, yes. And Bono is . . . I love Bono. He is my favorite artist. His lyrics are so perfect. He's the best."

"What a coincidence."

"There is no bigger fan. What's he doing here? Are they making a record?"

"Well, they are, yes. But Bono wanted to get away from the boys for a few days, so he rented a tiny studio to do some writing alone."

"Oh, that's so cool. What's he writing? Can I ask?"

"Nothing, actually. A bit of writer's block. Though he calls it 'heaven in peril.'"

"Bono gets writer's block?"

"This is a particularly bad bout."

"Oh my."

"Hey, would you like to meet him?"

"Seriously?"

"Yes. Bono likes meeting people. Certainly, he enjoys meeting fans, but someone like you who really appreciates him and his writing . . . he would love to meet you. It will distract him from the frustration. I've been with the band for a long time. I know how he works."

"Of course I would. Yes. How . . ."

"You could come up to the recording studio. This evening."

"Yes. Oh, my gosh. I, oh wait, I have an appointment at seven."

"So come at six."

"That's when I get off work."

"I'll meet you here, outside, and we can go over together. Just don't tell anyone. Really, you can't tell anyone."

"Okay. What will you say to Bono?"

"That I'm bringing a special fan to meet him. He'll be happy."

An hour later, Michel meets Eloise in front of Boucheron and helps her into the backseat of the Rolls Royce Silver Shadow parked at the curb. He drives them to a recording studio ten minutes away he has rented for the next four hours and escorts her inside.

"Please sit here," Michel gestures to the chair in front of the recording console.

Eloise points to the large glass window looking into the darkened live room. "Bono?"

"Is in there, yes. He likes the dark when he's writing."

"He's writing right now?"

"Yes. We record everything. Let me go and tell him you're here. You can hold that button down to speak."

Michel goes into the live room, sits on a chair in the dark, and presses the button that turns on the microphone.

"Hello dear, thank you for coming to visit me. Michel told me you're my biggest fan. You are too kind," says Michel in his best Irish-accented Bono impersonation. Two hours last night with Duke, and he had nailed it down pretty well.

"I am your biggest fan. Bono, it's so nice to meet you."

"Tell me your name."

"Eloise Tremblay."

"I'm trying to write a love song. But heaven's in peril. Tell me about your first love, Eloise Tremblay."

Eloise's hand flies to her mouth.

"You want to know about *my* first love?"

"Yes. The flush of your skin, the shy smile. It was something, wasn't it? Please, tell me. Save me from myself. Lead me back to her mysterious ways."

Eloise's smile widens. "I knew that was a love song."

"It's a life song, dear," says Michel knowing he has no idea what the song really means but trusting Duke's prepared lines.

"How young were you?" he asks.

"I was . . . we were . . ."

"Just go back to that time, let the memories flow."

As Madame Tremblay tells Bono her story, she loses track of time. And in the recording booth, Michel strums a guitar every now and again and, telling himself he's doing great, has no problem keeping up his Irish accent.

40

The Paris streets are bustling with cars, bikes, and a pastiche of locals and tourists trodding the sidewalks. Mace steps out of a cab in the center of Place Vendome under a colossal bronze column topped by a statue of Napoleon. All around are iconic stores. Their sparkling contents in shiny glass cases sit behind windows that are lit and inviting. Mace, in cuffed blue jeans, retro white Chuck Taylors, and white linen button-down shirt, watches the cab head off, then struts past Boucheron, around the back of Hotel Gaillard and into a small courtyard. She stops in front of a modern black metal door, pushes a buzzer and waits.

Benny, in black jeans, a black t-shirt, and an earpiece, opens the door. "Nom?"

"Bostick," Mace says, giving him an alias.

Benny nods, and Mace follows him in. The door sweeps shut behind them and closes with a heavy click.

At the end of a short hallway, Benny and Mace arrive at Louis and an elevator.

"This is Bostick," Benny says to Louis in English.

Louis, in an outfit matching Benny's, nods and pushes the up button. The elevator door opens, and Mace, Benny, and Louis step in. The doors close. Mace stares them down, her eyes unblinking beneath her slicked-back hair. Benny and Louis stare back. Then Bennie and Louis look at each other. *She doesn't look like the kind of person who could run Boniface and Prewitt,* Benny's squinting expression says. *In this game, you shouldn't judge a book by its cover,* suggests Louis's. Mace stands there wondering if they both have indigestion.

"Nice king snake flash," Mace says to Louis.

"Thanks, but it's a coral snake. They're poisonous."

"Are you sure?"

"Red touch yellow, you're a dead fellow. Red touch black, mimicry hack."

"What does that mean?"

"That's how you tell the two snakes apart."

Mace looks annoyed. "I guess I missed snake rhyme day in nursery school," she says.

The elevator opens to a large windowless room with two doors on the opposite side. Along the other walls are glass cases of jewelry; necklaces on busts, and rows of black velvet-covered fingers spiking up with precious stones of every color. In the center of the room is a square metal table with two lamps, two armless leather chairs, and a stool. Mace walks to the table and sits in one of the chairs. Louis takes position next to the elevator. Benny goes around the desk and knocks once on one of the doors. Then he stands against the wall beside it. Both watch Mace as she holds out her hand to examine the chunky silver ring on her middle finger, then uses the nail on her thumb to pick out something from under the nail.

The door opens, and Boniface comes through, followed by Amelie, then Ranger, who is carrying a briefcase. Benny closes the door.

"Good to see you again, Ms. Bostick," Boniface says in English. Everyone takes the cue and carries on in that language.

"You too." She stands.

"Monsieur and Madame Perreault," Boniface says to Ranger and Amelie. "This is Ms. Bostick."

"Bonsoir," Amelie says.

"Likewise."

"Madame Bostick, a pleasure," Ranger says. He notices there is one chair next to Mace. "Here my darling," he says to Amelie while drawing the chair back. "You sit. I am happy to stand."

"Thank you, my treasure," Amelie responds, batting her eyelashes. She turns to Mace, who has sat back down. "This is so exciting."

Mace fake-smiles at Amelie as Ranger affectionately pats Amelie on the shoulder.

The door opens again, and Pensee strolls in. She has costumed herself in a black business suit. Her hair is pulled into a tight ballerina bun. Little red and white checkered cat eye librarian glasses rest on her nose. Pensee settles herself onto a stool and clicks on both lamps.

"Madam Tremblay, these are the prospective buyers, the Perreaults, and our seller Ms. Bostick," Boniface says to Pensee.

Pensee makes eye contact with Boniface, waits, shifts her gaze to Ranger, then to Amelie, then finally to Mace.

Mace tries her best at a polite smile. Boniface takes a few steps back.

"Ms. Bostick, nice to meet you in person. I know this will go well. When you're ready, I'll appraise your items."

Mace nods. Pensee opens a drawer and takes out a loupe and a small rubber mat.

"After my appraisal, I'll withdraw so you may do your business privately. My security officers must remain in the room at all times." Pensee waves a hand to either side of her, motioning to Benny and Louis. "My fee is €5,000, paid by the buyer, whether they make a purchase or not. Okay?"

Mace nods.

"Excellent. Great outfit, by the way," says Pensee.

"I think so too," says Amelie.

Mace forces a tiny smile. "Thank you."

"I love fashion," says Pensee,

"I believe you," says Mace.

"There's a secure wireless connection in this room. Once I have verified receipt of my payment, and you have both verified any transactions, the elevator will become available again. Any questions?" Pensee says.

"None," Amelie says.

"Not for me, either. I'm excited to see something shiny," says Ranger, sounding convincingly like an idiot. "Can we take them out?"

Mace reaches under the hem of her button-down shirt and pulls free a flesh-colored waist belt. She sets it on the table, unzips the top edge and lays out the velvet jewelry roll that holds the Courtemanche jewels.

Pensee unfurls it onto the desk. She draws out the necklace first, lays it on the mat, and repositions one of the lamps.

Amelie feigns awe.

Pensee clips the loupe to the lens over her right eye and leans in. "Hmm."

After careful examination of each of the main jewels in the necklace, Pensee lifts the whole thing and drapes it around her neck.

"Oh, goodness!" Amelie exclaims.

"I must feel the weight, my dear. I must allow the piece to breathe freely and speak to me."

"Marvelous," Ranger says, trying a bit too hard.

Mace adjusts in her chair, but Pensee's oddity, which seems to work for the Perraults, keeps her from opening her mouth.

Pensee returns the necklace to the rubber mat and removes the rest of the jewelry one piece at a time. She hmms and oohs and ahhs, then wears, seeming to commune with them.

Finally, Pensee puts her tools away in the desk. Then using a cotton flannel cloth, she wipes away any trace of handling. Pensee arranges the jewels back into the pockets of the velvet jewelry roll.

"Well? What are the numbers?" says Mace.

"The cut of the stones, the composition of the metal, the craftsmanship, the rarity. My appraisals always reveal the true value." She looks up to the rafters. "That is my gift. Passed down to me from nomad ancestors who have bought and sold jewelry since the Renaissance," says Pensee, reciting her favorite line from the script Duke wrote for her.

"And these?" says Mace.

"As fine as the Tower Jewels."

"The numbers, please?" says Mace.

"So we may negotiate," Amelie says.

"These are real auction estimates, not insurance ones."

"Yeah, yeah. I get it," says Mace.

"I'll start with the rings. Each of them is €50,000 to €55,000. The pair of earrings, €70,000 to €85,000. The pearl necklaces, €85,000. The bracelet estimate is €100,000. And last, the sapphire and gold necklace, €410,000." Pensee stands, gives a little nod to each woman and Ranger, then starts toward the door. Benny opens it, and Pensee strides through.

Amelie looks to Ranger. "Honey, the laptop is in my bag."

"Of course, lamb." Ranger pulls a computer from his briefcase.

Boniface passes both Amelie and Mace a business card. "The network and password."

Amelie opens the laptop and starts typing.

Mace watches her and waits.

On the other side of the wall, Pensee sits beside Kat, who is typing on her own laptop. A bank website on her screen says, "Fidelity Bank Little Cayman."

"How is it going?" says Kat.

"Very well."

"I'm connected to Amelie's computer now."

"Good." Pensee grins and rubs her hands together. "We're gonna get this bitch."

Back in the room, Amelie makes a few more clicks then turns to Mace. "The appraiser has been paid."

Mace waits.

"€650 for all of them," says Ranger.

"€830," says Mace.

"€720."

"Hmmm. I won't take less than €800."

"Then you won't have to. I accept."

Amelie leaps up and places each of her hands on Ranger's cheeks. "I love you. I really do."

Ranger hugs her to his chest. "I love you too, Snooks."

Amelie then returns to her laptop and opens a funds transfer form on the webpage of Fidelity Bank Little Cayman. She angles it so Mace can see and types in the amount. "Routing number and account number for receipt of funds?"

"I'd like to do it," says Mace.

Amelie shifts the laptop down to Mace. It slides easily on the metal table.

In the office, Kat watches as the numbers appear in the database fields. "Here we go," she says to Pensee. The screen processes the false transaction and sends a confirmation to Amelie's screen.

Mace watches the transaction. "I'll check from my end too." Mace pulls out her phone.

There is a banging behind the second door. Then it rips off its hinges and crashes to the floor as the room goes dark. "Police," yells a gruff voice.

Red night vision beams sweep around the room.

"Merde!" screams Boniface.

"On the ground," the voice yells.

"Now, now, on the ground," barks another voice.

Mace lunges for the jewels, but hands are already pulling the jewelry roll from her fingertips.

"Don't hurt us, please. We can explain," yells Ranger, terrified.

"Halt!"

"Movement on your left."

"Halt! Or I'll shoot!"

A single gunshot rings out. Amelie screams.

"Restore the lights!"

"Give us the lights back, Unit Two."

Five seconds later, the lights come back on. Three members of the French National Police, two men and a woman, stand in full gear with guns drawn. One has his weapon pointed at Boniface, who lies slumped against the elevator door, eyes closed, bleeding from a wound on his side. "Paramedic!" the officer yells into his radio.

Benny lays on the ground by the blown-off door, unconscious. Louis is crouched by the elevator, arms over his head.

Amelie is huddled under the desk. "Oh no. No, no, no," she cries.

Ranger protects Amelie with his body. "Please, we surrender," he yells, cowering.

Mace, eyes closed, is crawling but runs into one of the officer's legs. She opens her eyes and sees him shaking his head at her.

"Handcuff everyone," an officer says as he removes a plastic-wrapped compress from his vest, tears off the wrapping, and steps toward Boniface. He crouches beside Boniface and applies pressure to his wound. Boniface groans in pain.

The female officer speaks into the handset at her shoulder, "Base, suspect hit. Ambulance to 26 Place Vendome." She walks to the table and pulls out two sets of handcuffs. "Hands up."

Mace puts her hands up.

"We can explain. Please," says Ranger, lifting his hands.

Amelie continues to sob. One of the officers gently pulls her out from under the table and puts cuffs on her.

From his position over Boniface, the lead officer turns toward Ranger, "Villeneuve, take the suspects to booking. I'll stay until the medics arrive."

The female officer cuffs Mace and walks her out through the busted doorway.

The other officer follows with Amelie and Ranger.

Once they are out of the room, Boniface opens one eye and looks at the officer leaning over him.

The officer takes his hands off Boniface's wound and speaks into his radio. "What's your status?"

"All clear," comes the reply.

The officer pulls Boniface to his feet and takes off his police helmet.

"Bravo, as always," Boniface says to Duke.

"How did the Courtemanches perform?" Duke asks, sweat pouring down his face.

"Excellent," says Benny as he and Louis both get to their feet.

"Ranger and Amelie were great. And Pensee gave her heart to the role," says Boniface, gushing.

Pensee and Kat come through the other door. Duke goes to Pensee and takes her by the hands. "And in your soaring performance, the playful in you is embraced by all wishing to believe," Duke says, smiling proudly.

Kat pats a beaming Pensee on the shoulder.

In front of the jewelry store, Lorelei loads Mace into the back of one of two police cars.

Duke comes out from the alley. He sees Ranger sitting in the back seat of the second police car where the other officer is helping Amelie in. He walks over to Lorelei.

"I'll ride with you," Duke says.

"Yes, sir," says Lorelei as she takes the driver's seat.

They depart.

In the other car, the officer unlocks Amelie's and Ranger's cuffs and takes off his riot helmet.

"I hope I didn't hurt you," Prewitt says to Amelie.

"Where were those three nights ago?"

Ranger's eyes go wide.

"I believe these belong to you." Prewitt pulls the jewelry roll from his tactical vest and hands it to Amelie. All three of them smile.

Duke and Lorelei stay silent as Mace stews in the backseat. All this hard work, and she's going away, she muses. Dirty rotten luck. And Boniface shot. Well, at least she got her money. "Turn in here."

Mace looks out the window. The cops have driven down a side street in a warehouse district. Her stomach drops. This is not how you get to a police station.

"Take a left. Park us behind that building there," says Duke.

Mace's life flashes before her eyes. Not really her life. More like fleeting scenes of great sex and the last time she had a perfectly cooked New York Strip at Gallaghers on 52nd. She reminds herself real cops aren't supposed to whack her. But what if this is the end? Mace takes a deep breath, hoping to find she's okay with that. Instead, she feels her stomach drop farther.

Duke turns around in his seat and addresses Mace through the metal of the cage. "Madame, we're going to remove your cuffs, then we're going to let you go because we know you had no knowledge you were dealing with criminals."

"Criminals? They were criminals?" says Mace, relieved and playing along.

"Yes. The man that was shot is a known con artist. His name is Boniface Beaumont."

Mace can't believe these cops think she's a square, that they don't realize she was fencing stolen jewelry. Nor do they realize her money was transferred right before they busted in. Now she's thinking about going for that steak as soon as she lands back in New York.

"But you'd better check your bank account because I don't think what you think is in there is in there," says Lorelei.

"Wait, what?" says Mace as the realization smacks her in the face like a wrecking ball swinging on the end of a long cable and leaving her soul ringing.

Duke and Lorelei nod and watch Mace.

Lava rises and turns her face purple.

"Breathe, dear, just breathe," says Duke.

"You motherfuckers. You mooouuutherfuuuckers."

"No, fuck you. You're the motherfucker," snaps Lorelei. Duke puts his hand over Lorelei's to settle her.

Mace stares at Lorelei as her head tilts down and her eyes tilt up, and her lower lip covers her top lip, and she looks entirely possessed. Then she gazes off into some fourth dimension of hell that somehow injects bitter acceptance into her brain. She finally looks back at Duke but remains silent.

"It will sting. For a bit. But you'll recover," Duke says as he reaches through a window in the cage and removes her handcuffs.

"You better hope I don't," says Mace.

"Time to get out of the car," says Duke.

Mace shakes her head and opens the door. "Fucking Prewitt, that bastard."

"You're the bastard. Fuck you, fuck you double," says Lorelei.

Duke squeezes Lorelei's hand, and she bites her lip.

"Until next time," Duke says, nodding respectfully.

"Yeah, yeah," says Mace as she steps out of the car and starts down the sidewalk.

41

Prewitt stands in the open doorway to Ranger's office. Earlier, he had joined the three fabulous du Courtemanches in the kitchen. Pensee had pulled a tub of ice cream from the freezer, and everyone went at it with their own spoons. Then Prewitt mostly listened as Amelie, Pensee, and Ranger shared their own personal highlights from an evening on the grift. Pensee, still on cloud nine, seemed the happiest, but there was also a closeness between the siblings as they fell into a childlike, carefree banter. Sitting there, Prewitt imagined them as the kids they each once were, laughing and enjoying long-forgotten, innocent times. He sat with them until the ice cream was gone and the stories had waned, and Ranger had gotten up to go to his office and attend to a development in the lawsuit he had "been happy to ignore all day." After another half hour with Pensee and Amelie, Prewitt had decided this might be a good time to talk to Ranger alone.

"Earl du Courtemanche, may I come in?"

"Yes," says Ranger, sitting at his desk.

"There's something I need to share with you."

"Not another surprise, I hope?"

"You know about the old letters in the basement safe?"

"I know there are old letters there. I don't know what they say."

"One of them is written for your ancestor, Benedict."

"Do we have to talk about my family Prewitt?"

"This is important. The letter is signed by the King of France. And the date aligns with William Wallace's trip through France, to Italy, to petition the Pope for help."

Ranger seems to be following, though he stays quiet.

"There is another, more well-known William Wallace letter, found in the Tower of London, which tells Wallace he can receive help from a French agent."

"I know who William Wallace was," Ranger says.

"I believe the letter in your safe is connected to William Wallace."

"In what way?"

"It identifies Benedict du Courtemanche as the French agent who was helping William Wallace. And there are other papers in your safe from the king that support the connection. Ranger, I believe if you allow these papers to be studied by a historian, it will prove your ancestor was given a secret mission seven hundred years ago by his king to aid Scotland in their fight for independence."

Prewitt looks into Ranger's eyes to see what he's thinking. But Ranger is giving nothing away.

Prewitt continues. "Benedict was advised never to reveal who he was so as not to suffer the same fate as Wallace. He wasn't a coward who turned on his friends to become rich and powerful. He was a brave man who tried to help an oppressed people. And he let a cruel rumor hide the truth of why the king owed him a debt to keep his identity secret and protect those around him. Your family didn't do anything bad to gain their riches, as everyone believes. Quite the contrary."

Ranger remains silent.

"Ranger, do you understand?"

Prewitt watches as the weight of pain and shame seem to slide away from Ranger's body. And for a few moments, Ranger sits there processing Prewitt's discovery, his mind working to grasp completely what it has heard.

Then Ranger looks off with sadness in his eyes. "Doesn't change much, really."

"You can tell the press about the letters after the story is confirmed by historians. It will be news. People will know the truth. They'll stop thinking badly of the Courtemanche family. They'll think the opposite."

"Maybe. But I guess I don't really care what they think anymore. I want out of all of this, Prewitt. I want to sell the chateau, pay off my debts, change my name, and be free of it all."

"Where would you go?"

"I don't know. Maybe I'll open a little flower shop," Ranger says with a glum smile. He thinks another moment, then continues. "Pensee and Amelie. They are languishing here, too. They need to leave and live the lives *they* choose. And if they don't do that now, they may never."

Prewitt waits as Ranger looks around the room, pausing for a moment on the oil of Benedict above the mantle.

"No, Prewitt, the Courtemanche story doesn't need another chapter. It simply needs to die."

Before it kills you, thinks Prewitt as he meets Ranger's gaze with understanding.

Prewitt is at the bottom of the stairs when he pulls his phone from his pocket and dials.

"Prewitt?" says Sharon.

"I know the payment for Harvard is due in two days. I don't have it."

"Oh, Prewitt."

"I have to take your father's offer."

"What offer?"

"He wants me to walk away from you and Josh forever. In exchange, he'll cover Harvard and anything else either of you ever need in your life. If I break the deal, he stops paying."

"I didn't know that."

"It's the best thing."

"Not for Josh." There is silence on the line for a few seconds. "I'll tell my father you don't have the money."

"I'm sorry."

"For what? You are who you are."

"Then that's what I'm sorry for."

"I have to go, Prewitt."

Prewitt hears the line hang up on the other end, then stares at his phone's display as if a portal to all he cares about has closed and been replaced by numbers and little squares you click on to find nothing that matters.

Prewitt has known for years Honey Hair was gone. But standing there half a world away from her, somehow now he understands how gone she really is. *It's over.*

He walks down the main hallway and out the front door. Then he walks out to the grass in the middle of the driveway and sits on the empty plinth. Prewitt looks back at the castle. The big lights are gone from the roof now, and the chateau looks almost abandoned in the low light coming from the smaller outdoor fixtures. Prewitt gazes upon its high walls and the gray watermarks on the stone there, and he thinks about how the blocks staring back at him were placed by craftsmen dead more than six hundred years now. Then he thinks about how all their little problems are long forgotten. *My life and its little problems will be forgotten too.*

Prewitt hears a door open, and when he looks back toward the drive, he sees Amelie has come outside. Once she sees him, she walks until she gets to the plinth. "I'm going to pack up, then I'll stay in Paris tonight," says Prewitt.

"Take a little walk with me?"

"Of course," says Prewitt.

They start toward the backyard.

"I overheard your phone call on the stairs."

"Oh, about my son."

"I wasn't eavesdropping."

"It's okay."

"Is that why you did this? For tuition for your son?"

"Yes."

"Your father-in-law sounds like an ass."

"You have no idea," Prewitt says with a sad chuckle.

"Well, I'm sorry that's happening to you."

They walk a bit further in silence.

"I could fall in love with you, you know," says Amelie.

"You know what I do."

"Well, you said you only do it to bad people. And besides, you're very good at this. A bit of intrigue. It certainly wouldn't be boring," says Amelie.

"There are worse things than boring. What you need, what would be good for you, is not what I have to offer right now."

Amelie is silent for a moment as they walk the path through the trees along the side of the chateau.

"Love is timing," Amelie finally says. She leads them toward the riverbank.

Love is timing. And timing is luck, so it's all a crapshoot. It was Johnny who once said that to Prewitt. *Is it?* Prewitt wonders. *Or is there such a thing as fate?* It's hard not to ponder here in a place like this. Prewitt's always believed it's all a dice roll, knowingly hiding from the endless equation that teases his mind and says fate was behind all of it. Laid out every move.

"And life is short. No regrets, Prewitt. Who knows?" Amelie smiles as she says it.

Prewitt smiles back, appreciating her.

Love is letting go. Some stupid self-help poet. *Just sounds so lame. But love really is letting go.* Prewitt thinks it, and it seems to ease the blow. He looks over at Amelie and feels the warm comfort of wanting the best for another. It feels better than desire. It feels like love.

They get to the trees at the bank of the Loire, the water slipping by.

The river is swollen and heavy. Prewitt considers his life lately has been a series of rapids and eddies, and narrow escapes, and time wasted on frantic paddling to keep from going under. *That's gotta change.*

As they stroll along the bank under the trees, Prewitt feels the ground blanketed with soft needles and leaf fall. He imagines Francesco and Lisette walking right where they are, excited and happy. And young.

Soon Amelie stops. "I'm going to give you the money for your son's tuition," she says.

Prewitt hears the kindness of the gesture he could never accept and knows even more what a missed opportunity this is. And what a lovely, decent woman Amelie is.

"I would never let you do that. But thank you."

"Why?"

"Because."

"Wasn't that the point of all of this?" Amelie says with a smile.

"It's very kind of you to even say, but, well, first of all, you don't have that kind of money. But more importantly . . . I can't."

"But I do have that kind of money. I'm going to sell the jewels. Pensee and I discussed it. It will help our family, but there will be more than enough to help you, too. We'll write you a check for the first payment tomorrow."

"Amelie. You can't."

"None of us have kids, you know. It would be fun to put one through Harvard."

"I won't take it."

"I'll expect updates."

"You can't."

"Are you telling me what I can and can't do? Because I will send the money to Harvard myself. All you need to do is tell your son. And your father-in-law."

"Amelie, please."

"This isn't some desperate act to tie us together, Prewitt. You helped us. And we want to help you. It's what family does," Amelie says. Prewitt looks at her, confused. She takes Prewitt's hand, and he looks down at it. She waits for his eyes. "You wouldn't know about that, would you? No, you wouldn't," she says kindly. "There was a different life for you, Prewitt. And it had more love in it." She squeezes his hand gently. "And that's why I want to do this for you."

42

Prewitt returns to the third floor. He packs quickly. On his way down to the first floor, he thinks about Ranger and Duke laughing in the blue salon. Then he passes the dining room and remembers Boniface and Pensee dancing. He continues toward the kitchen. But before he gets there, he sees someone out of the corner of his eye. It's Bertrand. He's at the far end of the dining room, standing by the window and watching Prewitt. Prewitt stops, and they stare at each other. He thinks of walking over to Bertrand and apologizing again. But he knows he can't. He nods to Bertrand, who does nothing. Then Prewitt continues into the kitchen.

Standing in the dark, Prewitt looks at the door to the basement. He thinks about the safe and the letters that lay inside it. Then he pictures the empty wine racks and contemplates the losses this family has suffered, and the way fate intervened to stop him from being the final blow. *Fate?* He doesn't know. *Life really is strange.*

Prewitt walks out to the Peugeot, loads his two suitcases into the trunk, and closes the lid. But he doesn't want to leave. He looks off into the dark night. Prewitt can only sense the Loire beyond the trees. But in his mind, he sees its inky waters cutting a channel that arcs around the fertile hectares of vineyard and back through a thousand lives beyond the Courtemanche estate.

Prewitt turns toward where he and Amelie walked and says a silent goodbye to the ghosts of Lisette and Francesco. Then he thinks about the other Courtemanches resting up on the hill, Benedict and Lily, and Ranger's children. Again, he imagines men building this castle, and picturing it, stands there wanting to stay forever. So, he waits. Soon, he tells himself he can always come back, that he needs to leave, and it allows him to. He takes a step toward the car *and whatever comes next.*

Prewitt settles into the driver's seat of the Peugeot and notices a brown paper bag on the seat next to him. He opens it. Madame Farine has packed him a sandwich.

Prewitt stops for gas ten miles before getting into Paris. After filling the tank, he looks at his phone, 12:28 a.m. Boniface has sent him an address of a place he can sleep.

Prewitt drives through the heart of Paris toward the 18th arrondissement. He enters Montmartre and passes the Sacre Coeur, the glow from its white domes lighting the late Parisian night. The sidewalks are full of people, like his beloved Manhattan. Prewitt passes a few young men waltzing in drunken steps. He sees two older women holding hands and smiles at the lazy stroll of a pair of policemen scanning the night. *If only you knew the shit we pulled.*

He parks and walks up to a large apartment building. Prewitt pushes the exterior door call button to 6P, waits for the sound of the lock buzzing, then enters. The modern lobby is metallic and stark and a million miles from the charm of the Loire Valley. He gets in an elevator, which soon opens to a large sleek apartment. The place is packed with Boniface's troupe and nearly a dozen other revelers.

Is this another unpaid-for sublet? Prewitt would bet yes. *Let them steal the night.* He walks toward a champagne tower, and a woman holds out a glass to him.

"Here, take this one," she says. Prewitt recognizes her as the woman who wore tassels at the first party and served Boniface at the restaurant in the plaza. Tonight, she sparkles from neck to boots in silver sequins. "My name is Sun Cha Kim."

"Thank you. I'm Prewitt. Too bad we didn't get to work together."

"I was on my own job," she says with a dimpled smile.

"Maybe another time."

"If you don't mind working for me," says Sun Cha Kim in Texan English. "Of course, if you ever need the best sharpshooter since Annie Oakley, I'll freelance for ya." She raises her own glass in a toast and melts into the crowd.

Prewitt passes a huge, white marble island. Behind it, in the kitchen, he sees Michel holding a baking tray in both hands. "Canapes aren't meant to be hot, stupid."

"These are. It says on the box," Louis says.

"Then you bought the wrong kind," Michel says.

Louis, wearing oven mitts on both hands, takes a swipe at Michel's hair.

Michel screams, "Not the hair."

"Quit your shenanigans!" says an older, smaller woman in a red knit cardigan, her short wispy hair dyed a similar color. "Give me that tray, Michel. Give me those mitts, Louis. And if you so much as lay a finger on each other tonight, I'll send you straight home."

Both men obey instantly with cowed heads and murmurs of "yes, Grandma."

Prewitt smiles because what's not to like about Grandma? He walks toward an open wall of windows where clever glass doors have slid away to reveal a massive terrace. He is almost knocked over by a young couple wrapped in each other's arms and trying to kiss and walk at the same time. It's Henri and Lorelei.

"Prewitt!" Lorelei throws herself into Prewitt's arms. She hugs him, squeezing hard, then lets him go. Henri is dressed in a suit and looks handsome and happy.

"Hello, Henri, nice suit."

"Thanks."

"I bought it for him," says Lorelei, looking adorable in a vintage peach dress.

"She's got good style. And good taste," says Henri.

"Exactly," Lorelei says, then kisses Henri.

"You two having a nice night?"

"Oui, monsieur," says Henri as Lorelei kisses him again.

"I must thank you for bringing us together," says Lorelei.

"Is that what you are?" says Prewitt.

Henri smiles like Cupid's arrow is stuck in his chest.

"Where is your Courtemanche lover?" says Lorelei.

Prewitt pretends he doesn't understand the question.

"I knew you went for her even before Boniface told everyone."

"Everyone?"

"Of course," she says with a chuckle.

Henri gives a little tug on Lorelei's hand. "Just one more second."

Prewitt wonders at Lorelei, all bright and bubbly and as happy as anyone he's ever seen. *She knows more than I do about navigating this world.*

"I'm glad to have met you, Lorelei, *profiter de tout*."

"Listen to your own advice, Prewitt," Lorelei says in English, then stretches up and plants a kiss on each of his cheeks before springing back to Henri's arms.

Prewitt walks across the terrace and comes to stand between Duke and Boniface. All three look out across the Paris rooftops from the Sacre Coeur to the Eiffel Tour.

"Nice place you have here. A new client of Aime tes Plantes?"

"Perhaps," Boniface says. "Don't be the last one out."

"My plane leaves in eight hours."

"So, you're not going to be with Amelie? She's in love with you."

"That is a fantastic woman," Duke says.

"I agree," says Prewitt.

"But you are not in love with her?" Boniface says.

"I am, but it's complicated."

"*Now* it's complicated? Prewitt, you are soft. You are so soft," says Boniface.

"Yes, he is. And thanks to the heavens for it. More of us men need to look into our hearts to learn who is there, who is really there." Duke puts his thick arm around Prewitt. "This one is not afraid to find out. I'm proud to know him."

Duke turns. "He'll be back," he says and raises his glass to the glittering city lights.

"*Tomorrow, at dawn, in the hour*

When the countryside becomes white,

I will leave. You see,

I know that you are waiting for me.
I will go by the forest,

I will go by the mountain.
I cannot stay far from you any longer."

"That's beautiful, Duke," says Boniface, sounding sincere. "Who is it, Shakespeare?"

"Victor Hugo, my unread friend."

Duke raises his glass to Paris, and Prewitt and Boniface both smile as they join him. Then Prewitt looks at Duke, staring out over the city as if hearing applause from every street and every car and every building. Prewitt swears he can hear the applause too.

43

Across the ocean, and two weeks later, Prewitt walks into his small apartment with a drill in his hand. He's added a motion-activated doorbell security camera after another break-in attempt last night while he was out walking. His neighbor Ed told him this time there was a guy crouched and playing with the locks for twenty minutes. Ed had called the police. They never showed. Prewitt knows no one is getting through his door without an axe, but hopefully, the camera will let Prewitt see who he's dealing with, which may help him learn what he's dealing with. This smells not random.

Prewitt bends down and puts the drill in a box under his walnut bookcase. When he stands, he notices the slightly open second drawer, pauses, then lifts out a black jeweler's cloth and stares at it, thinking of Amelie. He opens the cloth, and there, catching the light, is a cabochon cut sapphire set in gold and suspended on a drop from an earring clip. It had come from France a week after he got back, and every time he looks at it, he can almost see da Vinci's hands placing it into Melzi's. Prewitt never expected Amelie to give him anything. Not money for Harvard and especially not one of the jewels. But when the earring arrived, he understood why she did. And that made him miss her. In the note that it came with, she explained how the rest of the jewels would soon be going up for auction to give the Courtemanche siblings a new start to the rest of their lives. The connection to da Vinci had put the estimates through the roof. He pictured the different pieces spreading out over Europe, separating, and eventually becoming lost to time. That made him miss her too. He looks at the earring again. *I hope she kept its match.*

Prewitt rolls up the cloth and puts the earring back in the drawer. He starts toward the door and stops at the kitchen counter to grab his keys and cell phone. Checking, he sees a text notification. Johnny has sent a thumbs up. Tomorrow he'll have breakfast with his friend for the first time since he's been back.

Stepping out into the night, Prewitt tries to spot whoever must be watching his place, but all he sees are the wet streets and sidewalks and the raindrops in the light from streetlamps. There's a bit of pain in his back, but since he had his physical therapy appointment earlier in the week, he's been doing his exercises and trusts it can eventually resolve, which makes it hurt less. He starts down the sidewalk. Prewitt's been walking every night to breathe and think and plan his next moves. He's hungry in a way he hasn't been for years. And he no longer needs some hustler like Mace to tell him where he's going next. He knows exactly where he's going. And exactly who he plans to meet when he gets there. Won't they be surprised.

He turns right to head north through midtown. The rain falls a bit harder, and Prewitt pulls his hood over his head. But his pace stays the same. He's got one stop to make before he meets Josh for a late snack at Action Burger in Brooklyn. They're going more for the video games than the food, though he expects they'll both probably end up chowing some extreme variation on the cheeseburger. Josh has thrown down a Galaga challenge Prewitt expects to lose badly. He's seen Josh every few days since returning home, both making an effort. Both clinging to the little time before he leaves for Harvard. Prewitt breathes in the warm, wet air and pictures a laughing Josh, biting into a mac and cheese bacon burger.

Twenty minutes later, Prewitt walks casually to the windows of an art gallery. Through the glass, he sees a large cast iron wind bell. Time has turned the surface a deep green. There is a gold foil vase featuring elaborate cherry blossoms and Kanji painted in black and a fine collection of lacquerware boxes. He looks beyond the various artifacts to a secure display case smack in the center of the space, then to the stately Black woman standing behind a desk. Other than her, and the two armed security guards by the door, the small gallery is empty. He pushes the hood of his jacket back and goes in.

"Welcome," the woman says.

"Hello. I apologize for being wet."

"It's fine. Feel free to look around."

"The collection in the window, could you tell me if the boxes are from Kyoto?"

"I believe they are. The gallery is currently showing artifacts from all over Japan. Most are for sale."

Prewitt walks farther into the space, passing the desk and smiling warmly at the woman. She smiles back then busies herself on a tablet. Prewitt browses around, reading the cards for each item, noting prices. They are all at the high end of his guesses for auction estimates. This woman is fair.

Prewitt stops at the display case in the center of the room. He's not far from the woman at her desk. He knows her name is Marigold Meens. She owns and operates the Meens Art Gallery by herself. But she's better known in the New York art scene for coordinating fundraising galas. The massive amounts of cash she can pluck from wallets with her silent auctions are legendary.

Prewitt looks down into the display case at a sword. He leans forward and reads the card: "*Sword owned by Tokugawa Ieyasu, Japan's first Shogun. Made by Honjo Masamune.*" No price. This item isn't for sale.

Marigold lifts her head from her tablet. "That piece has had a lot of admirers. Masamune is regarded as Japan's greatest sword maker. Did you hear about it in the news?"

"No, I didn't."

"Historians thought the sword was lost, but then it was plucked from thin air by a man they're calling a modern-day Indiana Jones, Dylan Watkin Standish."

"You don't say."

"I do."

"Must be quite a story there."

Marigold saunters out from behind her desk. "I expect so."

She takes a step toward him. "Is there anything else I can tell you more about?"

Prewitt leads Marigold to the front window display. "I'm looking for a birthday gift for my son. He did a semester abroad last year in Kyoto. I wonder if he might like the lacquerware boxes."

"They're in excellent condition and not so rare as to be beyond everyday use. They'd look nice on a bookshelf, or your son could use them to hold notes or special items."

"I think they sound perfect then. Do you ship?"

"Of course." Marigold returns to the desk and her tablet.

Prewitt pulls out his wallet and extracts a credit card and business card. He hands both to Marigold. "Send them to me at my office. It's local, but this way, I can keep them a surprise."

Marigold takes the cards and begins to input the information. "Mr. Peak, I see you work at The Plaza Hotel."

"Yes, just started there recently. I was at another Fairmont property prior."

"That sword is heading to the Plaza next month. It's going to be auctioned. A big to-do. It should fetch a prize. And some eccentric characters," Marigold says as she finishes Prewitt's purchase. She hands him back his cards.

"Keep this, please," Prewitt says, handing her the business card. "As fate would have it, we will be working together on that fundraiser."

"Then I look forward to that."

"Oh . . . me too," Prewitt says with an assured smile.

THE END

EPILOGUE

One Year Later

In a small kitchen in Paris, Bertrand and Madame Farine both lean into a cookbook and squint to read from a recipe for cherry pie. All around them are dirty bowls and spoons, pots, cutting boards, and knives.

"The crust must be a lattice," Madame Farine says.

"It can be a solid crust too. You use the tines of a fork to pierce it so the steam can escape during baking. That's what it says, Madame Farine."

"I'm teaching *you* to cook, not the other way around," says Madame Farine, laughing.

"I thought it would be nice to do it differently."

"Is that so? Are you trying to get rid of me, Bertrand, take my job?"

"I would never."

"I see the way you look at this stove."

"Madame Farine!

"Because I'm not going anywhere," she says, laughing harder.

"I would hope not," says Bertrand, with the slightest chuckle of his own.

***

Past the kitchen and down a hallway with aged, dark wood floors, a single glass door opens to a tidy balcony. Nestled against the facade of the old apartment building, the balcony is buttressed by the awning of the ground floor below.

On the balcony is Ranger du Courtemanche, Earl of Orleans, Viscount of Blois. Except to his neighbors, mostly older and mostly friendly, he now is simply Ranger, the beloved owner of Benedict Floral Shop, known especially for its roses. Ranger wears a wide-brimmed hat to protect him from the rather bright sun shining down today. He wears it other days, too, unless he's going riding with Duke. Those days, he wears his riding helmet while on the horse and for hours afterward until dusk. It's the same cap he used as a young man, the leather straps worn and darkened, the black velvet fraying at the brim. Though instead of riding pants and a polo shirt, he favors the soft denim trousers and linen button-down he is wearing now.

Ranger reaches into the middle of a Queen Anne rose bush and grasps a stem, carefully avoiding the thorns. With the other hand, he inserts nippers, and prunes the withered, pink bloom.

Around him in a sea of color, the blossoms from a dozen varieties of roses sip the warm air and breathe out aromas of fruit, musk, and clove. They climb the apartment building walls and stretch across trellises. Below Ranger on the sidewalk, sometimes someone, if they bother to look up, stops and marvels at the quaint beauty. Today they would see Ranger Benedict feeling at home, his home, for the first time in his life. Ranger prunes the leaves of a rose. It's a pretty one. And when he looks down, he sees another, even prettier.

Other books by
ADDISON J. CHAPPLE

The Man Who Would Be King

In this hilarious satire on American exceptionalism, two Midwestern idiots travel to Somalia, impersonate Navy SEALs, and steal money from pirates . . . what could possibly go wrong?

Rambling with Rebah

When a leading travel blogger returns to a bed-and-breakfast she blasted years ago, the owner must go to extreme—and hilarious—measures to ensure her stay is perfect, or risk going bankrupt. Even sworn enemies can fall in love in wine country.

Santa Ana

A wildly irreverent and hilarious story about an insurance clerk who is a savant when it comes to mathematical probabilities but a failure at personal relationships. As the Santa Ana winds blow, he decides to spend his life's savings to impress his classmates at his 25-year high school reunion and then commit suicide. But when he arrives, he's mistaken for a drug kingpin and drawn into a hilarious and sprawling battle for his life.

Stay up to date with Addison J. Chapple:

Follow Addison on Amazon & Goodreads

https://amazon.com/author/addisonjchapple